Astral Odyssey
Virgil Knightley and Jay Aury

Copyright © 2024 by Virgil Knightley and Jay Aury. Permission to publish audio, ebook, and paperback editions granted exclusively to Royal Guard Publishing.

All rights reserved.

No portion of this book may be reproduced in any form without written permission from the publisher or author, except as permitted by U.S. copyright law.

Contents

1. Chapter 1 — 1
2. Chapter 2 — 22
3. Chapter 3 — 46
4. Chapter 4 — 59
5. Chapter 5 — 71
6. Chapter 6 — 86
7. Chapter 7 — 105
8. Chapter 8 — 115
9. Chapter 9 — 131
10. Chapter 10 — 144
11. Chapter 11 — 154
12. Chapter 12 — 179
13. Chapter 13 — 190
14. Chapter 14 — 204
15. Chapter 15 — 217

16.	Chapter 16	233
17.	Chapter 17	253
18.	Chapter 18	269
19.	Chapter 19	290
20.	Chapter 20	301
21.	Chapter 21	312
22.	Chapter 22	325
23.	Chapter 23	340
24.	Chapter 24	349
25.	Chapter 25	366
26.	Chapter 26	380
27.	Chapter 27	398
28.	Chapter 28	408
29.	Chapter 29	424
30.	Chapter 30	445
31.	Chapter 31	456
	Links	470

Chapter 1

THE SECOND OF THE twin suns set on the horizon. With that, the air cooled considerably, and Dorian Hawke wiped a streak of sweat from his brow. Sunset had found him hanging up laundry for the innkeeper, Grouse, exactly like he had been this time the day before. And before that. And that.

He didn't resent it. Well, not much. Not really. The denizens of the feudal estate and its residents had been kind to him since he was a boy. So long as anyone could say, he had been an orphan with no claim to any family, but there were those who tried to make him feel welcome, or at least like he belonged on some level. Grouse was one of them.

Growing up without family meant he often filled in for tasks with various folks around the Clemmen estate, gaining competency in a wide variety of jobs. If a net needed mending for a fisherman, he was willing to lend a hand. If a field needed plowing, he could do that too. If the blacksmith needed someone to really hammer out the shape of a sword because his rheumatism was acting up, then Dorian was his man. Hell, he even helped some of the knights up at the castle spar to keep them limber thrice a week, just in case of a raider attack or gods forbid, one of the king's many enemies declared war.

As it happened, he was quite good at...well, all of it. He took to every task like a duck to a pond, gaining proficiency in record time. As such, his fellow denizens of the estate weren't shy about asking for his help.

He could hear all their voices now, taking him for granted whether they meant to or not. "Dorian, m'lad, Tilda's thrown out her back. Would you mind helping us out with dinner up at the manor?"

"Dorian! So good to see you! Actually you're just the young man I wanted to see! Would you mind helping my husband tan his leathers today? He's got a big order coming in next week."

"Dorian, boy, there's a tournament up at the capital this weekend, and I need you to help me bring my jousting up to the next level. Mind putting on that armor and letting me wail on you for a few hours?"

"Sure," he'd said with a smile and a hidden sigh—to all of them. Because that was him. Helpful Dorian.

Grouse had a bit more gratitude than most. He even let Dorian live in the backroom of the inn, and had been strongly hinting that if he played his cards right, he, Dorian Hawke, might be looking at a fulfilling career as a stableboy or, dare he dream, even a bouncer throwing out the drunken fishermen after lights out.

Which was...great...he guessed.

Dorian sighed and finished hanging up the last shirt. He took a moment to admire the loose flutter of the clothes under the hot pink rays of the setting suns. Another job done. At least he could rest.

With a roll of his shoulder, which came with a slight pop, he made his way to the inn's fence and sat on the post, fetching out his pocket knife and a piece of wood. The blade bit into the block, carving off chunks as he looked down the hill at the main road leading to the wharves, the fishermen making their way along the path and towards the tavern.

Carving wood. That was the one thing he was *really* good at. A number of his pieces graced the mantles of various homes in Clemmen, and Lord Clemmen had even gotten one. Though, that had been because he'd been frantic for a last minute gift after forgetting his wife's birthday. Again. But it seemed she'd at least been mollified by it, seeing as the guards hadn't come to break down Dorian's door and drag him off to the dungeons for failing his lord and master. Not that that happened all too often.

It did happen, though.

He sighed again as another chip of wood came off. He was of majority age, now. Maybe he should head to the capital? See if there was work for a man who seemed to know how to do most anything? Every trade seemed to come to him naturally, but none inspired him. The closest to peace he'd ever felt was when he was invited on a fishing trip with some of Lord Clemmen's friends. Not to fish, of course. His job had been to serve drinks and take a turn on the oars heading back. But taking in the vastness of the sea, he felt like he'd discovered a key to the missing truth of himself that he'd sometimes drunk to fill, but never felt quenched. Nothing else really inspired much of anything resembling contentment in him.

Save for carving. *That* he enjoyed. He seemed to have a knack for finding the true shape within the wood and bringing it out. Maybe he could be a carpenter? Whittler didn't really seem a viable career choice...

"Boy! Is the laundry done?"

Dorian lifted his head and glanced back at the tavern as Grouse waddled out the back door. Wide, like the man had eaten one of his own wine barrels and lived to tell the tale, Grouse had beady black eyes and a large apron that flapped over the slope of his gut with every swaying step.

"All hung up," Dorian replied, nodding at the lines of cloth.

"Hrm! So I see. Good work, lad. Good work. And those barrels are down in the cellar?"

"Yes."

"Firewood chopped?"

"And in the firebox."

"Hmm..." Grouse said, one eye screwing up suspiciously. "You sure?"

Dorian mentally rolled his eyes, but just smiled. "Of course."

"Hrmph. Well, good lad. Good lad..."

Grouse nodded and looked out over the hilly village with Dorian. "Glad to see things in order, of course."

"Of course," Dorian grunted, wiping some sweat from his brow on his sleeve.

"Mmm...Good. Well, take a breather, I suppose, but the cook needs some help with peeling the potatoes for tonight's stew. You can do that, right?"

Dorian repressed a sigh. "Sure. Can do." Just when he thought he'd finished his day's work.

"Good lad."

Dorian smiled, then frowned as he turned back around, staring at the darkening horizon. Just another day. A day that was getting...brighter for some reason. That didn't seem right. Hadn't the suns just set?

Dorian lifted his head curiously towards the glow fluttering over the sea and clinkered roofs of the village. At first, he thought it was a shooting star that he was seeing. But then it got bigger.

Much bigger.

"Gods above!" Grouse gasped behind him, and Dorian couldn't deny the epithet as a screaming mass of fire and sparks tore through the sky above the village. The passage ripped clothes from the line, sending them flapping through the air like startled birds. Dorian's head swiveled, following the blazing ball until it passed over them, dropping behind some distant fields.

An explosion shook the earth and sent up a plume of fire and smoke.

"Gods! A falling star!" Grouse gasped, making a sign of the hammer on his chest.

Dorian rose to his feet, stunned at what he had just seen. Gods! It was the most interesting thing that had happened since farmer Townsend grew that potato as big as a pig—but this?! This?!

"Where are you going, lad!" Grouse gasped as Dorian's feet started carrying him in the direction of the anomaly.

Dorian hadn't realized he'd started moving, but even as the simple fact came to his attention, he knew he had no desire to stop. "I'm going to check it out."

"Lad! That's a fool's errand! Could be a sky demon or some nonsense! Let the knights get it. Lad!"

But Dorian was already jogging, no, *running* down the path and towards the hills, his heart leaping in excitement, his veins singing with exhilaration he couldn't quite explain.

Gods. Whatever it was—a sight it would be! He just knew it, just sensed that this was something special. A chance, perhaps. A way out of his desperately directionless situation, maybe. Directionless was even too kind a word. Motionless was more like it.

...And even if it was *neither* of those things, well at least it was a distraction and an excuse not to spend his evening peeling potatoes with a cantankerous geriatric cook who was more likely to smack him with a spoon than thank him.

He vaulted over the low stone walls which divided the paddocks from one another, the acrid smell of smoke growing stronger by the second. He reached the mound of earth thrown up by the star's impact, and only then did he slow, hesitating as logic warned him of the danger, but he didn't come to a full halt. He felt drawn forward as if by magic, cautiously approached the lip of the crater, and peered over.

At first, he couldn't understand what he was seeing. It looked like...well, like a boat, though quite unlike the fishing vessels he knew. It had a keel and curving bottom, the wood charred and torn as if it had come through an almighty storm. A large sail lay tattered at the top, and jutting from the side was a limb like something between an oar and a bat's wing. The entire vessel lay tilted on the ground as if beached by a receding tide. Parts of it were aflame, burning with a strange, violet fire that spit and crackled sparks.

Wow.

Much more interesting than peeling potatoes, indeed...

Dorian stepped over the edge of the crater and slid down towards the ship. Its hull had been torn apart, and a large hole ripped in the underside. Through it, he saw strange flutters of light and heard something over the crackle of flames. Smoke filled his nostrils, and he coughed.

The sensible thing, Dorian knew, was to back off and wait for the knights and guards to arrive. It might indeed be a monster or a sky demon for all he could tell, one of those strange creatures fabled to haunt the heavens and come down to the world to prey on sinners and children who didn't eat their vegetables. But good sense seemed in short supply at the moment, and as if hypnotized, Dorian drew even closer.

More sounds came from the hole—a clang of metal and a strange, humming sound like a thousand bees busy at work. Ducking near the ragged gap in the ship, Dorian peered inside.

It took him a moment for his eyes to adjust, but soon he made out the interior. A mess of what looked like copper piping tangled through the hull like the roots of a tree, all of it radiating from some vast contraption of brass in the middle of the ship like a recumbent octopus. Glass domes, windows, and portholes covered it, swimming with a kaleidoscope of violets, blues and greens.

And in front of it was a woman. A gorgeous one.

Dorian stared at her, gobsmacked. Yep, she was decidedly a woman just going by her lithe, attractive silhouette, but *human* would be stretching it. Some tight leather leggings clung to her hips and a similar jacket hung off her shoulders. A pair of goggles were perched atop messy long brown hair, from which jutted what looked like the ears of a deer. Another deer-like feature was the small tail that poked out of a hole cut into her pants, and what looked like hooves clip-clopped as she worked on the strange machine. Plus, the antlers. She had...antlers.

"Come on...Work with me you stupid...son of a...grnnnn!" the woman groaned with an attractive high-pitched voice, heaving on a wheel set in the machine. When it failed to budge, she took a step back, bouncing on her hooves like a pugilist. "So, you want some more, eh? Well fine! Have some of this!" she cried, banging the wheel with a wrench.

"What in the..." Dorian breathed in disbelief. Then he felt something cold, long, and very sharp slide against his neck.

"Like the view, human?" asked a voice as cold as winter's frost.

Dorian very, very slowly turned his head.

A woman stood behind him. Dressed in tight black pants and a shirt tied under her rib cage that flattered her figure's waist and rounded breasts. She also wore a somewhat tattered earthen colored jacket with copper buttons and pauldrons with gold lace. She was slim, though not lacking in curves, and her hair seemed to shimmer with colour, though mostly reds like she wore a crown of flames. Two long, pointed ears jutted from the sides of her head, and her features were delicate, lovely—and looking down at him with deadly seriousness.

"I—uh..." Dorian sputtered, trying to figure out just how to reply to a blade at his throat.

"Shut up," the elf said, which at least took that burden off his shoulders. Her narrow sword gave a twitch. "Stand."

Dorian obeyed, the alternatives few and not exactly appealing. He raised his arms to show he was unarmed.

"I—"

"Quiet," the elf snapped, the colours of her hair flaring red again. She looked past him. "Fuck. I don't have time for you. Fable! Have you got the core yet?"

"I'm working on it, Melia!" the woman in the ship said. "The crash bent the damn hatch. Just let me...Aha!"

The humming drone suddenly faded, along with the shimmering lights behind Dorian. He dearly wanted to look, but didn't want to lose his head, so settled for examining his captor a little closer. Now that the initial shock had faded, he noted that her outfit looked a bit more tattered than he'd initially given it credit for, ripped, smokey, and even singed here and there. Some light cuts decorated her face and slashed the fabric of her loose jacket, but her eyes remained steely.

"Got it!" Fable shouted. "When are we—whoa! Who's this cutie?!"

"An excellent question," Melia growled, pushing the edge of her blade a bit harder against his throat. "Who are *you*?"

"Uh, hi," Dorian grunted, finding the most logical path forward to be dependent on his agreeableness and manners. "I'm Dorian. Dorian Hawke. Nice to, uh, meet you. And I live here on the Clemmen Estate."

The elf smirked. "Funny. You don't seem like a simple peasant boy."

He heard a gasp from behind him. "Oh fuck! We didn't crash on your house, did we? Stars and burns, I'm so sorry! We totally didn't mean to. We were just looking for a place to land after that nether ray gutted the engines and—"

"Stop apologizing," Melia hissed sharply.

"But we wrecked his house!"

"No, we didn't."

"We didn't?"

"Of course not. He just said he lives on the feudal estate we passed over."

"Oh. Then...whose house did we smash?"

"What?" Dorian mumbled blankly. It was a filler word in this case, giving him time to process this unfolding madness before he uttered a real reply.

Melia rolled her eyes, but Dorian noted the shimmering red of her hair had faded to a softer violet. "Let me do the talking," she said to her friend, then redirected her attention his way. "Now, you. Human. What do you know of dragons?"

"Dragons?" Dorian asked, perplexed. "You mean the big, scaly lizards that breathe fire?"

"Well, not just fire," Fable corrected him with a giggle. "Certain species have been known to breathe other elemental forces. It's hypothesized that their scales and breath responds to environmental factors and—"

"Yes," Melia said, cutting off her companion. "Dragons. Are there any around?"

Dorian stared at her, flummoxed. "Dragons? I mean, not in these parts. Not for generations. There's rumours they still exist across the Circle Sea and in the Mountains of Mourn, but..."

Melia sighed. "Blast," she muttered. "Fine. Is there a port nearby?"

"Er, well, the village is part of the Clemmen estate, which is known for its fishing, so yes. There is one."

"Fantastic! We can charter something off planet," Fable piped. "Once we find ourselves the navigator here."

"Navigator?" Dorian muttered in confusion.

"Fable. *Shut up*," Melia snapped. "The less the groundling knows, the better."

"Aww, come on! Maybe he could help us find him," Fable said. "I mean, he lives here, right? And he's so cute!"

Under siege of such unprompted compliments, Dorian had a hard time feeling any negative sort of way about what was going on, blade to his throat and all. He gulped.

The elf looked sourly at her friend. "No. He knows too much already. We have to...deal with him."

Dorian's eyes popped open. That changed things. "Sorry?"

"We're *killing* him?" Fable gasped, appalled. "Melia! No! I'm not standing around and letting you kill him! He's too hot to just off! Plus, even if he does know too much, he's just a peasant. What is he going to do, tell his Lord how to find us out in the Black?"

Melia blew a frustrated huff from her nose. "Dammit, Fable!" she snapped, her attention flicking over Dorian's shoulder at the faun. "We have to make sure he—"

The slip of her attention was the opening Dorian needed. Sir Pentus had taught him well, and his hand sprang up, slapping the flat of Melia's sword up and away from his neck. The elf's eyes whipped back to him, but before she could respond he'd bulled forward, slamming a shoulder into her midriff. Melia gasped, doubling over his back, and he threw her over him.

The lithe elf flipped over and landed hard on the ground, driving the wind out of her. Reaching down, Dorian snatched up the fallen sword and whirled about, blade up and ready.

Fable stared at him, jaw slack and what looked like an orb of shimmering light clutched to her chest. Melia, to her credit, was fast, and almost instantly sprang back to her feet, a dagger drawn from her belt and at the ready.

"Um...Maybe he's not just a cute peasant," Fable said.

"No one's killing me," Dorian declared. "My life may not be great, but it's the only one I've got, so I'm going to keep it, thanks!"

Melia growled, her hair again shimmering red like fire. "Cocky son of a—"

Fable smacked Melia on the back of the head. "Great job, Melia!"

Melia winced. "I wasn't really going to *kill* him," the elf said sharply. "Just...tie him up and leave him while we get out of here."

"Then you shoulda said so," Fable huffed. "Honestly, you are the worst negotiator. Not everyone wants to gut us. Your chest thumping and temper tantrums always cause things like this, you know."

Melia grimaced, straightening slowly, though Dorian noted she still held her dagger guardedly. "Fine," she said, glancing back at Dorian as some of the fiery hue faded from her hair. "Look, human, we just need to find the navigator around here and leave. That's all we need. If you let us, we can be out of your hair in an hour."

"And where is this navigator, exactly?" Dorian demanded suspiciously, lowering the saber but keeping a tight grip on it.

Melia glanced at Fable, who brightened and held up the orb. "We can find him with this! A ship's core always seeks the nearest unclaimed navigator. Just need to make it...Hang on."

Fable whispered some words to the stone, the sounds sending sudden tingles racing up Dorian's spine, making him straighten sharply. The orb pulsed in Fable's hands, the colours swirling, shimmering and beginning to glow.

And so was Dorian.

"Gah!" he gasped, jumping back, sword instantly back on guard as his skin shone with gold and red like a living torch. "What did you do?" he demanded.

Fable was staring at him, slack-jawed, and even Melia looked stunned. The faun turned to the elf, beaming. "See?" she said. "See! That's why we don't try and kill everyone we meet!"

"I see," Melia murmured, sighing and reluctantly putting her dagger away. "And I don't try and kill everyone we meet," she added somewhat peevishly.

"See? See what?" Dorian demanded, looking between the two strange women. "Why am I glowing? What's going on?"

"Duh! It means you're the navigator, cutie!" Fable said eagerly, fairly bouncing in excitement. "In you flows the blood of dragons. Which means you can steer our stellar ship through the wyrmways and the void between worlds. Isn't that fantastic?"

Dorian stared at her.

"Steer what between *what*?!"

Chapter 2

THE DOCKS OF CLEMMEN lay sleeping under the stars, wrapped in the silent security of the fact that nothing at all interesting ever happened to them. The fishermen's boats gently rode the waves, the masts and rigging creaking softly in the breeze, scented of salt and the sea. A picture of calm. Of quiet.

And Dorian dearly hoped to keep it that way.

That was largely why he'd agreed to help the two strangers find a boat. He hardly trusted them, even after Fable had wrapped up the so-called 'core' in some strange fabric, which had blocked the light and, mercifully, made him stop glowing too. Melia had been short about it, just commanding him to get them a ship so they could leave the world, which certainly appealed to Dorian. He didn't much relish the pair hanging around

Clemmen. Their crash had done enough damage. He didn't want to find out what their continued presence could do.

Especially with what else Melia had said.

"Why should I help you?" he'd demanded.

"Because the ones who grounded us very well might burn this little feudal estate to the ground if they find out we're stranded here," Melia had said with grim finality, donning a hood which masked the glow of her hair and long, pointed ears. "So if you don't want that to happen, we need to be gone. The sooner the better."

"They really will," Fable said as she pulled on her own hood. "Please. It's for the best, cutie."

He'd wanted to argue, but a look again at the damaged ship had shut him up. He didn't know where they'd come from, but he knew damage from sea and storm, and their burning ship had suffered wounds that no wind or rock would give. Again he thought of the sky demons and the terrifying legends of their ravages. Something had made Melia and Fable crash, and whatever it was, he had a grim feeling Clemmen could ill afford to meet it.

Thus they lurked in the shadows of an alley, between the chandler's shop and the Fitzgbibbon family's home, where Dorian, on Tuesdays, was typically asked to milk the goats. There was no one about. Everyone had gathered on the hill outside the village to gawk at the smoke still pluming into the sky. A small mercy, but a welcome one. It made this part easier.

"What about that one," he said, pointing to Walter Belt's old craft, tugging at its mooring rope with every lick of a wave like a dog looking to run away.

Beside him, Fable tapped her chin, frowning as she appraised it seriously. "Mm. No. Too small."

"Well, how large do you need?" he asked, exasperated.

"Bigger than those," Melia grunted. "The biggest you have."

"Why?"

"Air," Fable quickly said, her hands tracing a round shape. "The oxygen bubble formed by a void ship is determined by the mass of the ship itself. If it's too small, then we won't have enough oxygen to reach the next world or beyond. Or we will, but we'll have to get used to cutting it close and stopping at every air station we can."

Dorian didn't understand more than half of what she said, but her reasoning did seem logical somehow—and she'd know better than him. He again glanced at the orb she cradled at her hip, slung in the strange dark fabric. It was odd, but though he was relieved to be out of its glow, he somehow...missed it too. It wasn't a feeling he was too fond of. It felt weird, but right, and the less he dwelled on it and got these two strange women gone, the better.

"We mostly just have fishing boats here," he said with a shrug. "Besides his lordship's yacht, *The Windlass*, anyway."

"And where's that?" Melia demanded.

"Over there, in its private dock," he said with a nod, then sent a sharp glance their way. "Wait, you can't mean to steal that!"

"We must. All three of us," Melia said.

"Why do you need me?" Dorian demanded. "I'm just the local handyman."

"We need you to steer us through the Black," Melia informed him hotly, jabbing a finger into his chest. "We don't have any other navigator but you, nor anyone else who can fudge the job."

"I've never even been outside Clemmen!" Dorian protested, his brows pooling with sweat. Him? Steal a ship? And take it where, exactly? Into the sky, wherever they came from? Into the...the Black? Whatever that was...

"Doesn't matter," Fable said brightly. "Those with dragon's blood can feel the courses of the wyrmways without fail, not to mention work with a ship core way more smoothly than anyone else."

This was madness. "I don't have dragon's blood!"

Melia laughed shortly. "If I hadn't seen the glow, I'd be inclined to believe that."

"There'll be time to explain things once we're netherborne," Fable said. "For now, just trust us."

"Trust you?" He scoffed. "I just met you. And one of you threatened me with a sword. Besides, why should I want to leave?"

"Oh yes," Melia said mockingly and gestured at the village. "Who could imagine leaving all *this* behind? Such a wonderful life you have here, mister handyman. Tell me, navigator, do you eat anything outside of potatoes in your one room hovel? Or is that only during winter while you wait for the cold to kill you?"

"There's more to life here than that," Dorian shot back, but he felt the sting of how close to truth she was. "Fine," he growled, starting off down the dark street. If he didn't agree to their terms, they'd be stuck here, which meant he'd be inviting their pursuer to wreak havoc. "Let's just...let's get you out of here."

Melia snorted and Fable murmured some admonishment to her companion, but Dorian listened to neither woman. Gods above, this had been a hell of a night. And he could tell it wasn't over yet, either.

He led them along the rocky shoreline, until the castle formed a humping shape in the distance. Down from it, at the bottom of a small inlet lay the pier, and at its end sat *The Windlass*. A fine ship. The finest Dorian had ever seen, which, admittedly, wasn't an immense number. Sleek as a blade, the sails were furled, oars docked and the wood sound and solid. When needed, the craft served Lord Clemmen to fish, sail to the capital, and occasionally to hunt the odd pirate around the craggy shores. Dorian had helped fix it up a few times, so knew the ship fairly well.

And as he'd dreaded, it was guarded.

He peeked from the cover of some boulders down at the docks. Several men at arms stood on the pier and deck, looking in the direction that the comet had fallen, but sadly too disciplined to go investigate what had happened. Dorian cursed the bad luck and glared down at them, counting their numbers the best he could. *No chance of sneaking aboard*, he mused sourly. They were too keyed up after the crash.

"Not bad," Melia said from behind him as she scrutinized the ship. "It will do."

Dorian winced. Was he really going to do this? Well, not that he was particularly fond of his lordship on a personal level, but he knew too well if he did, he was basically saying goodbye to his life in Clemmen.

Which was...sad.

Right?

He sighed, realizing he'd made his decision the minute he decided not to instantly go to the guards and fork over the two women. There was something strange about them, true. But familiar as well. Almost more familiar than the village he'd spent his whole life in. As if he'd always lived in a foreign country, and had just met visitors from his homeland. Curiosity urged him on. He wasn't afraid of admitting his ignorance, and he realized that whatever these two were involved with was far, far over his head.

And yet, despite everything, he wanted to see how far up this madness went.

"Alright," he said. "We'll have to deal with the guards."

"Simple enough," Melia replied with a nod, nodding at the sword he had taken from her.

"Without killing them," Dorian added sharply. "These are people I know, maybe a few of them by name. If you can't give me that assurance, I won't help you."

Melia glared at him, but Fable elbowed her sharply in the side, and the elf sighed. "Fine," she growled. "But give me my sword back."

"That'll leave me unarmed," he noted.

"Then grab a weapon from a guard," Melia said with mock sweetness and a harsh smile. "Besides, I know how to wield it better than you."

"Yet I took it off you," he pointed out.

Melia frowned at the reminder. "If I don't have it, then I'll have no choice but to kill them."

Dorian winced, but also wondered just how she planned to do that without a sword. Even so, he somewhat reluctantly handed over her rapier. Melia snatched it up eagerly, letting out a grunt of satisfaction as she sheathed the blade at her side with a nod of something like gratitude, but only barely.

"We'll go down and I'll get us close," Dorian said. "Then we take them by surprise, get the ship, and sail off. Any issues?"

"None," Melia replied.

"We're good," Fable said, her gaze fixed on the boat.

Dorian nodded and looked down once more at the waiting ship. He felt again the subtle tug of uncertainty, then shrugged it off and rose. "Let's go," he grunted, and started down the path.

His plan wasn't exactly genius. Then again, it didn't need to be. The guards to the Clemmen estate knew how to use their weapons, but they'd be edgy and nervous after the fireball overhead. Many would be wondering if it was a sky demon, and if they'd be called up to deal with it. But once the guards realized the crashed ship was just that, they'd fan out and search the village and surroundings for the intruders, and Dorian had no illusions that the pair would be found, and would not go quietly. This was the best choice, he reminded himself, minimizing death and damage to all parties. And it certainly wasn't because he was curious about them and where they wished to sail, or because he found the pair of them uncommonly gorgeous.

Nope. Not that at all.

At least...he wouldn't admit that aloud.

Their approach hardly went unnoticed. As they neared the edge of the dock, several guards hurried forward, blocking the way.

"Halt!" the lead one barked, a middle-aged man bearing the plume of a captain in his helmet. "Identify yourself!"

Dorian groaned internally. *Oh lovely.* That would be Captain Terrance. The man had a reputation, and for good reason. A more swaggering, bullying prick of a man had never set foot in Clemmen, and of course he had to be on yacht guard duty tonight of all nights. Big and brawny, he distinctly didn't like Dorian for the simple fact that he was good at everything, and made his dislike known in a million little ways that those with a smidge of authority over others always did. Commanding him to clean privvies. Polish chainmail. And generally inconveniencing him however he could.

Well, at least Dorian felt a bit less guilty for what was about to happen.

"Captain," Dorian grunted with a nod.

Terrance proffered an ugly smirk, curling a lip under his thin mustache. "Well, well! Look who it is. The potboy from the inn. What are you doing here? And with...rather interesting company," he said, eyes moving over Fable and Melia. Particularly the latter, whose scant and tight-fitting garb left little to the imagination.

"Guests of his lordship," Dorian said. "He wished for them to be given a tour of his ship."

Terrance scoffed. "Ha! You must think I was born yesterday, potboy. As if his lordship would ask you to take on such a task, and with a faun no less! Hm, but then, I might be open to it all the same," Terrance said, leering at Melia. He reached out, grabbed her arm and pulled her close, grinning. "How's about it, milady? Shall we show you the...lower decks?"

Melia smiled sweetly. "Delighted," she replied through a saccharine smile.

Then her knee slammed into his crotch.

Terrance's face seemed to tighten around itself, his eyes rolling back and a sound like someone squeezed a bag of air escaping him. His legs buckled inward and he toppled to his knees.

"O-oy!" one of the other guards gasped, bringing down his spear.

Fable gestured at him, a word that seemed to vibrate in the air leaving her lips. A ball of light burst from her palm and slammed into the guard's chest, flinging him back like he'd been kicked by a mule. The man flew through the air and off the dock, hitting the water with a heavy splash.

"Attack!" the other guard shouted, drawing his sword.

He rushed forward, and Dorian realized the man was coming right at him. He twisted as the guard swung at him, the blade whistling harmlessly past, and then Dorian followed it up by slamming his fist into the guard's nose.

There was an audible crunch and the man toppled back, moaning and pawing at his face. Shit! Well, he was committed now. Dorian snatched up the fallen sword, just as several guards from aboard the ship rattled down the gangplank. There was no space for regret anymore. If he stayed, this offense would see him hung.

Dorian parried a slash from the first man onto the dock, the clash of swords ringing loud before he kicked the man in the chest, sending him tumbling over the edge of the pier and into the waters with a loud splash.

"Not bad, navigator," Melia said, suddenly beside him and meeting another slashing blade with her narrow rapier, deflecting the clumsy blow with ease before smashing the hilt of her sword into the wielder's face.

"Thanks," Dorian grunted, his blade meeting another guard's. The man tried to bull Dorian over with sheer momentum, but he swiftly sidestepped, tripping the guard as he did so. The man yelped and went headfirst over the side and into the sea, his splashing audible as he tried to swim in the heavy armour.

Looked like those years of taking beatings from the knights paid off after all, he internally mused as adrenaline surged and he felt a hidden strength come out to play. He did hope the guards would all make it to shore without drowning, but there wasn't much he could do about that now.

The sudden bellow of a horn split the night. Dorian looked sharply aboard, spotting a guard blowing on a horn for all he was worth. Dammit! That'd have every guard in the castle coming down the hill in minutes!

Charging up the gangplank, Dorian leaped over the gunwale, landing with a bang on the deck. The guard with the horn retreated, still furiously blowing while his other hand fumbled for his sword. Dorian swiped, cutting the horn in two and the bellowing off with a sour note before he grabbed the man by the front of his tabard and flung him overboard.

Ignoring the resulting splash, Dorian turned about as Fable and Melia raced aboard after him, the faun already unrolling a scroll and pulling the core from its bag. "Here!" she shouted, tossing the glowing orb to Melia, who caught it with ease and hastened to the ship's wheel.

Dorian kicked the gangplank free and into the water and peered up at the castle. He could see torchlight, threading down the path to the docks in packs, illuminating a number of guards. "Hurry!" he called. "We got company coming fast!"

"Working on it, cutie!" Fable said as she took up her place at the prow and turned about, unrolling the scroll. She began to chant, the strange words singing up Dorian's spine as swirling lines glowed on Fable's skin, seeping down from the scroll, across her arms, down her legs and into the ship like a spill of swirling ivy paint. Dorian skipped back as the designs squiggled under his feet, but they didn't touch him. Though he did feel...odd.

But not as odd as when Melia hammered the core into the center of the ship's wheel.

It felt like a blast of wind hit him each time the hammer fell on the glowing stone. He whirled about in shock. "What are you—"

"Unbind us from the docks. Hurry!" Melia cried as her hammer fell again.

Unsure but out of options, Dorian did so, his sword slashing the mooring ropes. As the last came free, he caught a glimpse of movement on the docks and looked up to see Terrance straightening. The captain's eyes were murderous as they glared at the distracted Melia, his jaw tight as he unslung his bow and fitted an arrow.

Dorian's eyes widened and he lunged towards Melia just as the guard captain drew back the string to his ear and let fly.

The arrow hissed through the air, and with a frantic motion Dorian's sword ascended, slicing through the projectile mid-flight. The head flew wild, thudding into the deck near Melia's feet, yanking her attention back to the present. Both she and Terrance stared at him in shock, and even Dorian was surprised at what he'd pulled off. But it was Melia who recovered first, her hand darting to her belt and drawing her dagger once more. She flung it with unerring skill, the blade flashing through the dark before it thudded into Terrence's shoulder. The guard captain dropped his bow with a strangled cry, clutching his arm and falling to his knees.

With a snort of satisfaction, Melia gifted Dorian with a short nod of thanks, then gave her hammer a final swing, slamming the core harder into the wheel. The stone flashed, and Dorian jolted as he felt the impact as if the blow had been hammered into his own chest.

"Done!" Fable cried from the other end of the deck, rolling up her scroll.

"Good! Now, you!" Melia barked, grabbing Dorian and pushing him towards the wheel. "Fly us out of here. Now!"

"F-fly? What are you talking about? I—"

An arrow thudded into the deck. Dorian looked back sharply as dozens of guards stormed the beach, several already loosing from their bows. Black arrows hissed through the air, several planting themselves into the deck.

"Fly! Now!" Melia barked, shoving him to the wheel.

Reflexively, Dorian grabbed it. It was the only thing that made sense to do, if only to buy him a reprieve from Melia's shouting.

And then...everything changed.

He jerked upright, his eyes widening as the core flashed to life. His skin flared golden and red like living flame, the light spreading across the vessel, tracing the contours of the swirling ink Fable had enchanted across the craft. Dorian sucked in a gasp as scales grew across his arms, his fingers changing to talons, gripping the wheel in their powerful grasp.

He needed to fly. And he knew just how.

Dorian realized this like a bolt from the heavens. Understanding seemed to rush into him like a flood of information distilled right into his mind—not even that. Into his...soul. And he felt everything as though the yacht itself were a part of him.

He felt the wood of the ship and the kiss of the waters on its belly. The feel of the wind against the sails—and something more. Like threads of light spun around them, arcing up into the night sky above, beckoning them on.

He could make *The Windlass* fly.

In an act as instinctive as breathing, he willed *The Windlass* to sail. A great groan echoed through the night. The guards paused in their assault as the six oars on either side of the ship pushed themselves free. The swirls of paint seemed to shift the wood, growing it over the oarlocks and stretching out the paddles, warping and thinning them into long, narrow fingers like those of a bat's wings. No.

Like a dragon's.

Dorian's chest swelled with nameless happiness and pride as light shimmered like a membrane of gold over the ship. He leaned forward as if to physically push *The Windlass* on, and in answer the winged oars swept at the air, hurling them forward.

What a rush.

Exhilaration burned in Dorian like he was filled with light. He widened his stance, firming his grasp on the wheel as the wings of oars beat the air again, the prow of *The Windlass* rising, water skimming along the wood as it lifted into the air. More shouts came from the guards and arrows flew once more, but most too short. A few thumped into the back of the ship, a feeling tingling against Dorian's senses dimly, as if he were aware of every inch of the craft he piloted.

But it mattered not.

The wings of *The Windlass* beat again, *again*, lifting the craft finally clear of the sea and into the sky. The whirls of paint glowed gold along the ship, fading from the initial blaze until they'd burned themselves into the ship like veins of light. Dorian threw back his head and laughed aloud as the ship swept into the heavens, soaring like an eagle into the night.

"It worked!" Fable cheered, jumping up and down with glee, her hooves clicking against the ship's deck.

Melia laughed too, wild and free, her hood thrown back and hair streaming in her wake like a banner of brilliant blue flame. Dorian looked at her, shocked at her beauty in that moment, his awareness so taut and sensitive it was like he could sense everything around her. Like she glowed with life and radiance as they soared, the quickening of her pulse and beating of her heart like music thrumming in the air.

The elf turned to him, her eyes glowing as bright as her hair as she grabbed him by the cheeks, squeezing them and beaming at him. "Wonderful. Wonderful!" she cried. "I could actually kiss you!"

"But...you haven't," Dorian noted breathlessly.

Melia grinned, flashing pearly whites and pronounced canines. "No," she said, giving his face a fond squeeze. "But there are many voyages ahead of us, navigator."

"Hell, I will!" the faun hooted as she hopped into place between them and planted a smooch on his cheek. "We did it!" She then gave an identical kiss to Melia and returned to her own celebrations.

With a clopping sound Fable began to dance about the mast, her thumbs in her belt and her hooves skipping over the deck, her gentle voice singing a song in a language Dorian didn't know, but whose tune reminded him of sea shanties the fishermen would sing in the tavern after a long day.

Oh, we set our sails for cosmic seas, The Starbound Sloop and her trusty crew. Off to the stars, on the threads we flee, To the endless void, to the Black we flew.

Oh, sail with me through the Wyrmway fast, Through the glimmering passage, our fortunes cast. With hearts so brave and the cosmos vast, I'll return with gold, to my love at last.

With a laugh and a wink, Melia skipped away, joining the faun in the jig, her heels clicking as the pair noisily sang the robust tune, their relief and joy so infectious Dorian couldn't help but grin until his cheeks hurt.

And even as he did, he turned his eyes to the night sky as *The Windlass* soared towards the darkness above, a realm beyond his imagining. Already Clemmen felt far behind them, and in his heart he knew he was leaving behind the village, likely for good. The past was well and truly behind him. As the starlit future glowed ahead, he wondered with, yes, a trace of fear, but ever more excitement, just what the future might hold in its stead.

Chapter 3

As he sailed on into the starry horizon, the initial exhilaration began to fade for Dorian, replaced by a feeling he couldn't quite name. The jigging was done, and Melia had gone below to see what the ship had in stock for supplies. Fable was wandering about the deck, examining the markings made in the wood from the scroll, and Dorian was beginning to grow a little concerned.

"Ah," he said as the starry blackness grew before them. "You mentioned that whole...air bubble thing. How exactly do I go about making that? Seems important..."

Fable giggled, clopping up behind him. "Don't worry about that," she said, planting her hands on his shoulders, instantly making him jump. "You're doing great! The enchantment and the nature of the Black itself will conspire together to automatically form an air dome, or bubble, around the ship. The real worry would be failing to break the atmosphere."

"What happens then?" Dorian asked.

"We plummet to the surface in a ball of screaming flames," Fable said conversationally.

"Oh. Uh..."

"Don't worry about it," Fable teased him lightly, her fingers beginning to dig into his shoulders with slow, soothing motions, which was somewhat surprising, but Dorian wasn't sure what, if anything, he should do about it. "Really, you're doing great. You're a natural at this—a quicker study than I expected, honestly. Just keep the prow pointed at an angle like you are. Maybe lift it just a nudge. Not too far though. We're still held in the planet's gravity field. Once we're free, the core's pull will anchor us to the deck, but until then if you angle us too far, we run the risk of falling off and being pulled down towards the planet below, wailing like banshees as we disintegrate through reentry."

"I'll uh, keep that in mind," Dorian said, gradually relaxing, even enjoying the faun's touch.

"Awesome! We're honestly super grateful to find you. Really!" Fable cooed, accidentally poking the back of his head with her antler as she rubbed his shoulders harder. "And we do appreciate all your help. Things were pretty dicey there, but you pulled through. You even saved Melia, and she can be slow to trust people, so that probably helped a ton."

"Happy to contribute," Dorian chuckled, reflecting on the change in demeanor that Melia showed him after his deft deflection of Terrance's arrow. "One more question, though."

"Mhm?"

"Do I need to hold the wheel the whole trip? You made it sound like this would take a while."

Laughter echoed from the hold as Melia came up it, hoisting a crate of clinking wine bottles. "Hardly!" she said with a teasing smirk, her hair rolling with merry pink and blues. "We'll need you there until we break atmosphere, then you just set the course and keep an eye on things."

"I am new to this," Dorian reminded her.

"Too true," Fable said brightly. "But given how good you are at it so far, you'll forgive us for forgetting. See, the void is huge. Bigger than you could imagine! Scholars have spent centuries trying to understand and map it, and have gotten about as much as a grain of sand's worth on that beach you lived near. Huge expanses exist between systems and worlds, filled with things you'd never dream of! Comets and planets and moons and asteroids. Creatures that feed on and lurk between stars...Astral behemoths, stellar dragons, void gorgons and so much more!"

"I suppose we can travel faster than this then. Right?" he asked nervously.

"Nope! Well, just a bit, probably, once you get a hang of things. But that's fine, thanks to the wyrmways."

Dorian glanced back at Fable, looking at her face over her shoulder. Gods, but she was even prettier close up than she was from a distance. "The wyrm-what?"

She giggled, planting a hand on his head and turning it back around. "Eyes forward, cutie."

"Sorry."

"Anyway!" Fable continued as her hands resumed their soothing motions on his shoulders. "Wyrmways are tears in space opened by stellar dragons—beings of amazing power and intimate knowledge of the Black. And our ships can travel through those wyrmways too! It makes trips between systems take days or weeks instead of decades. The science isn't super clear, and we don't even know if dragons are sure how they do it. It's almost instinct for them, best anyone can tell."

"Dragons like my supposed ancestors?" Dorian asked with a dubious smirk. He wasn't sure he bought that part of their story just yet, that he was somehow connected to these entities they spoke of.

"Yep! You're probably not descended from a stellar dragon, but all dragons have knowledge of the wyrmway in their blood—and somehow so do navigators like you. So it's not just dragons in there. In fact, dragons are very rare. You're much more likely to run across pirates, or raiders, or space monsters."

"Or Elven Imperialists," Melia said before biting down on a cork and ripping it from a bottle with a bit more force than necessary. "They think the universe belongs to them and their empress, since they claim they're the heirs of the High Empire that used to rule a bunch of the galaxy, but the only authority they really have is their guns."

"Which, to be fair, gives them a fair bit," Fable admitted. "Even outside their core worlds."

"Are we going there?" Dorian asked.

Fable scoffed. "Of course not! They claim they police space to keep order, but the High Empire collapsed millenia ago. And outside of them, most ships will just ignore each other passing through. Usually more trouble than it's worth to try anything, but some will take shots at each other. There's dangers everywhere. Some pirates fly ships specially made to grapple and board."

"Is that what happened to you two?" Dorian asked.

There was a tense silence with that. "No," Melia said before taking a swig from her bottle, wiping her mouth on her sleeve. "We were hit by some dwarven miners guarding an asteroid ore deposit. They probably thought we were there to try and steal their prize, but we were just hiding from some pirates. Didn't matter," she said, shaking her head. "They still attacked us."

"And that's what happened to your last navigator?" he asked.

"Yeah," Melia confirmed bitterly. "Poor old bastard. Bit it on the first salvo. He barely managed to steer us towards your planet before he was lost. The rest of that crew didn't last long either."

"I'm, uh...sorry," Dorian said.

Melia shrugged, rising back to her feet, the tails of her tattered jacket fluttering. "So it goes out here," she said as she paced over to the side, gripping some rigging ropes as she gazed out over the curve of the world and into the twinkling beyond the firmament. "In my heart, it's always been just Fable and me against the rest of the universe. We never got close to our crew aside from each other." She wagged a finger at Dorian as she noted his expression. "Listen, no one said the Black was safe. At least it was quick for them. And there's worse ways to go. Like running out of air."

"That's a risk?" Dorian said.

"One of the biggest," Fable replied. "Many wrecks you find in the Black are from the crew running out of oxygen on their journey. Without that, the crew dies, of course, and their ship drifts until someone finds it, or it crashes into something. But we don't need to worry too much. There's enough air on this for us three to last at least a month. WIth that kind of time, we'll always manage to find *somewhere* to dock. An inhabited moon, another planet, an air station, or something similar. Our maiden voyage will luckily be very short." She nudged him playfully, draping her arm around his shoulders rather than continue to massage them. "How about it, cutie? Feeling a bit more confident?"

"A bit," Dorian said, and realized it was true. Sir Pentus had told him often that most fear was born from facing the unknown, and the more he learned of the realm he was entering, the less he found his unease. "But it is a lot to take in," he admitted, both to the women and himself.

"That's okay. Just focus on flying for now," Fable said, patting his shoulder. "We're almost out of the atmosphere anyway. You'll want to speed up a little bit here so we can properly leave the planet's gravity."

"Right. Sure. And ah, how do I do that?"

"Speed depends partially on the power of the navigator and on the cosmic winds that radiate between worlds. Navigators describe it like a stream they can ride a bit. Since you're dragon-blooded and were so eagerly acknowledged by our ship core, I'm positive you'll figure it out with just a bit of intention."

Recalling the threads of light he'd been seeing, Dorian gingerly adjusted the wheel, their craft drifting slightly to the right and closer to one of the shimmering strands. As they did, he felt the faint rush of acceleration as the oar wings caught loose ebbs from the great ribbon, spurring them on faster.

As the world behind them fell away, he felt a subtle tugging, like a net trying to pull a fish back into a boat. He set himself more securely on the deck, his scaled hands tightening on the wheel as the pull grew stronger, like a halter around his shoulders. Then, suddenly, it was gone, and he gasped as they soared free of the world behind them.

...And into the vastness of the dark beyond.

For a moment, Dorian could only stare in wonder at the expanse before him. More stars than he had ever seen lay out there, and among them shimmered colours like the one he'd leaned into to speed up. They flowed like great ribbons of violets, blue, purples and blacks, expanding through oblivion like riverways in the nothingness—a canvas of colours stretching across eternity.

"Wow," he exhaled, his voice breathy, not really able to conjure up enough volume to properly speak the word due to his awe.

"I know," Fable said. "I got the same feeling when I first went into the Black. There's really nothing like it."

Dorian had to agree. A dark cluster in the distance caught his attention and he looked that way. "What's that?" he asked.

"The asteroid belt," Fable said. Her hands went off his shoulders and he glanced back, seeing her pull a spyglass from her belt. She tweaked some of the strange copper rings set in it and angled it towards the distant shapes, easing it in front of Dorian's eyes. "See?"

She put on her goggles as Dorian raised the spyglass, squinting as the shapes jumped into view. It looked like huge rocks floating amongst each other in the great distance, tumbling slowly in a silent dance. Here and there, he thought he could make out the flash of lights.

"Dwarves mine them?" he asked.

"Sure do," Fable said brightly. "Must have found a really rich vein of gold or iron. There's no law out there, but every idiot knows not to get close to dwarves when they're mining. We re-learned that lesson the hardest way imaginable."

"Will they come after us?" Dorian added nervously.

"Unlikely now that we're back in space," Melia said as she leaned on the rail, glowering at the distant masses of stone, their faces pockmarked like lava rock. "We're out of their view now, and won't seem a threat or worth a chase. So long as we keep moving, anyway."

"You're, uh, sure about that, right?"

"Of course," Melia grunted, taking another drink from her bottle, then glancing back his way. "They have ships designed for navigating asteroid fields, and we don't. They wouldn't go out of their way to harass us. They'd lose their advantage. Why?"

"Because I think something is coming straight our way."

"What?" Fable yelped, pulling the telescope from his eye and putting it to hers.

Melia straightened, tense once more, one hand gripping her sheathed saber as her hair fluttered violet with worry. "What is it?" she asked, her voice higher than the norm.

Fable gulped. "He's right," she said. "One of the asteroids just fell from orbit, and it's heading right toward us!"

Chapter 4

DORIAN COULD FEEL THE panic that seized the pair. Though he couldn't quite understand what was going on around him, he felt that panic too—perhaps sympathetically, perhaps instinctively. What he did know was that his heart was beating like that of a hummingbird, adrenaline howling through his veins.

Fable hurried to the railing and passed Melia the spyglass, the elf peering through it. Dorian rushed over to join them, not sure what else to do. He wasn't sure what she saw, but by the way her hair turned from an agitated red to a sickly green he suspected it wasn't good.

"Is that normal?" he asked. "The asteroid thingy doing that, I mean."

"No," Melia answered frankly, lowering the spyglass. "Not one fucking bit. Back on the helm, navigator! Angle the bow of the ship upward!"

"How?" he asked.

"*You're* the navigator! *You* know how, not me," she hissed, her hair glowing red again. "At least you'd better, or we're well and truly boned."

"I..." Dorian trailed off just after starting to protest, interrupted by the fact that he suddenly realized he *did* know. He returned to the ship's wheel and rested his hands on it, and the scales covering them emerged up to his elbows. The moment he thought of his intention, the ship seemed to sense his want like a spouse of fifty years, the oar wings tilting subtly, shifting their course so the ship flew at a higher angle.

But much to Dorian's growing alarm, the space rock seemed to adjust its flight too. It was near enough now that he could make out its movement without the need for Fable's spyglass.

"What is that thing?" he asked as Melia and Fable scrambled behind him.

"Probably a golem," Fable said. "The dwarves must have dug too deep and woken it up. It happens."

"Fuck," Melia growled. "I wish we had some fucking weapons! I feel so useless!"

Dorian ignored Melia's frustration to focus on what he needed to know. "Why's it coming after us?"

"Who cares!" Melia barked, striding across the deck. "Philosophize about it later! So long as we get far enough from the field that spawned it, it'll probably give up the chase. And since we don't have any way to defend ourselves in this giant bathtub, that means we need to go faster!"

"Faster?" Dorian asked.

"As fast as you can, navigator! Or it's going to break this ship like we sailed into a cliff swinging haymakers!"

Melia certainly knew how to motivate someone, Dorian mused. He gripped the wheel tighter, tensing as he urged their craft to speed up. He shivered as he felt a tingle race through him and the sense of acceleration grow, *The Windlass* soaring through the void with the sudden sense of giddy speed.

"Holy cogs and bottles!" Fable gasped in amazement. "Look at that!"

"What?! What now?!" Dorian asked frantically, looking around in case they now had a flight of dragons on their ass or some demon made of pure darkness crawling along the hull, but then he noticed that Fable was pointing at him. "...What is it?" he said again, this time uneasily.

Melia too was gawking, but she simply pointed behind him. Dorian glanced back and stared in wonder at what looked like a pair of immense translucent dragon wings stretching out from his back, outlined by motes of light like a constellation of shimmering gold and fire growing from his body. "Holy shit!" he muttered.

"He's got horns too!" Fable squeaked in amazement, the faun's eyes filled with more stars than the void around them.

"I do?" Dorian said. "Is...is that normal?"

"Never heard of it before," Fable breathed in awe. "Never seen...anything like this. How do you feel?"

"Terrified!"

"Good! That's good to know. Oh gosh, I gotta get my notepad!"

"Less note taking, more flying!" Melia barked, snapping out of her trance and pointing back at the asteroid golem. "Fable! Quick! Unfurl the sails! We need more astral wind!"

Fable jumped. "Oh! Er, right! Sure. Right away!"

Dorian watched as the pair ran together to the mast and hurriedly unfurled the sails. The great canvas fell with a rattle of the boom, bellying almost at once as it caught the cosmic wind that surged them onwards. Dorian jerked at the sudden burst of speed *The Windlass* caught, soaring ever faster.

"Where am I flying to?" he asked breathlessly.

"Away from the elemental. The most direct path we can take," Melia said as she finished securing the sail. Dorian tried not to be distracted by her ever-changing mane of colour, keeping his eyes on the wheel and what lay ahead of the ship's bow.

"And try to keep in mind what you're feeling!" Fable added giddily as she clopped across the deck. "I'll be quizzing you later! Unless we're dead. In which case we don't have anything to look forward to. So, try and avoid that, please!"

"Very motivating," Dorian said through gritted teeth as the hairs on his nape pricked up. Ahead of them, he made out shapes in their path. It looked like a vast field of rocky debris. He tensed, shifting the wheel sharply as one flew towards them, *The Windlass* swerving past it and ducking another tumbling mass of interstellar stone.

Dorian dared a look back, and one look was truly enough. Even with all their haste the asteroid was catching up. He could now see six immense holes in the face of the stone, all glowing like some inner forge blazed with hellfire. Below these, a maw opened in the rocky face. Teeth of jagged stone gnashed and huge arms formed from the sides, batting aside smaller asteroids that spun in its path.

Dorian turned ahead once more, ashen faced. And yet...exhilarated. Grinning. Almost laughing.

Which was insane. Utterly so. An immense stone monster from beyond the stars was trying to turn him into paste, and yet he'd never felt more alive, nor more sure of himself. His body sang like he himself was flying. His skin tingled. Energy raced through him and quickened his pulse, surging like a cauldron boiled within his belly. His head felt light. He felt good. *So* good! He felt like he could do anything at all!

Specifically, he felt as though he could outrun the monster behind them.

He dared to look back another time and his heart jumped into his throat at the sight of the creature suddenly so close that the fire of its eyes lit up the rear of the ship. It raised an arm of crags and rough stone, reaching for them. It let out a roar like the end of days.

"Dorian!" Melia cried, grabbing hold of the mast as the sails blew in the astral wind. "Please, Dorian! You can do this!"

"You're goddamn right." Dorian turned ahead once more. His talons tightened on the spokes of the wheel. He tensed as if to bodily shove the ship forward. He drew on the heat that seemed to fill him, his body blazing with golden light. "**Move!**" Dorian roared at the ship, gripping the wheel tighter and tighter. "Move your fat, wooden ass, *please*!"

A burst of speed ripped through him like the answer to a prayer. The golden veins that threaded the ship flared like a new sun dawning, and *The Windlass* soared forward so fast Dorian barely had enough time to spin out of the way of another asteroid.

Melia shrieked as her grip failed and she tumbled, falling against the rail, clinging onto it for dear life. Fable yelped, knocked off her hooves and slid across the deck before hitting the mast again, hugging it for deer life.

A bellowing roar of rage denied came from behind them and Dorian risked a final look back. The asteroid golem was being left behind. Moreover, it was receding. The lights that glowed in its eyes had begun to dim and grow small, and its reaching arm fell, molding itself once more against the bulk of its form.

Panting, Dorian sagged against the wheel, his hands still clinging to it for dear life. *The Windlass* began to decelerate, slowing to a more manageable speed, though still fast enough. The wings of light behind him seemed to dissolve like mist, breaking away until the glow around him had dimmed. Suddenly, Dorian felt terribly drained, like he'd been the one physically pushing the ship that last great burst of distance.

"Where the hell did that speed come from?" Melia gasped as she got her feet back under her.

"S...search me," Dorian managed, a feral grin splitting his face.

Melia laughed breathlessly. "Looks like this one's full of surprises, Fable."

"I'll say," the faun said. Rising, she skipped quickly to the back of the ship and fetched her spyglass out, training it on the space behind them. "Either way, looks like our craggy friend's given up. It's drifting back towards the asteroid field. See, golems are normally locked to the spawning zone where they were created. Which means they-"

"Fan...fantastic," Dorian interrupted. "Maybe. ..maybe give me a second here first. Just...just need to catch my breath..."

Melia chuckled and moved across the deck. Dorian turned his head as she came up behind him and gently touched his scale-covered hand, tilting the wheel. "Here," she said. "See that glow? That bright star just to the right of the prow?"

Dorian looked ahead quickly, feeling a different kind of heat rise in him as Melia's soft breasts in her tight shirt pressed into his back. "Er, yeah?"

"Set our course towards that," she said, her breath warm in his ear and scented faintly of wine. She was doing this on purpose, he was sure, though she'd never admit it. "It'd take ages to fly directly to a distant star, but somewhere close, between here and there, is where we need to be. Once you have your trajectory set, you can get away from the wheel for a bit as it should be smooth sailing from here."

Dorian did as asked, straightening a little as he adjusted the wheel. "Like that?"

"Perfect," she hummed, then stepped away from him, suddenly slapping him on the back. "Now let go of that wheel and join us. It's time to party!"

"As one does when one survives a scrape with death!" Fable giggled.

Dorian did so slowly, his fingers gripping the wheel so hard he fairly had to peel them off one by one. As he released the wheel at last, most of his scales receded, returning his hands to normal, save for some lingering stragglers. He turned them over curiously and gave a push of his will. To his amazement and delight, the scales regrew, along with his talons. That would be a useful trick, he mused. He looked up at Melia. "Sorry, party?"

"Damn straight!" Fable cheered as she popped the cork from one of the bottles Melia had brought from below. "P. A. R. T. Why? Because we simply *must*!"

With that cheerful declaration, Fable tipped back her bottle and took a long swig, her doe-ish ears flicking in delight. Dorian couldn't help but laugh as he accepted a bottle from Melia. "Well," he said, growing a talon once more and using it to yank the cork from the bottle. "Lord Clemmen did always have great taste in wine, so I hear."

"That's the spirit," Melia said, clinking her bottle against his, her fluorescent hair swaying behind her shoulders. "Drink up, navigator! We're alive and free, and in this business, that's always good enough reason to have some fun!"

Chapter 5

THOUGH HE MAY HAVE found himself sailing through the stars instead of the seas, one thing Dorian discovered that was the same was that when it was time to drink, it was time to tell stories.

Dorian took another swig as he listened to Fable and Melia spin another yarn of the strange sights they'd seen among the stars. He found every word they spoke captivating—and not just because they were so damn pretty and he was getting a bit into his cups. This current tale was about a small world borne on the back of a turtle, covered in trees, with rivers running through the cracks between the spots of the turtle's shell.

"And the whole world was flat!" Melia said.

"Right!" Fable giggled. "Well, not flat *exactly*. It was kind of like...A bulge!" Absent-mindedly, perhaps, she pointed at the crotch of Dorian's pants and continued on, innocently enough. "It was almost as weird as that planet where the grass was blue and everyone had one eye."

"One eye? Come now, you're just making random shit up at this point," Dorian accused her with a chuckle and a punctuating swig.

Fable trilled with laughter, her hooves kicking the deck in amusement. "Stars and garters! If you think that's crazy, you're in for some real shocks out in the Black!"

"But fine, navigator," Melia said as she downed another gulp of wine. She pointed the neck of the bottle at him. "You tell us the craziest thing *you* ever saw in your peasant existence. Hm?"

"Something crazy?" Dorian repeated, though this time like a question, scratching his chin thoughtfully. "Hmm. Well, there was this one time two goblins in a long coat came into the inn and tried to order a beer."

Fable choked on the wine she'd been drinking. "Two goblins in...what!" she giggled.

"No no! Really," Dorian said, chuckling. "The top one was even wearing a fake beard! And he introduced himself as Hugh Mann. We felt so bad for them we just gave them the drink and didn't even charge. Seemed like they had a rough day."

Fable hooted, slapping her thigh with mirth and even Melia let loose a ribald laugh at the thought. "Not bad, navigator. Not bad," Melia said. "But doesn't exactly compare, does it? You'll find plenty of goblins out here in very different circumstances, I assure you."

Dorian shrugged. "You're right, of course," he agreed with a sigh. "But less than a day ago, I was just worried about hanging laundry and how to cook tomorrow's potatoes. So this has all been a bit overwhelming for me, truth be told. More's happened to me in the last few hours than in my whole life, it seems like."

"That's the Black," Fable chirped merrily. "You're never sure what you're gonna get out here! And there's plenty more where that asteroid golem came from, I promise. But it's not all bad, and the whole universe is at your feet! That's the benefit of being a navigator. You'll get to see as much as you want!"

Dorian took another drink of his wine, feeling pleasantly warm and relaxed in the pair's strange company. "Are all navigators dragon-related?" he asked.

"Lots of them, yeah," Fable said happily, always apparently glad to expound on some facts. "But there's other ways to venture into the voids even if you're not. True dragonbloods are not exactly common, so we find other ways to get around it when there's a scarcity, which there often is. Some navigators are just powerful mages that manipulate the etherium to sail. Others use tokens stolen from dragons, like their blood, or stored souls. Some even use ships melded or bound to creatures able to naturally travel the wyrmways. Others use mined mana crystals to enable their passage."

"That's one of the most dangerous ways," Melia said, her hair shimmering to a dour grey like stormy skies. "The radiation from using the crystals causes them to start sprouting on their skin. Our old navigator, Bilford, used them. He had to file them down everyday, but it was already getting really bad. We were actually looking for you to replace him. If he'd kept using them, within a few years they'd start growing internally, and kill him."

Dorian shivered at the thought of such a horrific fate. "And he *chose* to do it? Why?"

"You kidding? Look at this," Fable said, gesturing at the starlit void around them, threaded with ribbons of shimmering hues. "Plenty of people would pay near any price to venture out among the stars. For a natural-born adventurer, it's the height of the game."

Dorian tilted back his head, taking in the endless expanse around them. Despite himself, he found he agreed. Had he known what lay beyond the skies of his homeworld, would he not have done most anything to see more? It was a giddy thought, he mused as he took another drink from his bottle.

"I suppose so," he admitted.

"Of course!" Melia scoffed. "Out here, we're truly free. Free of every bond and chain to keep you down. Though there are those with long arms and far-reaching eyes, you can hide among the stars pretty much forever if you know what you're doing."

"You've never thought of settling down?" Dorian asked.

Melia snorted and took another swig. "Not with as many enemies as I've made," she said with a fierce grin of fang, her hair tinting back to a smoldering red. "Shouldn't stay too long in one place lest they find you. Eventually they might forget their grudges. Maybe someday it'll be possible, but not now."

Dorian glanced between the pair. "What is it you two do, exactly?"

Fable fluttered her hands. "Oh, this and that. Shipping, bounty hunting, smuggling, salvaging. Most anything that keeps us in the skies and well fed."

"You're criminals?" Dorian asked warily. "Have I fallen in with criminals?"

"That'd imply there's some sort of law up here," Melia snickered, shaking her head. "And if there's one thing you learn fast in the Black, it's that the only laws are the ones that you can enforce from the other end of a sword—or arcane cannon."

Dorian wasn't sure what he thought about that. But then, he was new to this whole world (well, worlds), so decided to keep it to himself.

"But enough talk," Melia grunted, slamming the butt of her bottle down on the deck, grinning at them both like the saltiest sea dog Dorian had ever seen. "Who wants some *real* fun?"

"What kind of fun?" Dorian asked.

Fable merely rolled her eyes.

Melia chuckled as one hand snuck into her jacket pocket and came back out. "I'm talking...d ice!" she declared, fingers uncurling and revealing a handful of six sided dice.

"Dice?" Dorian muttered in confusion. "Sounds...simple."

"We'll play a game called High Rollers," Melia said, her hair lightening to a playful blue flutter. "We each roll and try to guess if the other person got higher or lower than our roll."

"And the stakes are?" Dorian said.

"This'll be good," Fable said with a wink his way.

Melia grinned wider. "The loser has to take a shot of whiskey. And drink it from the winner's mouth!"

Dorian's eyes popped at the suggestion. "What?"

"We don't even have whiskey," Fable said.

"Sure we do! There's a bottle down below," Melia quickly rebutted.

"We're not doing that," Fable huffed, a suspicious gleam in her eyes. "You're too drunk and horny. You'll regret it tomorrow."

"Er, how about the loser just takes a shot from the wine bottle?" Dorian suggested before Melia could process what Fable just said. "Keep things simple."

Melia scoffed, then hiccuped. "You're both boring. But fine! We'll play it your way."

Dorian sighed in relief. Not that he didn't find Melia's suggestion intriguing in a very tangible way, but with how buzzed the elf was already, he had a sneaking suspicion she might have punished him for jumping on the idea once she sobered up. And he suspected that Melia wouldn't take it too well if she lost, either. Considering how eager she'd been with the sword on their first meeting, Dorian reasoned it would be wise to temper the merriment a bit until they knew each other better.

The dice and cups to hide them were passed out between the three of them and the rolls began, and as they played, Dorian learned something else about Melia.

She was a terrible gambler.

"Fuck!" the elf cursed as the cups came up once more to reveal everyone's dice, and her as the loser. She always played against the odds, relying on big gambles and her own luck to lead her to victory. It rarely did, and it seemed she had trouble hiding her true thoughts, thanks to the shifting hues of her hair.

"Drinkie time!" Fable cheered, looking flushed, but not half as much as Melia.

"I know," Melia said, her voice slurring just a bit, her face red and her hair swirling an even brighter pink. In fact, Dorian could swear he saw bubbles shimmer in those hues, like she was wearing a crown of carbonated pink drink. Melia snatched up the bottle and took a swig, slamming it down and making the dozen or so other bottles near at hand rattle and clink.

"You've drunk a lot," Dorian noted. "We should probably slow down."

"I've drunken more before," Melia said hotly. "Like that one time. Right? Remember that...time?"

"Uh...no?" Dorian said. "I just met you."

"Psh!" Melia said. "You're just jealous I can hold my liquor so good!"

"Oh yeah. We're suuuuper impressed," Fable giggled, elbowing Dorian with a wink.

"Shut up! And you!" she declared, rounding on Dorian.

"Me?" he said.

"Yeah," Melia growled, pointing at Dorian. "You think you're so...so hot and badass just because...because you're so sexy. Hm?"

"Uh..."

"Well you get...get punished now!" she said.

"How do you—"

He trailed off as Melia crawled across the deck towards him. He leaned back as the elf suddenly swung herself around and planted her ass in his lap. Dorian sucked in a breath as she leaned against his chest, looking extremely smug like she just taught him a lesson, her soft bottom pressing down on him in a very distracting way.

"There!" Melia barked, tossing her head and shimmering violet hair. "Now you...you're my chair for the rest of...of the night. Serves you (*hic!*) right!"

"I uh..."

Fable burst into giggles, her laughter so hard she actually toppled over, holding her sides as she cackled with naked hilarity at his predicament, also hiccuping every now and then.

"Yeah," Melia said, slumping against him, her head lolling a bit. "Yeah. How 'bout that? You're nice 'nd...nice 'nd soft 'nd...smell good 'nd..."

Dorian raised an eyebrow as Melia's head rested against his shoulder, a soft snore coming from the elf, her hair still fluttering with pink that tickled his nose. In his time working at the inn back on his homeworld, he'd had plenty of experience with drunken housewives, maidens, and the like flirting with him, but never something so brazen as this in front of other people. He was entirely clueless as to how to act. All he knew was that taking advantage of her in her compromised state was not something he would be doing.

"Hee hee...ha ha. Ha...Awww..." Fable giggled, having rolled onto her side and was observing him with a teasing smile. "Looks like someone got all tuckered out."

"Looks like it," Dorian agreed with a sigh, but he smiled. Melia had complimented his scent, but he very much wanted to return the compliment. She smelt sort of fruity, maybe partially owing to the sweet wine they'd had earlier and which she spilled on her clothes here and there.

Still giggling now and then, the faun swung her legs back under her and rose to her feet, her deer-like ears twitching and cheeks warm and pink. "C'mon, cutie. Let's get her to bed down below. You gotta carry her, though. You're the designated chair." She winked at him.

Dorian rolled his eyes, but did realize he was probably the only one sober enough for the job. He wondered how Fable felt about this beyond what she showed him on her red-cheeked face. Up until now, she'd been the main one flirting with him, and suddenly her friend was putting the moves on strong. Didn't she care or at least find it awkward? She didn't seem to be put off at all.

Looping his arms under Melia, he rose to his feet, the elf muttering and snuggling against his chest, which really wasn't helping his troubled libido. He forced himself not to look at the elf's breasts as they pressed against his chest, and he followed the tipsy faun down the stairs into *The Windlass's* below decks.

The cabin was fit for a lord, which was hardly surprising, with one large bed and another smaller one at the other side of the room. The glow of stars filtered through the large window at the back, illuminating the room of charts, a large desk, a table and more. Several paintings hung on the walls, one of which depicted Lord Clemmen heroically riding a steed along the rocky shore. Dorian made a mental note to throw it over the side the first chance he got.

Fable yawned largely and clopped unsteadily across the room to the smaller bed. "Finally," she murmured, throwing herself onto it with a groan of satisfaction, snuggling deep into the blankets.

Dorian carried Melia to the larger bed and carefully laid her down on it. Melia murmured as he slid his arms out from under her, and her hand came up and grabbed the front of his shirt.

Dorian froze as Melia's eyes fluttered open. "Dad?" she muttered softly.

"Uh..." he said uncertainly.

Melia murmured and tugged him closer. "Didn't think I'd see you..." she whispered, her hair shimmering a softer blue. "Don't go. Please."

"I'm not your father," Dorian said gently. "It's me. Dorian. Er, the navigator."

Melia's other hand rose, sleepily rubbing her eyes. She peered up at him, a bit more clarity in her glowing blues. "Mmm," she said with a strange smile. "You can hold me too, if you want."

Dorian swallowed thickly, but Melia merely laughed, then yawned, her hand slipping from his shirt as she rolled over, curling up on the bed. Dorian sighed and pulled the blankets over the elf, a contented hum escaping her as she snuggled into the sheets. A low snore soon followed.

The sound made Dorian chuckle and he shook his head, lightly leaving the cabin and closing the door behind him. The pair deserved a rest. He could stay up a bit longer and mind the ship, just in case. Still smiling, he strode back up onto the deck and took a seat in front of the wheel. In the silence of space, he looked into the canvas of stars, and mused what a change to a man's outlook a single day could make.

Chapter 6

Dorian was still awake when, several hours later, he heard the familiar clip-clop of Fable's hooves. Moments later, the faun emerged from below deck, looking even more disheveled than before, with brown pigtails further rumpled, goggles askew, and jacket sliding down arms to bare shoulders and a sleeveless white undershirt. The faun yawned into her hand, ears flicking as she spotted him and smiled blearily.

"Hey there," she said, her voice taking on a coquettish tone despite the tiredness lingering in her gaze.

"Sleep well?" he asked from where he sat before the helm.

"You know it! Aren't *you* tired?"

He shrugged, surprising himself as he thought about it. "Not really."

"Yeah. I've heard those with dragonblood can get energized by the mana streams of the heavens. It's how the stellar dragons managed to fly for so long on their migration routes. You might be good for days! Mind if I keep track of it?"

"Don't see why not," Dorian said.

"Attaboy," Fable giggled cheerily as she plopped down next to him, tilting back her head and gazing at the heavens. Looking up, she sighed. "Gorgeous view, huh?"

"It really is," Dorian agreed. "But...a bit lonely too."

"Yeah," Fable said, leaning back and kicking her hooves carelessly. "But lots of beautiful things are. The tallest mountains. The widest seas. I sometimes wonder, you know, if there's something kinda...inherent in those kinds of places. Right? Like, their loneliness and remoteness is what makes them beautiful."

"Maybe," Dorian mused.

Fable smiled at him, then nudged him with an elbow. "Did you enjoy our little celebration last night?" she asked.

He chuckled. "Very."

"And did you hold Melia like she asked?" Fable teased impishly, pantomiming a self-embrace and rocking her body left and right.

Dorian felt his face colour and coughed into his fist. "You, uh, heard that, huh?"

"I'm a light sleeper," she giggled. "But don't worry about it. Melia gets kinda maudlin when she gets drunk. Most of us do, of course, but she has some unresolved issues."

"I didn't know..."

Fable waved it off. "It's fine. It's fine. She doesn't like talking about it, but if you're shipping with us, you may as well know. Melia came from an agri-spire—a farming station, basically. They're like living trees in the void of space, and support elves like her, but also produce long-lasting fruits and veggies we voyagers use in our travels. They make for great improvised air stations if you can fly into their orbit and don't need to dock or resupply. They don't always welcome random visitors."

Dorian looked at her with an arched brow, trying to take it all in. "Sounds interesting," he said noncommittally.

"Anyway, she'd been training to be a tender for the tree, before her parents got sick."

"Sick?"

"Yeah," Fable said sadly. "It was bad, and the medicine was rare and expensive. She jumped on the very next ship to try and earn the gold to pay for their treatment."

"Did she?"

"She did," Fable said softly. "But by the time she had the gold, they were gone."

"Oh," Dorian muttered, able to guess well enough what she meant by 'gone'.

Fable nodded. "Yeah," she said. "And the thing about tenders is that they have to be with the tree. Break the connection once, and it's almost impossible to repair. When she skipped out on her training, she couldn't just plug back in—especially not in her brokenhearted state. So when she came home, there was nothing left for her but to mourn her parents. So she just kept going through the stars. It was all she knew to do."

Dorian mulled over this information, feeling the weight of it. He could barely imagine such a decision, or the devastation of discovering its futility.

"I see," he said at last. "She makes a bit more sense all of a sudden. As rough as she often seems to be, I mean."

Fable patted his back. "Yeah. She has a good heart, really. Just a bit…rough around the edges. But she'll open up eventually. Just give her time. And, you know, keep this to yourself. She wouldn't be too happy to find out I let the catgirl out of the bag, but you should know."

"Right," Dorian said, then glanced at the faun. "And, what about you?"

"Me?" she said, brightening with a smile.

"Yeah. I mean, what do you do around the ship? Where are you from? Anything I should know, I guess."

"Aw, you're such a flatterer!" Fable giggled, giving his shoulder a playful shove. "Well," she said, drawing herself up importantly. "I'm an auramancer, which means I sense the auras around living things."

"What's an aura?"

"It's kind of like," Fable began, wiggling her fingers expressively. "the presence living things have in magical space. You, me, the stars, they all have auras to varying degrees. And magic does especially. Now that we're away from your planet, I can finally get a good sense for where the wyrmgate is."

"Which is the entrance to the wyrmway, I assume?" Dorian said.

"Bingo bango! You got it. We're lucky it's so near your world. I can sense that baby like a beacon. And auras are also super handy at spotting things like enemies and the like. But that's not all I can do. I'm also a minor enchanter and arcanoengineer."

"Er..."

"Means I work with magic machines," she said with a twinkle of a smile as she tapped the telescope in her belt. "Like this! Made it myself. And the engines for our old ship. And when we're looking to upgrade this one with new enchantments someday down the line, I can aid with that, too! The auramancy really helps with it. I can even sense the moods of those I read. Well, sometimes. Unless they're really good at hiding it. But I can't read synthetic life, like that golem from before."

"I see. I...think," Dorian said.

She patted his hand. "Don't worry about it if you don't yet. You'll see what I can do soon enough. And you've already seen what Melia can do. She's our combat specialist. Great with a sword and a cutting remark, as you may have noticed."

Dorian rubbed his neck where Melia's sword had been not so long ago. "I did."

Fable giggled. "Yeah. But she's great to have on your side! And so am I. I've got lots of skills I learned over the last century."

"Century? As in...a hundred years?"

"Sure do. I'm pretty spry for an old lady, eh?" Fable giggled impishly.

Dorian shook his head in wonder. Fable barely looked his age, and with her height, maybe even a year or two under twenty. But a century! It stunned him at the thought. "That's...wow."

"Yeah," Fable sighed with a lazy smile. "I'm just full of surprises."

It was then that Dorian noticed that the faun was leaning against his side, her head resting on his shoulder, her ears giving a playful flick. Her head was angled so that her antlers wouldn't poke his cheek. It felt very intentional. The warmth of her body tingled through him, and he found himself looking down at her soft face and round, lidded eyes. He felt his throat grow rough and cleared it. "I ah..."

The clop of footsteps coming up the stairs had Fable suddenly ease off him and stand, smiling as if nothing had happened just as Melia appeared from below deck. The elf looked annoyed, her face drawn and frowning, her hair flickering like embers of flame as she climbed aloft. But she looked more rested than she had when he'd slid her into bed, and the lightness of her steps attested to that.

And was it him, Dorian thought, or did something almost happen there? Had Fable really been so close, and then eased off when her friend arrived? The tension might have been his imagination, but Dorian wondered about that.

"Got a headache like a dwarf with a hammer thinks there's mana crystals in my skull," the elf growled as she moved onto the deck.

"Aw, come on," Fable said lightly. "You always recover fast once you get moving. Besides, if you knew it'd happen, you shouldn't have drunk so much!"

"Ugh, don't remind me," Melia groused. "Everything from last night is an absolute blur." She peeked one eye at the pair of them, leaving the other closed, as though she was trying to gauge whether or not they'd bought what she'd just claimed.

"Oh really?" Fable said skeptically, her hooves clopping and arms clasped behind her back impishly. "Then, I guess you don't remember stripping down to your skivvies?"

Melia glared at the faun. "I did not!"

"So you *do* remember!"

"No, I just know I'd never do something like that."

"But you did call Dorian 'daddy,'" she added with a grin.

Melia's eyes flashed to Dorian and a light blush coloured her cheeks. "No I...Ugh! Forget it! Are we at least on course for the wyrmgate?"

"Mhm," Fable hummed happily. She rose to the tips of her hooves, bending a little as she balanced herself, for a moment reminding Dorian of a very pretty weathervane. "Mmm...Yes! Should be there within a day. We can take it to the Guldraka system and land on Sphere within the week."

"Finally, some good news," Melia sighed. "And I've got some more," she added, lifting the bag she'd brought from below. "This ship was overflowing with food supplies. Mostly jerky, some barrels of fruit, and the bread'll probably start going sooner rather than later, so we'd better get on that. But for now, who wants some dried meat?"

"Me! Me!" Fable cheered eagerly. "Finally! Booze is wonderful, but it's just not that filling after a nap," she told Dorian with a wink.

Only then did Dorian realize how truly famished he was. He wondered how he didn't notice before, but given all the danger and excitement, he supposed it could be excused. Gladly, he took a number of strips from the bag, settling on a barrel near the other two as they ate in comfortable silence.

"This is nice," Dorian said after swallowing his first bite of jerky. "Sharing a meal with crewmates, I mean. It's a new feeling."

Fable glanced up at him. "Nice?" she said around two pieces of jerky.

"Nothing. I'm just enjoying it. I don't know. Feels...homey," Dorian said, then laughed at himself.

Melia snorted. "Don't buy too deep into it," she said. "This life goes through people like a meat grinder. They die, move on, get jobs elsewhere, move to a pioneer planet, whatever. It's a risky life. But the pay is good, if you live to spend it."

"Is that what we're going to this...Sphere for?" Dorian asked.

"Mhmm," Fable said, swallowing and patting her chest. "Yep! This ship isn't bad for a fresh groundling conversion, but we should outfit it with some extra equipment to make it a real void sailer. Some weapons, better food, and maybe some auxiliary sails, engines, and enchantments. But all that's gonna cost money, and Sphere is the place to get it!"

"By stealing it?" Dorian inquired warily.

"Ha! I wish. That'd make things easier," Melia said, shaking her head. "No. But Sphere always has plenty of people with work for privateers like us. We'll get a job and some gold easily enough, now that we have a real navigator."

"Glad to be of help," Dorian chuckled, taking another bite.

"You'll be more than a bit of help," Fable said brightly. "We're going to be relying on you a lot. But hey! The perks are pretty great. You get to hang out with us! Plus whoever else we pick up. We'll want some more bodies to fill out the crew—maybe just one for now should be enough."

"So what is Sphere like, then?" he asked.

Melia and Fable exchanged a knowing look. "You'll see," the faun said teasingly.

Dorian frowned, but neither of the women elaborated further. And they had plenty of tasks to keep him occupied afterwards. He was made to man the helm, Fable tweaking their course until they were properly on route, and then the three of them did an inventory of the ship's goods. It was pretty good, which didn't surprise Dorian. Lord Clemmen liked his ship ready to go whenever he felt the whim to travel, and there was even a fair bit of clothes, arms, armour, food and fresh water aboard. Fable approved of some of the fabric, noting they could sell some, and teasingly remarking about some lingerie she found in a hidden drawer. Melia took stock of the weapons, muttering about their quality under her breath. He couldn't tell if she was pleased or not.

During this, Dorian was at the helm, practicing his presence with the wheel and the flow of magic. It felt good, he noted with some surprise. Natural even. As if the means to pilot the ship had been a part of him all along. He'd always been fast to pick up new skills, but he was pretty sure flying a ship through space should take a bit more than an afternoon to become adept at. He eyed the core embedded in the center of the wheel, watching the hues shimmer across the sphere.

He wondered...

A sudden crash yanked his attention back to the present. He looked sharply amidship to see Fable standing over the ruins of a crate she'd dropped. Her eyes were faintly glowing, locked on the horizon, her body trembling like a sounding pole that had struck the bottom.

"What?" Dorian asked.

"Something's coming," she said breathlessly. "A lot of somethings!"

Dorian looked in the direction she'd indicated. He left the wheel, joining Fable as the faun hurried to the side, pulling her spyglass out and training it on the distance. Dorian peered out at the shimmering hues of space, and realized he could make out some dim, distant shapes.

"What are they?" he asked.

As he did, Melia bounded from below decks, rapier already drawn, hair blazing with violet agitation. "What happened? What's going on?" she demanded.

Fable's tongue stuck out the corner of her mouth as she adjusted the spyglass, and suddenly a grin split her worried face. She laughed in relief, lowering the spyglass. "Stars and cogs! Just a convoy," she said.

"Convoy?" Dorian repeated the word as a question.

With a grin, Fable passed over the spyglass. Taking it up, Dorian trained it on the distant shapes.

A train of ships jumped into view, but unlike any vessel he had seen before. Great, sweeping things with four long shapes like some sort of fish trap built around a central block like an immense wooden rectangle, sails sprouted all over the radiating crafts, bellying in the astral winds that ferried them forward.

"They look...odd," Dorian said.

"Merchant fleet," Fable explained lightly. "Those ships were built exclusively in space. No need for a proper hull or to take gravity into account. They ply the wyrmways between stations, dragging cargo along and selling it at premiums. Lot of them too."

"Should we be worried?" Dorian asked as he handed her back the telescope, the crafts now near enough he could make them out with the naked eye.

"Probably not," Melia said, walking up beside them and peering at the strange vessels cruising towards them. "Looks like they're heading to the wyrmgate too. Must be on a transport run."

Dorian nodded along, watching as the ships drew in closer. One in particular caught his eye. The lead vessel resembled the others, but instead of a central block, it appeared to have been built around something like an immense slug. The creature's faintly translucent skin shimmered with light, its body fluttering like it were propelling itself onward through the motions of the many fans which lined it.

"What is that thing?" he breathed.

"Star Scallop," Fable told him. "Real docile creatures, and good at finding their way through the wyrmways. They must not have a navigator, so they tamed it to guide them."

As she said this, one of the smaller ships in the convoy broke off, speeding towards them. Dorian tensed as the smaller craft hovered near, the ship resembling more their own than the huge crafts plowing through the shimmering sky, and over the rail that ran along its deck appeared a diminutive figure…who didn't get much bigger despite their proximity.

"Hello there!" the halfling cried. Dressed in a fine purple vest, he lounged back on his heels, his portly belly straining the bottom buttons of the fabric, tousled brown hair on his head and a heavy gold medallion riding the slope of his belly from a chain around his neck. "Fine day for a cruise."

"Sure is," Fable said jovially. "What's shipping?"

The halfling laughed, his belly wobbling. "Why, most everything, my dear! But especially space jellies. Off for processing! Why, you can make most anything with them. Soap and food and more than you can dream." He tapped two fingers to his brow jovially. "Mebus Clamber! Captain of the *Pot Skimmer*, at your service."

"Fable of *The Windlass*," Fable said, hooves clopping as she dipped in a merry bow before gesturing at Dorian and Melia. "And this is Dorian and Melia."

"Heading our way?" the halfling asked. "Safety in numbers and all that, and we'd be delighted to have you along."

"Gladly," Fable chirped back, kicking up a hoof as she leaned on the guardrail.

Mebus gave them another lazy salute, and his ship cruised back into the swarm of the rest of the vessels.

Dorian watched him go uncertainly. "You're sure about this?" he asked Fable.

"Absolutely," she said, beaming. "He had a good aura. Trustworthy and kind-hearted, not guarding his nature at all. We can trust him. At least to travel."

"He's really doing us a favour," Melia said, albeit somewhat begrudgingly. "Safety in numbers indeed. Especially near a wyrmgate. Pirates and worse sometimes stake them out and prey on ships just as they're heading into the gate. Bring us in close, Dorian," she said. "But...keep an eye out. Just in case."

Dorian nodded, returning to the helm. Scales flowed over his hands as he gripped the wheel, easing *The Windlass* closer to the great hulls of the convoy of ships. As he did, he marvelled at the scale of them and their journey through the stars. Like a school of fish in the company of whales. And he knew with utter certainty that this was going to be a sight that would stay with him all his days.

Chapter 7

THOUGH AT FIRST WARY of the strange ships, Dorian quickly found a benefit of their presence beyond the oft repeated "strength in numbers" boon. Having them so near allowed him to converse with Mebus, and getting the perspective of someone other than Fable and Melia was quite refreshing.

That, of course, was not to say he didn't trust the pair, but the halfling had less reason to be cagey about any information Dorian wanted as he didn't expect to live with the consequences of saying too much. Even better, he was surely eager to share all he knew.

"Years?" Dorian said in amazement. "Like, literal *years*?"

"Oh yes!" Mebus said as he sat on the rail of his boat, smoking a curving corncob pipe contentedly as his comically large feet idly kicked the air. "Some people don't set foot on a single world for decades—it's just air stations and commercial hubs for many of us. Why, I've known some who've been born among the stars and never known the touch of a single true planet. Many simply have no need! Why, they'd find the sheer size of such a thing truly outrageous!"

Dorian shook his head in amazement, leaning on the rail of *The Windlass*. "Do you miss it? Your own world, I mean, assuming you came from one."

Mebus shrugged. "I did, and I still do from time to time. Still, I'm happier in the astral playground, coasting through the Black from place to place. Traveling with a convoy is the rare sort of aimless lifestyle that knows exactly where we'll be from week to week or month to month. To each their own, says I. There's little reason to miss it in many ways. I—"

"Mebus!"

Mebus jolted and twisted about as a stocky female halfling in a spattered apron stomped out of the ship's cabin looking as angry as a tipped cow.

"Ah!" he said uneasily. "My dearest little Cookie! What is the problem?"

"Don't you Cookie me, you homebodied son of a sourdough starter!" she huffed shortly as she stomped towards him. "I was just going through our supplies, and what do I find? That we're all out of biscuits! And where, I wonder," she demanded, poking him in his admittedly rotund belly, "might those have gone, hmm?"

"Ah, well, you see," Mebus said hastily. "It's really a—uh...a ringing endorsement of your culinary skills, my dear Cookie. For you see, I knew that it would prove very—err—distracting for the crew to know there were some of your delectable—"

"Work some of it off, you fat lump!" Cookie said, and shoved the startled Mebus over the rail.

Dorian gasped, lunging forward as if to catch the halfling. "No!" he shouted as the fat merchant tumbled end over end off the railing, hurtling towards the fathomless void with a yelp....

...Only for his path to slow, holding him suspended perhaps five yards below the ship, rising back up until he deftly landed on the underside of his own ship.

Dorian gaped, uncomprehending as the halfling tromped back along the hull of the ship as easily as if he were off on a stroll about a field. "What..."

Fable giggled, coming up behind him. "Surprised?" she said teasingly, poking Dorian's cheek. "You shouldn't be. We told you! A ship's core forms its own gravity. He couldn't fall off like you wouldn't fly into the atmosphere by jumping on your home planet."

"O-oh. I see," Dorian said, wiping the sweat off his brow with a shaking hand. The shock of it had sent his heart racing, and he watched in amazement as Mebus pulled himself back over the rail to receive more berating remarks from the irate Cookie. Dorian shook his head. There was so much he still didn't understand about this new existence.

"Alright," Melia called out, striding up with a clap of finality. "Time to get back to the helm. We're getting near the wyrmgate, and the astral winds can get a bit wonky. We don't want to crash into anything if there's a holdup."

"Yeah. Suppose so," Dorian agreed as though he knew a damn thing about any of this. And it looked like Mebus wouldn't be much good for conversation now anyway. Though he'd returned to the deck, the halfling appeared to be busy trying to placate his irate cook, his pleas growing more desperate and humble when the prospect of 'no dessert for a week' was mentioned. It was getting hard to watch.

Chuckling, Dorian turned and returned to the helm, grasping the wheel with another growth of scales and claws. As he did, Fable clopped up behind him, smirking with mirth. "Mind if I touch your scales?" she asked.

"Sorry?" Dorian grunted, almost laughing with surprise at the forwardness of her sudden inquiry.

"For scientific reasons, of course," she added, though the lightness of her tone seemed to suggest a different sort of curiosity.

"Fable, leave him alone," Melia groaned as she stalked by, carrying a crate of something or another.

"I don't really mind. I can probably steer as long as she's not too violent about it," Dorian said. "Besides, company is nice."

Melia scoffed. "I bet it is," she growled under her breath.

Dorian shot her an uneasy glance. The tension in the air was palpable, like Melia was dragging a storm in her wake. He wasn't an idiot. There hadn't been many good men around Clemmen, and he'd gotten a fair bit of attention from the fairer sex, which hadn't endeared him to a number of men near his age or slightly older.

Still, that wasn't the problem up here. It was competition among the ladies for his affection that he'd likely have to concern himself with. He had always been popular with women for his looks, his physique, and for his ability to basically help with whatever needed doing. Despite the fact that he was literally worlds away from Clemmen now, it seemed some things were universal—even in the Black.

Fable rolled her eyes as she draped herself over his shoulder. "Don't mind her," the faun said as her fingers traced their way down his arm and began lightly rubbing the golden scales of his hand. "Melia's just a little protective. That's all."

"You sure that's all?" Dorian said.

"Maybe," Fable giggled teasingly. "She is maybe a little worried you'd do something naughty. Defile me or something. But you wouldn't do that. Would you?" she asked, her blue eyes sparkling, her breasts pressing into his back and her ears flicking playfully.

"Well..."

"Because I warn you," Fable added, leaning in closer, her breath warm against his ear as her fingers slid down his scaly hands, rubbing the space between his fingers. "I'm not gonna let you have it all your way. I am a lady of science, you should know. But if, say, we were looking into how much of a dragon you could turn into, I would have to insist you strip totally. To be sure I got a perfect view."

Dorian chuckled throatily, amused despite his better judgment. "Would you, now? And, would you strip down as well? You know, so I didn't feel uncomfortable?"

"Naturally," Fable giggled. "I am a professional, of course. And that means getting really in depth. Very...studious. Very hands on."

"I also love certain depths." Dorian sucked in a breath as he felt her gently press her hips into him, grinding against his thigh. He was suddenly very glad the wheel was in front of him, and covered him from his chest down. "Being an engineer, capable of building such technomagical marvels as that telescope of yours, those hands are probably very skilled."

"Absolutely," Fable cooed with a light giggle. "You know, Dorian, I'd love to get my hands on your...tool."

"Fable!"

Melia's bark of a voice made the faun roll her eyes and Dorian slump his shoulders. "Yeah?" Fable called back.

"How close are we to the wyrmgate?"

Fable pursed her lips and squinted, closing her eyes. When they reopened, they glowed softly with the strange blue light Dorian had seen before. "Mmm. Coming up soon. We should be able to see it within an hour or so."

"Finally," Melia growled from near the helm, her hand holding some rigging for balance as she leaned forward, gazing into the encompassing void ahead, her hair fluttering red like flame.

Fable blinked, the light fading as she patted his hand. "I'd better get to work prepping things for our passage through. The enchantment I inscribed on this ship was a bit hasty, and the wyrmway doesn't excuse sloppy work. We'll pick up this little discussion...later," she said.

"Will we?" Dorian asked, his eyebrow lifting with interest despite his best instincts.

"Count on it," the faun replied with a wink, slipping away before he could ask a follow-up question.

Dorian watched her go, and maybe it was just him, but she seemed to put a bit more swing in her hips, her small tail flicking teasingly from the hole in her pants. He shook his head, chuckling. What would it be like to hook up with a cute faun like her? There were many mysteries still waiting for him in space, but he was looking forward to investigating that one real soon.

Chapter 8

As Fable had predicted, within a few hours, the wyrmgate came into view.

The sight rooted Dorian where he stood, awe gripping him. The wymrgate stood open like some great wound in the sky—a tear in the black canvas of stars, within which swirled a multitude of hues and colours like ever-shifting paints running amongst each other. It was a cyclone of reds and purples, like the winds of magic had been drawn into a tempest—a window into a reality of chaos beyond even the strangeness of space.

Dorian stared at it as it grew with every passing mile. His hands tightened on the wheel and his heart beat faster. A strange sensation filled him. A sense of anticipation, yes, but something more than that...Something familiar and stunning. He couldn't seem to look away from it. It was like it called to him, like a siren song beckoned him onward.

"Pretty impressive, isn't it, cutie?" Fable chirped as she clopped back up beside him.

Dorian nodded dumbly. "It's amazing," he said, his words a soft exhalation, like he had all but given up on taking a breath ever again.

"That it is. Only the biggest, strongest, oldest dragons can make tears like that," Fable said. "Most are much smaller, and though those ones do close up eventually, the breach never really goes away."

"But what is it, exactly?" he asked.

"Mmm," Fable hummed. "It's kinda like...space between space. Right? No one knows if dragons made it, found it, or what, but it sort of exists like a shortcut between locations. Only dragons actually know how to work it, though. And only dragons can open them—new ones, I mean. There's been all kinds of efforts to do it independently, but it's never worked, and usually just winds up with the mages exploding."

"Exploding?" Dorian said, shocked.

"Very messy," Fable muttered, nodding. "Those are the rumours, anyway. So better to just piggyback on a dragon's hard work, I say!"

Shouts began to come from the other ships in the convoy, crews hurrying to and fro, battening down sails and hatches as they prepared to venture through.

"Should...should we do something like that?" Dorian asked.

"You should watch the helm and your stomach," Melia said as she strode up towards them with a wry look. "First time going through the wyrmgate, everyone gets sick."

"So if you do need to run over to the rail, don't worry about it," Fable said, patting his back. "We won't think less of you. But we do reserve the right to tease you for a few weeks afterwards."

"How kind," Dorian remarked, though he was grinning. Not even the imminent possibility of throwing up in front of two gorgeous women could dampen his spirit, and he watched with eager anticipation as the rift in space grew before them. As they came nearer, a sound began to grow.

A low moaning, like the wind as a storm built around the cliffs. Dorian felt a shiver work through him, and noticed his skin was glowing brighter, the gold and red of its normal shimmer becoming more potent and vibrant.

The convoy slowed as it neared the rift, ships gathering around the larger vessels. Many were throwing ropes to anchor themselves to the one built around the Star Scallop.

"They don't have navigators," Fable said, noticing his attention. "The wyrmway constantly shifts its space and the location of exits are never quite the same. Only draconic navigators like yourself can find their way through reliably. If one of those ships without a draconic navigator or at least a specialized mage drifts even a bit from the convoy, the wyrmway would tear them apart in seconds. If they were lucky."

"And if they were unlucky?" Dorian asked, eager but horrified to hear the answer.

"They'd drift," Melia said grimly. "Lost in the wyrmway until their ship ran out of oxygen and they all suffocated. Or until they were preyed on by the horrors that lurk in the deeper parts of the wyrmway. There are countless unexplored routes, and the dangers that fester in those deadends are worse than you can dream."

Dorian was starting to wonder if Melia relished revealing that kind of information to him. She seemed to have a penchant for it.

But he took the warning to heart, bracing as the convoy slipped through the gap in space, gliding onwards into the strangeness of the wyrmway. Dorian tensed as the nose of The Windlass slipped through, the swirling markings along the ship shimmering with colours, the gold glowing brighter and the air around them tinting in the iridescent hues. The walls of the wyrmways were pockmarked with tunnels delving through them, some as big as moons, others looking too small even for their ship.

Dorian shivered, licking his lips as a tremor of something strange surged through him. He felt like the ground beneath his feet had suddenly shifted, like his body was being submerged in something light as water, his skin soaking it in.

It felt...good.

This, evidently, was hardly universal.

Melia grabbed the railing of the helm, gritting her teeth as if in pain. Her hair shimmered, turning an unpleasant green before returning to a more composed violet.

"Ooh boy," Fable said from beside Dorian, the faun swaying on her hooves, eyes momentarily rolling as she stumbled.

Reflexively, Dorian reached out with one hand, catching the faun and pulling her against his side. Fable tumbled into him, her head rocking with vertigo.

"You okay?" Dorian asked.

Fable blinked up at him and gave her head a shake. She grinned. "Yeah, thanks. Hoo! Wow, you handled it like a champ! That was a rough one for me, cutie!"

"I bet it was," Melia said with a glare their way, her hair flickering to red again. "Now, both hands on the wheel, navigator."

Once he was sure Fable was fine, Dorian (somewhat reluctantly, he would admit) took his hand off the faun and grasped the wheel again. As he did, he felt a throb from the core of the ship. Before his eyes, like spindles of light weaving through the shimmering expanse, gold threads came to be, spinning away and through the strange realm they found themselves.

"Whoa," Dorian breathed.

"Good. Now, we need to go to Sphere," Melia said.

"Sphere, right," Dorian grunted. Even as he did, one of the spiralling threads of light seemed to glow brighter, giving a subtle tug to his hands. He turned towards it, following the thread of light.

"What are you doing?" Fable said with a puzzled frown as she reached out, tapping the core in the wheel. "You need to channel the pilot rune in and then let it guide—"

"It's that way," he said, nodding in the direction of that single thread. "About...ten hours travel from here."

Fable and Melia stared at him in shock. "How...the hell could you possibly know that?" Fable asked.

Dorian shrugged. "I just...do."

"Um, no. You can't. That's not possible," Melia contested, hands resting on her hips.

"But...he isn't wrong," Fable muttered in disbelief. "Weird."

The pair exchanged a look, then again stared at Dorian as he gently tweaked the helm. Dorian shifted uneasily under their stunned faces.

"Isn't it normal?" he said. "How many dragonblood navigators have you known?"

Melia did a quick mental tally. "Dozens," she said.

"Hundreds, maybe," Fable added. "I mean—I've only flown with a handful, but—"

"And none knew how to do what I just did?" Dorian asked.

"Not to the hour," Melia said. "And not without channeling first. They needed a pilot rune to know when to turn off. And you just...know?"

He shrugged. "Seems so."

"Amazing," Fable murmured, hastily fumbling out a notepad from her pocket, her ears twitching as she quickly scribbled inside. "Incredible!"

"How do we know it's accurate?" Melia demanded.

"He nailed the time estimate, so I say we trust him. It won't be long until we find out one way or another, will it?" Fable said happily.

Melia shook her head, giving Dorian a scrutinizing look. She folded her arms under her breasts, lips pursed and hair fluttering a wary purple. "How much did you know about your parents again?" she asked.

"Very little," Dorian said. "My mom supposedly died when I was a baby. No one ever knew my father."

"But—"

"I really think I need to focus on piloting," Dorian said, not seeing anything useful coming out of continuing this interaction.

***

MELIA OPENED HER MOUTH to protest, but Fable snuck up behind her and pulled on the elf's sleeve.

Melia scowled, but allowed Fable to tug her back across the deck and near the rail.

"What?" Melia hissed.

"Let it lie for now," Fable snapped right back. "We don't want to lose him!"

"What are you talking about?" Melia growled in an undertone.

Fable grabbed her friend's shoulder and pulled her in closer, stealing a glance at Dorian as he carefully navigated the shimmering tunnels. "Look, he's obviously not just some peasant from a feudal world. He's strong, fast, learns things quickly—and remember those wings and horns? That is not normal! Neither is this."

"Exactly! So why should we—"

"No, not *exactly*," Fable hissed. "Don't screw up a good thing, Melia! This is better than striking gold. He's like striking the motherload! Remember our last navigator? Bilford had to go half this speed, and it was like riding a cart over a road filled with boulders! This has been the smoothest and quickest journey of my life! Dorian's not just some dragon's fourth generation bastard son of a bastard. He's gotta have a dragon soul locked in him with its memories intact. At least! He's our secret weapon, Melia! With him at the helm, it's going to make jobs a breeze."

Melia scowled, her lovely face pinching, but as her hair shimmered from a reddish violet to something more blue, Fable knew the other woman saw her point.

Fable patted her friend on the shoulder. "We can quiz him later," she said. "Get the info more casually. Right? For now, let's just accept it and keep things moving. Don't scare him off with the Imperial inquisition treatment, yeah?"

Melia sighed, running her hand through her shimmering hair. "Fine," she said.

With another encouraging pat, Fable let go of her friend and clopped back over to Dorian.

***

"ANY TROUBLE?" DORIAN ASKED, never looking away from the shifting horizon as he heard Fable's hooves approach.

"Nope! All good. Just girl talk," Fable said impishly.

Dorian glanced at the faun, but that pretty smile was more impenetrable than a castle's iron gate. He shrugged. "Interesting moment for it. It really is amazing in here, though," he added.

"Think so?"

"Absolutely. I mean, it would be so easy to just run away in here. Just pick a gate and vanish if you're being chased. There are hundreds of them, and they all spit you out into a different system. It's all just so...incredible."

"Mm. You could try to run like that," Fable said. "But they wouldn't get far, honestly. Not with auramancers around. Ships leave echoes of their passage in the wyrmway for a while, so someone like me could track them if I knew what to look for."

"Sounds like you're pretty useful," Dorian chuckled. "I guess I should..."

He suddenly trailed off. A shudder seemed to wrack the walls of the wyrmway, sending the violets and reds convulsing as if in pain. His eyes flashed about, then went down as in the distance, the wall of the wyrmway suddenly split open with a tearing sound. Fable whipped about and Melia ran up to the deck. Shouts came from the caravan near them, every ship slowing, halflings pointing and several grabbing weapons.

Then the tear widened, and the source came through. Huge iridescent wings seemed to fan out, blotting out the horizon. Scales that shimmered as if reflecting the wyrmway right back at it pushed through. A proud, horned head with a long maw. Limbs tipped in claws big as men, the creature dwarfed even the largest ship in the convoy as it soared into the wyrmway like a titan striding into its home.

A dragon.

A real dragon.

But this was no wyrm like the legends spoke of in Dorian's village. Fables of monsters that lived beyond the sea and in distant mountains. Here was a creature as impressive as the galaxy which housed it. Light coursed over it like a violet star burned within its chest. The beat of its wings sent the walls of the wyrmway shuddering and left in its wake a shimmering wave of astral light. Compared to it, the fleet of ships were like mice before a tiger.

Fable grabbed Dorian's arm as if to anchor herself to reality, her body trembling at the sheer scale of the creature before them. Melia clutched her sword even as she felt the futility of that weapon before the immensity that soared through the wyrmway overhead. Had it the inclination, it could destroy the entire fleet of them without even a thought. Just its presence buffeted the ships, threatening to throw them off course.

The dragon's wings beat again, carrying it over the caravan. But then it slowed. Its wings shifted, and the dragon's head began to move, scanning the fleet.

"Oh gods," Melia breathed. "Fuck, no. No no no, please..."

Fable murmured something that sounded like a prayer in a language Dorian didn't understand. He swallowed hard, scaled hands tightening on the wheel, wondering if he should try and accelerate like he did when chased by the asteroid elemental. Something inside him urged him not to.

The dragon stopped, hovering before the caravan with lazy beats of its wings. Its head suddenly stopped moving, and Dorian felt its gaze on him. Its attention seemed to sear him, nailing him where he stood.

And then, he thought he detected something like a smile.

The dragon's wings suddenly gave a great beat, and the creature soared over the tiny fleet and beyond them. Every head turned, watching the iridescent underbelly shimmer as the dragon passed them, soaring deeper into the wyrmway before vanishing into the distance.

Dorian took a shuddering breath and quickly looked at the pair. "Everyone okay?" he asked, scanning them instinctively, even though nothing worse than a scare had befallen them.

Fable let out a gasp, sagging against Dorian as she clutched her chest. "Oh gods," she breathed. "Oh gods, I thought that was it. I thought it was gonna kill us."

"We're alive. Dear gods we're alive," Melia breathed in amazement.

Dorian nodded, looking back at where the dragon had vanished. He didn't have to ask if that kind of interaction was standard. Somehow he knew that seeing a wyrm in the wyrmway was rare indeed—he just sensed it, or felt that truth in his blood. He felt again the shiver of awareness from the dragon's scrutiny as he reflected on it.

Fortunately, it seemed everyone else had been too awed to realize it was looking straight at him.

He wondered what that smile could mean...

Chapter 9

Dorian was relieved to get back underway and was hardly surprised the feeling was shared by his lovely crew. Though the sight of the dragon had been awe-inspiring, the sheer terror of that moment impressed itself on him even more in quiet reflection. To think such a creature existed in reality! And he was soon to realize that was but one creature that lurked in the wyrmways.

They passed a number of them as their ships ventured on into the shimmering expanse of the surreal depths. Huge things that looked like squids made of ethereal mist with a multitude of eyes and hooks at the end of their tentacles. Vast whales nearly as big as the dragon had been, their skin fluttering with hues like the northern lights made flesh. They spotted schools of horned, cycloptic bat-like creatures and kept a wide berth from them, and skirted shoals of suspicious rocks suspended in the void and strange, ancient buildings that seemed like they'd been ripped from some distant world and flung, suspended for eternity in the depths of this mysterious passage.

And soon, they also came across other ships as well. Dozens of them, moving along or in groups, many of make like *The Windlass*, others of that heedless construction that dismissed the need of gravity like the halfling's convoy. A number of them were built on or into creatures of the astral realms. They passed a school of creatures like dolphins with something like an immense conch hitched to them like horses carrying a chariot. Another time, they saw a sea turtle whose shell was made of iron and sported small windows like a bunker.

And there were those who could only be pirates.

Dorian watched one warily. It was a ship much like theirs, though its hull was painted red and the entire front of the ship was metal beaten to resemble a skull. Dorian watched them closely, and saw a number of figures returning the same look on that craft.

"Why don't they attack?" he asked.

"Safety in numbers," Fable reminded him. "And we'd be able to outrun that hulk in the wyrmway easily."

"They could cripple us," he noted, eying what looked like harpoons built into the eyes of the prow's skull.

Melia snorted. "They could try," she said, arms crossed.

"Distance is almost impossible to properly figure in the wyrmway," Fable informed him. "Maybe not for you, but for them, certainly. Firing off those things in here, they'd be more likely to hit nothing even if we seemed to be right in front of their nose. And forget using magic! Aside from navigators and auramancer skills, other spells play havoc when you try and cast them in here. They'd be more likely to blow themselves up than us if they tried."

"Gotcha," Dorian said, daring to relax a little.

"But the risk is still real," Melia opined darkly as she watched the deadly craft cruise past, her hand gripping the hilt of her rapier and thumb rubbing the pommel. "If you can get close enough to another ship, you can still board it. If your oxygen bubble melds to another ship's, the distance is the same as it would be outside the wyrmway."

Dorian grimaced. "Good to know," he said. "Do people live in here, though?"

"In the wyrmway? Sure!" Fable said. "Some do. More than we probably know, actually. Some say whole civilizations exist in some of the unexplored bends of the wyrmway, but that's a bit much. Still, there are a few places. The Hole is the biggest we know of. Whole network of ships bolted all together like a floating city! It's super fun. We'll have to take you there one of these days," she said, nudging Dorian playfully. "And you can buy almost anything there!"

"Except arcane weapons. For obvious reasons," Melia said. "Which is why we're heading to Sphere. Presumably." She tossed another suspicious look at Dorian.

Fable gave Dorian a knowing smirk and rolled her eyes. As she did, some music became just audible. Dorian glanced towards the fleet of the Halfling's ships, noticing a number had fetched out instruments and begun to play a jig, the jovial music echoing through the wyrmway in a strange, but far from unpleasant way.

Fable laughed, her hooves clopping as she began to dance. "Wanna dance, Dorian?" she asked, skipping before the helm with a look of gleeful mischief.

"I probably shouldn't leave the wheel," he said with a grin.

"In that case," Fable said, twirling before him, her hoofbeats accompanying the strum of the band, "I'll dance for your viewing pleasure!"

"Wouldn't say no," he said, grinning.

With another giggle, Fable pranced back, the midship her stage as she skipped and jigged, her coat fluttering around her and hair tumbling around the crown of her antlers. Her eyes sparkled and laughter escaped her with joy as she moved.

Dorian chuckled, finding himself tapping his foot to the music as he switched his glance between Fable and the swirling tunnel of the wyrmway. And as a result, he couldn't be quite sure just when Fable's dance became a little more...provocative.

Her hooves still clopped to the thrum of the fiddles, but her movements had become more suggestive. Her jacket slipped down off her shoulders, revealing her bare arms and the firm globes of her breasts, trapped within a sleeveless white undershirt. She whirled, her hips swaying pendulously, emphasizing their curves while her chest undulated.

Dorian's eyebrows rose with interest as her hands began to move over herself, outlining her figure, her eyes growing lidded, watching him with a soft, simmering heat that made his throat feel dry and pants a size too small.

"Oh for the gods' sake," Melia groaned with a roll of her eyes.

"What? What's wrong with...a little...dancing?" Fable asked with a grin.

"Yeah, sure. That's what you're doing," Melia said.

"You jealous?" Fable asked as she spun.

Melia folded her arms, glaring. "Of course not," she growled.

Dorian glanced at the elf's hair, which had changed from cold blue to fluttering red.

"Sure." Fable grinned.

"As if I am," Melia said, turning to Dorian and striding across the deck. "See? Dancing? That sort of footwork is fine on a ship, but elves have perfected the art. What you're seeing is little more than child's play compared to what we learn in the cradle."

"Then why not...show him?" Fable asked.

"You really don't have to," Dorian said quickly, feeling the tension tighten in the air.

"Of course I don't need to," Melia huffed as she came up behind Dorian. "Why would I? Besides, the elven arts are far more refined. For example, we are masters of the twenty pressure point massage."

"Er..."

"See?" Melia said, her hands landing on Dorian's shoulders, fingers digging in.

He sucked in a breath, stiffening up reflexively, but then her deft fingers began their work and he let out a groan as the tension seemed to melt off him like steam off a stewpot. "Oh gods," he breathed. "You weren't—mnn—kidding."

Fable's hooves rapped out a final step as she came to a halt, lips pursed as she frowned at the helm and the two on it. "Oh, is that what we're doing?" she asked, strutting up and swinging herself up onto the wheel's pedestal, her breasts suddenly directly in Dorian's line of sight. "We're massaging him? Fine with me. I call his temples."

"I—uhh..." Dorian said, but too late to stop Fable from reaching out, her fingers resting on his head and beginning to gently rub soothing circles into his brows.

"You think he likes that?" Melia asked. "Ha! You're just piggybacking on my work. As usual."

"As usual?! As USUAL?! We'll see about that!"

Dorian was pretty sure he shouldn't be enjoying the moment as much as he was. Then again, he also knew it would be a sin not to. "Mmm. What did I do to deserve this?" he murmured aloud.

Melia's fingers stilled on his shoulders. "What are you talking about?" she said, her voice peaky. "This is totally normal for—"

"Oh come off it, Melia," Fable scoffed, rolling her eyes and practically pushing Dorian's head into her breasts. "We've been netherborne for years barely without break, and the last guy we had aboard either of us were willing to even work alone with was a geezer with rocks growing out of his face—may he rest in peace. But this hunk?"

Dorian felt Fable's hands move from his brows and to his cheeks, tilting his head up to look at her. "Me?" he said with a laugh. He was loving this.

Fable smiled down at him, the colors of the wyrmway shimmering in her brown hair and through her antlers. "That's right, cutie. You're a damn fine catch. And not just for that tasty body. You're a hell of a natural navigator, a good fighter, a smooth talker, and our ticket to not scraping the bottom of barge work for the rest of our careers. So personally, I think we'd like to keep you around. And I think Melia feels the same way, whether or not she wants to admit it."

Dorian glanced backwards at the elf, and this time it wasn't just her hair that was red. Melia's cheeks were flushed and when she caught Dorian's eyes, her own flicked away as if looking for an escape.

"N-not at all. I mean, of course I would be, well, happy if he were to stay on as navigator. I think we should be on good terms, of course. It's just the three of us. Of course. So, I mean, well..."

Fable laughed aloud. "Oh really? Then more for me!" she said, and this time really did pull Dorian's head into her breasts. "Go ahead and spoil yourself, big guy!"

Dorian's shock didn't lessen his delight at the position he suddenly found himself in. But by the sudden tensing of the elven fingers in his shoulders, he knew he'd better not indulge in it too long. He quickly pulled his head back (not without some regrets) and cleared his throat.

"Er—ladies? Not to say I'm not, of course, very flattered, but I...think the two of you aren't yet on the same page. Not to say I'm not willing to indulge. Gods no! But maybe we should take it easy for the sake of harmony among the crew—at least until we know where everyone stands. We are supposed to be working together. And I don't really want to be the source of fighting between you two, so..."

Fable pouted at him, then sighed and gave her head a toss, brown hair fluttering as she let her hands slip off Dorian's head and onto Melia's hands, still gripping his shoulder like an eagle snatching up a particularly fine salmon.

"I guess," the faun said. "And I definitely don't want drama between us, Melia. I'm sorry if I went a bit too far there."

Melia said nothing, her face ashen, her hair a pale white tinted with greys. She yanked her hands from Dorian's shoulders, turning on her heel and marching away, rubbing her hands as if they'd been burned. Dorian watched her go uneasily, Fable doing the same, but with a hint of melancholy sadness.

"Is...she going to be okay?" Dorian asked.

"Eventually," Fable said, slipping off the wheel's stand with a clop of hooves. "She's tough on the outside, and...also on the inside. But like a s'more, there's a delicious, gooey middle that can get riled up. I'll go talk to her. Don't worry. It's not your fault. Well, I mean, it kinda is. This'd be so much easier if you weren't such a cutie."

"Sorry," Dorian muttered.

"Never apologize for being hot. I sure don't," Fable said. "Vavoom!" she added with a playful swing of her hips.

Dorian couldn't help but crack a smile at that. "If you say so."

"You feel up to sailing on your own for a bit?" Fable asked.

Dorian looked ahead again, tracking the threads of golden light that guided him as he sailed. "I think so. I'll be breaking off the convoy soon, I think, so I'd better stay at the helm."

"Awesome! Give 'er, big boy. I'm gonna go talk to our favorite elf. Be back soon! Don't crash into anything."

"I'll be careful," he said.

"I know ya will, cutie," Fable chirped, then leaned up and stole a quick kiss on his cheek.

Dorian blinked in surprise, turning his head to stare at the faun, who leaned back, shyly touching her lips with a playful smile and a soft, rouging blush. "I know I shouldn't," she giggled. "But it was too good to resist. Bye!"

He stared as Fable spun about, her tail flicking as she skipped down into the hold, leaving him alone on deck. Dorian sighed, looking out at the guiding threads of the wyrmway's maddened hues. Navigating the stars was turning out to be far easier than navigating the feelings of his fellow crew.

Chapter 10

MELIA LAY IN HER bed, staring at the cabin ceiling as if the knothole in the beam could reveal some hidden truth to what she should do. Had she remained as a tender of the Mother Tree, perhaps it would have. But that bridge had not just been burned, but scorched, buried, and used as fertilizer to grow some bitter fruits.

But she was not so deep in her melancholy (or booze, though she was tempted to make a visit to the store room) not to hear Fable's hooves coming down the steps. Nor the way they paused at the door, and then the gentle rap of a knock.

"It's open," Melia sighed, turning over to stare at the wall. She knew she was being childish, and she hated the feeling. She had hated feeling this way ever since childhood had so abruptly ended, when her parents contracted the Green Rot and she had to venture out on her own—and what did she have to show for it? She shuddered at the memory as the door creaked open and Fable walked softly towards the bed.

"Hey, Mimi," Fable said.

"Hello, Fable," Melia answered, voice half muffled by a pillow.

She felt the blankets shift as Fable climbed into the bed behind her, the faun's short figure molding itself against Melia's back as the other woman gently hugged her. "How're you doing?"

Melia gave a bark of a laugh. "Oh, just dandy. Or was that not apparent by how I stormed off like a fucking brat?"

"Well, you weren't the only one acting up," Fable said, her hands gently stroking Melia's arms. "I'm sorry for teasing you like that. And for catching our mutual love interest in the crossfire. Dorian's right. We shouldn't fight. Agreed?"

"I guess," Melia sighed.

"We've always stuck together, right?" Fable said. "We had to. Two sexy women out among the stars, in the void, no one to rely on but each other.

It's why we used to only crew with female captains and navigators. Not that that always worked out. Remember that time that shit-head captain thought I stole her makeup?"

"I remember you telling her you'd never because she needed all the help she could get," Melia said.

Fable giggled. "That was probably the bitchiest moment I had with that crew."

"I can name more," Melia teased, smiling despite her best efforts.

"I bet you could. How about that time that writher tried to convince you to come on his crew, even though he was trying to feel you up with his tentacles as he made the pitch?"

"Yeah. Right until I dumped that bottle of grog on his head."

"And don't forget the little faun who tossed a lit match on him," Fable added.

"Oh, I'd never forget that," Melia said, her hair fluttering blue with pleasure at the memory.

Fable giggled. "Right? The most guys we had around as crew was that last one. And only because one was an impotent, rickety crystalmancer, another was a golem so didn't count, and the last was a goblin more obsessed with putting cogwheels and gears on things than anything else. Let's face it. Dorian's a bit of a step up from that, huh?"

Melia sighed. "I know he is," she admitted. "And...alright. I do find him...appealing. But I don't know if there's, well, feelings there right now. It's all been so fast..."

"You always overcomplicate things," Fable said, nuzzling the back of Melia's neck. "It's okay to just have fun sometimes."

"But we barely know anything about him! What if it makes things weird?"

"We're grown-ups, Mimi. We can figure it out," Fable insisted. "You have to admit, what we do know about him is pretty exceptional. He's a skilled navigator, not bad with the sword, not a creep, and was actually aware of the drama we were heading for up there and defused it when he could have just had his way with me on that helm. He's not just here to fuck us and fly off. So, I dunno. I wanna jump his bones, just putting it out there, but if there ends up being even more to this whole thing. Well..."

Melia felt her face heat again, her hair glowing a faint pink with desire. "I...I do admit I've thought about it."

"Well, duh. You do have eyes last I checked."

Melia bit her lower lip. "Fable, I mean...since he came aboard I have been, you know. Thinking about it. I've been a bit...pent up, I admit. But..."

"I know," Fable murmured, her hands gliding down Melia's body, stroking the firmness of her stomach. "Do you...want some help?"

Melia frowned, turned her head a bit. "Fable, I'm not, well, into women like that."

"I know," Fable said with an impish grin. "So maybe let me help narrate a bit. A little fantasy. You can take care of the physical part yourself."

Melia squirmed a little, but didn't resist her friend's embrace. "Huh? You..."

"Just close your eyes," Fable said, leaning up, her lips near Melia's ear, tone soft and enticing.

"And imagine it's Dorian down here, just you and him."

Melia blushed hotter, but her hair burned a hotter pink. Still uncertain, but growing more enticed with every moment, her eyes slowly slid shut.

"That's it," Fable breathed as Melia's fingers toyed with her own belt, easing it open with a clink. "Imagine he came down and found you all alone on your bed. You're a bit startled, but then he sits down beside you, cupping your cheek. You're uncertain, skittish like a deer..."

Melia snorted at the image and from whom it came, but found herself following Fable's instructions. She imagined Dorian beside her, but maybe not in a shirt...His taut, muscled form so near to her...The heat of his body radiating against her as he touched her, her cheek easing into his palm. That feeling of closeness melting into an embrace—sexual, raw, fueled by animalistic lust that might one day become something more. She wanted it.

"And he leans in close," Fable murmured, catching up with Melia's needy mind. "He kisses you. Firm. Tender. His lips so soft, his tongue teasing your lips as if asking to enter. You let him, of course."

Melia shivered as she teased down her trousers, revealing the soft white of her panties. She felt her finger stroke herself through the thin fabric, a streak of moisture already there betraying the intensity of her hunger. A quiver radiated from her core and thrummed through her mound, swelling up into her chest. Her lips parted with a gasp, imagining Dorian's lips locked with hers, his hot breath mingling, his tongue pushing into her mouth.

"He kisses you. Easing you back. You tremble, and his other hand catches yours, your fingers tightening in his grasp, but you don't fight it as he rolls you onto your back—straddling you. Kissing you deeper and longer."

Melia moaned softly, her finger at first hesitant against her tender entrance, then bolder, stroking herself, imagining it was Dorian's hand doing it. Would he be as sure as he was when piloting the ship? Would he be able to sense all the places that made her moan as he seemed to know the wyrmway's eddies?

He would.

She imagined he would.

Melia whimpered, her hips bucking, riding her finger, which had at some point or another delved inside her panties. She barely needed Fable's narration as she found herself sinking into the fantasy completely. Letting herself be free. Surrendering. The thought of giving in to such an experience was both terrifying and thrilling.

"I bet he'd be good," Fable giggled as Melia rocked to the motions of her own hand, strumming her tender inner walls, teasing her way up to the peak that made her gasp and whimper in delight as it was rubbed so purposefully. "I bet his cock would feel so good in you. As he fucked you into the bed. You'd call his name like a slut as he thrust inside you. Your hands would go around his back or his neck—the mattress bouncing as you let him inside again and again, never wanting him to pull out. Imagine...Your hand squeezing his as he just...stripped away the last bit of the maiden inside you and made you his personal whore. Just fucking you into a puddle of your sweat and cum. Your legs wrapping around his waist to try and pull him into you faster. Harder. Would you lock him in there when he was going to spill? Would you do it, Mimi?"

"Oh f-fuck," Melia gasped, sweat beading her brow, her hair burning like a pink inferno of color as she rode her hand towards the inevitable peak of climax. Her breath came in hot. Short. The blankets tangled around her writhing legs. Moisture leaked and lightly squirted, the sounds of her squelching pussy filling the room. "Fuck, Fable!"

"Bet you'll cum first," Fable giggled, her hands stroking Melia's tummy as her friend gave in to the fantasy. "Bet he can hold off until you give in. Until you moan and whimper and just...fucking...*cum* for him..."

"Oh. Oh! Oh nnnnnn!" Melia groaned, her whole body tightening, her inner walls squeezing her fluttering finger, a cry of ecstasy escaping her lips as she surrendered to the moment—the climax. As she came with a groan of blessed relief, a sensation like a hot wash of water splashing over her carried away the tension, pain, and uncertainty.

Panting, Melia sagged into the bed, breathing hot, fast, and hard. Fable smirked, her own cheeks warm, but she could find her own relief later. Preferably straight from the source.

Snuggling up against Melia's back, Fable felt her friend sigh and slip away into comfortable silence, and a nice, long, relaxing snooze.

Fable sighed contentedly and giggled. "I'm such a good friend."

Chapter 11

Dorian watched Melia and Fable closely as they came onto the deck once more. They must have had a deep conversation, considering how long they'd been below, but both seemed much better for it. The pair looked a little rumpled but much more relaxed as they approached the helm and him.

"Closing in on Sphere soon, I think," he said, nodding to the swirling tunnel they sailed down. "Should be any minute."

"Great!" Fable cheered, clopping up beside him and leaning forward. She shaded her eyes for dramatic effect, Dorian suspected, even as the blue glow of auramancy filled her vision. The faun grinned and leaned back. "Yep! He's right. It's just ahead. See? Told you we could trust him."

"You did," Melia said, giving Dorian a lazy smirk. "Not bad, navigator."

"Just doing my job," he replied, feeling relieved beyond measure the tension from before was gone. At least for now. Well, if it came up again, he'd deal with it then. For now, he'd just appreciate the return of a more genial camaraderie between the three of them.

Fable suddenly pointed ahead. "There it is!" she cried.

Dorian quickly turned his attention directly in front of him, marveling as the wyrmway narrowed ahead, and indeed, he could see the end. Another tear in the fabric of the shimmering space lay before them, opening up into the familiar canvas of stars and darkness of reality, like a great eye peering into the galaxy of mortals. As *The Windlass* closed on it, Dorian felt something almost like reluctance to enter realspace once more—as if the wyrmway was more familiar than the realm beyond. But he buried the feeling, knowing it to be foolishness.

They were hardly alone either. What seemed like hundreds of ships went through the wyrmgate. They ranged from the colossal ships like the halflings had piloted to smaller crafts like his own. With care, Dorian cruised their vessel around the traffic, the wings of the oars creaking as they shifted *The Windlass* to and fro around the hulls of great barges and narrower ships. He had to dodge through some cabling that tethered a number of smaller ships to a great bulk like a wooden castle with sails as it passed them by.

Then they were out, passing through the gate once more. The strange sensation of shifting footing rocked him again, but Dorian rode it with far greater ease than before. Both Fable and Melia seemed to do likewise, only brief swaying and flickers of distaste betraying their return to realspace.

"There it is," Fable said grandly, beckoning ahead. "Sphere!"

Dorian stared ahead, and he didn't have to pretend to be impressed.

Sphere was like nothing he had seen before. Once, it had been a moon, or perhaps an immense meteor of such a scale. But that had been long ago, before something had hollowed out much of the planetoid. Layers were cut in the vast surface of the former moon, split from each other by columns of stone and mined rock. Docks stretched out from it like thousands of stubby, grasping tentacles. What looked like palaces took up some tiers, while taverns, inns, and other buildings crowded others. Rings of life built atop each other until they covered the former planetoid like sores of wood, metal, stone and what looked like even some ships welded to the surface.

"Wow," was all Dorian could say, his eyes struggling to comprehend the full vastness of the thing.

"Not bad, huh?" Fable said smugly, arms crossing as she looked down at it proudly, like she herself had a hand in its creation. "The hub of a hundred worlds! Sphere! You can get anything there, and all for a reasonable price, so long as you know how to barter. And we're headed down there!"

"Um," Dorian grunted as a bulk moved into their path. "Maybe...not quite yet."

Melia cursed as she spotted the ship bearing down on them, and Fable paled as well. Dorian had seen many ships in his short time in the Black, but the one before them was a new sight indeed. It was both a thing of beauty and elegant brutality, with a narrow prow and sails projecting from the center. What looked like two engines burned at the keel, and all along it ran flowing gilt, as if waves of gold were ferrying the ship onward. From between the gilt could be seen gunwales of cannons, and upon the prow a pair of turrets that looked like they'd been built on the back of two gorgeous women leaping from the wood, lifting the barrels dramatically. And now they rotated so their barrels aimed squarely at *The Windlass*.

"Elven fucking Imperials," Melia cursed.

"Halt!" boomed a voice through the vastness of space. "Do not resist, or face the consequences."

Dorian glanced at the cannons, having a grim premonition of what that might entail.

Melia patted his arm. "Let me talk to them," she said. "They listen to other elves."

"You sure?"

"Oh posh," Melia said in a sudden drawling, aristocratic tone as she ran her fingers through her hair. "It'll hardly be the first time, my dear."

Dorian snorted and tried to hide a smile as Melia's fluttering hair reformed into a beehive. The elf strutted towards the rail as *The Windlass* glided alongside the gilded ship of white and gold. Along the other craft, Dorian made out a number of sailors in tight white and gold uniforms, rifles held at attention, hair fluttering blue and combed back behind golden circlets.

Their captain was impossible to miss, and it was a wonder the man could move under so much metal and gilt. A captain's jacket hung off him, weighed down with medals all over his chest. A sharp mustache jutted out on either side of an upturned upper lip like two needles. His collar squeezed his neck and epaulets that looked heavy enough to drag him down hung from his shoulders.

His expression, Dorian mused, wasn't even a sneer. Peasants sneered. The look on that too pale face was one of such aristocratic contempt it looked down on not only Dorian and his ship, but his last six generations.

"Mmm. Good day," the captain said, his mustache glowing golden as he rubbed it between two fingers wrapped in immaculate white gloves. "I am Captain Clambell Spruceling, the fourth. Master of this fine vessel, *The Star Nymph*."

"A pleasure, captain," Melia drawled, curtsying politely. "It is an honour to meet a man of such renown as yourself, and have them inspect our sad little vessel."

"Hmm. Yes. It is, isn't it?" Clambell said, his chest puffing out a little more. An impressive feat, given the man looked skinnier than a starving dog.

"May I ask, sir, why you grace us with your attentions?" Melia said.

"We have noticed that your vessel is not within our registry," Clambell said, as if this were a personal affront to his dignity. He snapped his fingers, and a young elf scuttled forward, expression schooled and pale as his captain's as he fetched out a scroll, pen poised above the page. "And we seek to rectify that forthwith."

"Our greatest pardons, captain," Melia said with a breathy sigh. "I'm afraid our last ship was lost in a tragic accident with the uncouth *garungir*. We crashed on a simply miserable little world, and did the best we could to get into the sky once more."

"Ugh! The dwarves," Clambell sighed. "Such miserable creatures. I swear, every day they seem more bold. They should stick to their holes and leave the stars to those with the experience and appreciation to behold them."

"So true, captain," Melia drawled. "But one does what one can."

"So I see," Clambell grunted, his eyes raking *The Windlass* as if he'd be doing the universe a favor by torching it. His eyes halted when they beheld Dorian, who clamped his lips tight to suppress his laughter. "And...your navigator would be..."

"Oh. Him. Pish posh. A new helmsman," Melia said with a dismissing flick of her fingers. "Hardly even worth mentioning."

"Indeed. Humans tend to be. And yet, we must for the proper registration."

"Must we?" Melia said in surprise. "My my! This has never been asked of us before."

"New regulations, I fear, madame," Clambell said with an almost apologetic bow of his head, which seemed more profound due to the copious feathers in his hat flapping around like a nest of birds trying to escape the stitching.

"Well, if we must," Melia sighed, but Dorian couldn't help but notice a flicker of red in her hair before it schooled itself back to calm blue. "I believe he said his name was Dorian."

The page beside Campbell rapidly scratched the name, his pen returning to its taut poise immediately after. "Indeed," the captain said dryly. "And his navigational method?"

"A common mage," Melia said. "Navigating as best he can. But merely human, of course. A crude passage, I must admit, and quite the uncomfortable journey. I intend to hire someone more refined and skillful on Sphere if possible."

"A no doubt wise choice," Clambell said. But Dorian didn't much like the intense look the foppish captain gave him. The intensity of it belied the man's decadent drawl. "...A mage you said?" Clambell mused.

"So he tells me," Melia said smoothly.

"And, how long has he been navigating?"

"Not long, I dare say," Melia sighed. "Seems he barely comprehends how to pilot a ship. Personally, I rather suspect he'll explode before too long with how crudely he weaves the astral paths. And I must say, if he was not so new, I would have tied him to the mast and scourged his back for the roughness of my journey!"

"A fair decision," Clambell said thoughtfully over the scratching of the scribe's pen. His eye lingered on Dorian. "Hmm. I suggest you quiz him with the lash nonetheless, madame, before turning him loose."

"I have been meaning to. I haven't dared try and apply the makeup appropriate to an elf of my standing while we rattled through the way."

"Indeed? Well, madame, I assure you that you are lovely all the same. And with the proper treatment, you'd be utterly ravishing."

"Captain! Please," Melia giggled, coyly turning her head with a bat of her hand. "You do me such honour. Why, your own morning toilet clearly must be extensive."

"Three hours," Clambell said proudly, preening with a rattle of medals.

"But worth every moment, Captain. Assuredly," Melia replied sweetly.

Clambell smirked anew, tweaking his mustache, burning a bright brass of pleasure. "Mm. A woman of fine taste. Now, if you wouldn't mind, we would need to board your ship, in case there's some contraband..."

"Oh dear. Must you, sir?" Melia sighed. "For, I fear that this ship I acquired had little...amenities, and I have been in direst need of a bath and shower. I would normally demure, captain, but as a man who understands the needs to be seen at their best, surely you can appreciate why I would wish to reach Sphere and properly...compose myself."

Clambell bowed deeper this time. "My fellow elf, I understand completely! Do forgive me, there are times I let the seriousness of my work interfere in my better judgment."

"Oh not at all, captain. Not at all! A man as cultured as yourself can be excused for appointing himself with such seriousness. It is a grand thing. A thing to be lauded, captain!"

"You are kind, my lady. Very kind indeed. You may go. And please! Next time we meet, it would be my pleasure to see you aboard for dinner, once you can attire yourself to your satisfaction."

"Truly, it is a pleasure, captain, to meet a man of such culture and generosity after so long. Like a whiff of fresh air, scented with finest rosehip."

Clambell preened again, the feathers of his hat and medals on his chest fairly quivering like a personal brass band. With a final curtsy, Melia gave Dorian a quick gesture, and he gladly willed *The Windlass* into motion, the winged oars on either side beating at the air and spurring them away from the gilded ship and towards Sphere.

Once they were some distance away, the three of them burst out laughing.

"Hahaha!" Melia gasped, wiping a tear from her eye as her hair settled back into its wild flutter. "Did you see him! How could he move with all that crap?"

"Hee hee hee!" Fable giggled, bent over the rail of the helm, her laughter so hard her legs threatened to give out under her. "And you! 'Oh do forgive me, sir. My perfume is all used up!' Ha ha ha!"

"Good gods," Dorian gasped, his ribs aching from mirth. "What a tool!"

"Absolutely," Melia chortled, shaking her head as she slumped back against the mast. "Oh gods. But they are dangerous too. That ship could have blasted us to driftwood with barely a thought."

"Yeah?" Dorian said, the last of his chuckles dying down. "What if he caught us in a lie?"

Melia shook her head, her smile fading. "You really don't want to know."

"Yeah," Fable agreed, hoisting herself back to her hooves. "Elven Imperials can get pretty testy. They don't technically have any authority, aside from what their guns give them. But they're so well armed—that's usually plenty."

"Do those stops happen often?" he asked.

"Not really," Fable said with a shrug. "But they do happen. And better watch out. The only reason Imperials can look that stupid is because they've got the power to make sure no one can tell them otherwise."

Dorian could believe that. Despite his lingering chuckles, he glanced back at the gilded ship as it cruised towards the wyrmgate like a shark. Elegant, beautiful, but beyond deadly. With a sigh, he shook his head, and returned his full attention to what lay in front of him.

Finding a place to dock at Sphere wasn't hard. Melia had him avoid the upper levels, which had been carved from stone and whose piers were huge, gaping maws built into the planetoid itself like vast drydocks. Many of those, apparently, were owned by very wealthy merchant companies or mercenary groups. Instead, they settled for some of the sprawling wood and metal docks of the expansive mid-levels, finding one crooked length that projected outward in front of a raucous tavern district.

Slowing *The Windlass*, Dorian brought it alongside the wooden walkway, and once they were near Melia nimbly hopped off the ship with a mooring rope and tied them off securely. Finally letting go of the wheel, Dorian stepped back, his scales partially receding on his hands and leaving him himself once more.

As he disembarked, he saw Melia talking to what looked like some sort of upright lizard in a long black cloak, a silver eye stitched into his hood and another topping the tall staff he carried. Some coins changed hands, and the lizardman turned, hissing something as he swept his staff at *The Windlass*.

A shimmer framed the ship like a bubble, and Dorian shivered at a feeling like someone had tightened the air around him. "What was that?" he asked as Melia joined him and Fable.

"Security warder," Melia said, showing off a stone with a runed mark on it she'd received from the reptilian mage. "He warded the ship and will keep it safe. Pricey, but worth every copper in a place like this."

"Like this?" Dorian muttered.

As he said this, the window of one of the nearby taverns smashed, a human flying through it backwards to slam onto the sprawling docks with a bang of wood.

"Yeah. This," Melia said.

"Ah," Dorian grunted as a number of what looked like humanoid rats in rags suddenly burst from the shadows, mobbing the unconscious human and ripping off boots before rifling through his pockets.

Note to self, Dorian mused as the girls bustled him towards the crooked avenues of wood, stone and metal. *Don't go to sleep off of the ship.*

But though grungy, the level of Sphere they were on quickly overwhelmed Dorian with awe. He'd never traveled far outside his home village, and even if he had, he doubted he'd ever have seen a place like Sphere. It was like walking into a cave that someone had crammed an entire port city into. Domes of magic light burned here and there in the ceiling, while taverns, chandler shops, and more fought for space. Some were built atop other buildings, reached by staircases that looked extremely unstable. Races of all kinds jostled for space between taverns and shops. He spotted orcs, goblins, elves and humans, but also even more outlandish creatures he'd never dreamed could exist. One looked like a human with transparent skin. Another was what looked like a bipedal rabbit, but so densely muscled he could stop arrows with his mere bulk.

So stunned by the sights before him, Dorian offered no resistance as both Fable and Melia drew him down the gritty street, the two women smiling at each other over his amazement.

"We'll get a drink here," Melia said, steering them towards a tavern. *The Moonshot*, it seemed to be called, sported the picture of a moon being dipped into a glass of wine. It looked about as good as any place to Dorian, and surely met their current needs.

The bat-wing doors swung open and dumped them in a common room as varied as the streets outside. A slew of creatures filled it, a number of whom looked to be quite literally devils, including horns and fangs. The motley array of races and creatures stuffed the common room near to bursting, the sound of their voices speaking a hundred tongues, sometimes with more than one actual tongue, filled the air, and the scent of bodies and booze finished the scene.

This, at least, Dorian understood. Though he'd never known Grouse's inn to be so crowded, the atmosphere of boisterous joviality was the same as the old man's inn during those days when the catches came in and the sailors and fishermen spent their coin on ale to warm them.

Fable clopped merrily into the room, Melia close behind and Dorian dragging after. He tried not to stare at one denizen who seemed to have two heads, four arms, and no patience as he bellowed at a man without ears or eyes, but wore straps of leather and blades crossed over his shoulder.

Fable found the way to the bar and took a seat, raising her hand to the bartender, who appeared to be an octopus wearing a red uniform, arms handling dozens of taps and mugs with ease as he served the entire bar.

"Three of your finest, cheapest, biggest drinks, my good cephalopod," Fable declared, holding up three fingers and sporting a grin that would make a wise man check his wallet.

The bartender made a sound that was either an affirmative or it was choking on something. The former, Dorian guessed as three tentacles swiped up some mugs, filled them from a tap one after the next, and served them up on the bar so fast they rattled, yet never spilled a drop.

Dorian cautiously took his mug. The drink was fizzing, popping, and quite purple. He glanced over at Fable as the faun scooped up her drink, smacking her lips greedily before downing a great quaff of it.

"Hoooeee!" Fable gasped, slamming the mug down with a shake of her head. "Damn! That's the stuff. Moobin Ale! Made from fermenting deddon mushrooms! Try it, you'll like it," she added to Dorian.

Dorian had his doubts, but the girls hadn't steered him wrong yet—at least not as far as he knew. He lifted his mug in salute to Fable.

...And had a huge, hairy hand grab it from his own.

"'Ere! That's too good for humies!"

Dorian turned his head as he looked up at what appeared to be a literal demon with skin red as a rash and leather straps crossing his chest, currently straining under the heaviness of a pronounced gut. Tattooed on one shoulder was a stylized skull sporting two cutlasses buried in the eye sockets. Two horns peaked a head that strongly resembled a pig. The demon was huge and bulky, with a leer of fanged teeth and blurry eyes that spoke of too much drink—or maybe a brain injury. Very possibly both, Dorian mused as the demon took a pull from the stolen mug.

With a guffaw of foul breath, the demon leaned in, leering down at Dorian. "What? You gonna be mad humie?"

"No, not really," Dorian sighed as though bored. He'd had enough experience with regular belligerent drunks to know not to escalate whatever was going on here.

"What? Why not? You not gonna fight back 'r nuffin?" the demon slurred.

"Thanks, but no thanks," Dorian chuckled, pivoting away. His heart was beating fast with warning, but his own ego got the better of him, and he turned his back on the demon and started off.

The drunken devil suddenly grabbed him by the side of the shirt and pulled him close, whipping him back around. The horned head leaned down and grinned meanly. "And what if I don't give ya a choice? What if I wants a fight, yeah?"

"Well, if a gentlemen requests..."

"Dorian," Melia hissed, throwing her face into her palm and gritting her teeth. "That is not how we do things here."

He glanced at her, wondering if there was some faux pas he'd missed. "It's not?"

"Of course not. This is!" Melia shouted, and punched the demon hard in the face.

The demon reeled back with a sound like a squealing pig. As the pugnacious devil swung back forward, he found Melia had already sprang onto the bar and was now behind him. Her arm looped around the rolls of his neck and tightened in a choking headlock.

The demon gagged, his fat fingers reflexively reaching back, which left his front tragically open. This fact did not go unmissed by Fable as she bounded forward and drove her knee up and into the fat monster's crotch.

The demon wheezed, leaning forward again and doubling over. Even Dorian winced sympathetically. Hoots and shouts of delight erupted as the patrons quickly formed a circle around the combatants, tonight's evening entertainment evidently decided on.

"Don't fuck with my navigator!" Melia shouted, raising a random stein from the bar over her head, then chugging it. The crowd exploded once more. Even Dorian almost got caught up in the spectacle.

He shoved his way back into the front of the crowd, arriving just in time to see another strange creature push its way through from the other side.

This specimen of inebriated pirate seemed to be of the same crew, judging by the skull and cutlass tattoo on its shoulder. It surely wasn't of the same species, as instead of a porcine figure, this one was tall and rangy like a mantis, sporting four arms tipped with three taloned fingers. Its face opened, revealing a segmented jaw of teeth as two of its hands grabbed a startled Melia from behind, wrenching her off the newcomer's piggy cohort and beginning to strangle the elf.

Rage flared like dwarven whiskey on a fire in Dorian's chest. He lunged out of the crowd, grabbing Melia's half-drunk ale and smashing the mug into the alien's face. The pirate's insectile head snapped sideways, then swung back around towards Dorian with a hiss, face soaked in the purple liquor as it continued to choke Melia. The alien's other hands moved to reach for its belt and the weapons there.

The fury in Dorian's chest grew hotter—blazed in him. He grabbed the alien's wrists holding Melia, talons growing from his fingers along with scales all down his forearms and biceps. The insectoid creature shrieked in pain over the crack of bones, its hands suddenly releasing Melia. But it had two other arms, and both drew wickedly serrated daggers.

Dorian didn't care. Fury consumed him. He bared his teeth, and felt them grow sharper with fangs. Scales peeled over his skin across his face and cheeks. The rage exploded in his gullet like the belly of a sun. He saw fear in the alien's face as its antennae wilted.

And then Dorian exhaled all his anger in a gout of golden flame.

The crowd fell silent in shock as the alien shrieked in agony, dropping its blades and grabbing for its burning face. Dorian released its broken limbs and the pirate staggered back, reeling through a hole that abruptly opened in the crowd.

The alien fled, careening out the doors as it frantically tried to pat out the flames consuming it.

Dorian heaved, breathing hard and fast with anger. But as the rage dissipated along with the flames he'd exhaled, he quickly became aware of the stunned looks from the crowd. Melia sat where she'd fallen, staring up at him in equal shock, and even Fable had stopped shoving the pig demon's head into a spittoon.

Dorian hastily straightened, clearing his throat, rapping a scaly fist against his chest and eliciting a burp of a fluttering flame.

"Er...excuse me," he said. "Strong ale. Right?"

Chapter 12

MELIA'S EYES FLASHED ABOUT the stunned tavern, her mind working fast. She suddenly sprang to her feet and grabbed Fable by the arm. Her other hand spun Dorian around and shoved him towards the door. "Okay!" she declared loudly. "Time to go, navigator!"

"Uh, I—" Dorian didn't really resist as he was bullied towards the exit.

"Shut up!" Melia hissed, her hair a fluttering mane of agitated purple. "We're on Sphere for five minutes and you cook someone's head in a bar fight! I swear, we can't take you *anywhere*!"

"But I—"

"Shush!" Melia hissed as she glanced back nervously. "We gotta—"

She was interrupted by something large and solid finding itself in her path. She bounced off it and looked up, then froze at what she saw. Dorian reached out to balance her, but his grip was limp when he looked up at the thing in front of them.

He'd seen orcs on his homeworld—but none like this one.

For one, he was bigger, near the size of the two ogre bodyguards flanking him on either side, his bald head studded with scars and what looked like plugs of ruby red stones and gold casings. For another, there was the dangerous gleam of not just cleverness, but raw intelligence in his eyes. He had a heavy, low slung jaw and a white, immaculate jacket that sat strangely on his bulky frame. The upper buttons were undone, revealing a red shirt beneath, along with a necklace of large, sharp teeth. One of his arms bulged, crudely artificial, made of thick, metallic blocks of golden material embedded with glittering stones all along its length, and ending in a pincer-like claw. The orc smiled at her, showing rows of sharp teeth that looked to be made of steel.

Melia quickly retreated, a keenly honed survival instinct saying offending the greenskin before her was a very bad idea. "S-sorry! Didn't mean to. Just um, heading for the door!"

"Wot? So soon?" the orc said in a voice like something between a bark and rocks breaking. "What a waste that'd be, when I's wanted so bad ta make yer acquaintance." He thrust forward the metallic arm, the crystals embedded in it gleaming. "Boss Grash Ironjaw, at yer service."

Dorian watched cautiously as Melia swallowed hard. He felt a shift in the crowd around them. Specifically a shift *away* from the orc. Melia exchanged a quick glance with Fable, who gaped in amazement. Dorian couldn't blame them. He got the feeling that the name was hardly unknown. Based on what he was seeing, he'd guess it belonged to one of the most powerful figures on Sphere. The elf and the faun probably recognized the big bastard the second they laid eyes on him.

"Pleasure," Melia said weakly, reluctantly taking the offered hand, and was relieved when the cold metal didn't squeeze hard as he shook it. "I'm Melia. This is Fable, an auramancer, and Dorian, our ship's navigator."

"Pleased ta make yer acquaintance," Grash said as his eyes drifted to Dorian, who instantly tensed. "No mistakin' indeed. This be a navigator, no doubt. Pretty powerful one, must say."

Dorian gave him a puzzled look. "How can you..."

Grash laughed. "Youz can always tell. It's tha scales, see? They stick 'round longer tha more powerful you iz. Never met one what had them still around after they left tha helm so long ago. You're interestin' my lad," Grash said with a leering grin.

Dorian leaned back a little, feeling uneasy about the attention. He much preferred being under Fable and Melia's heavy gazes. "Um...thank you?"

"Nah. Thank you! I gots ta see somethin' interestin' 'ere. In fact, I'd be most pleased if'n you'd join me in me private booth."

"Oh, uh, actually, we need to head out," Melia quickly said with the desperation of someone drowning. "Just stopped by for a quick break before looking for some work."

"Oh! Youz wantin' some work?" Grash said jovially, straightening the sleeves of his coat. "Well, ain't that lucky! I've got work, right ya are. More 'n you can handle. How's about we 'ave ourselves a little palaver, eh?"

"How...generous. We'd love to," Melia replied, grinning, but Dorian noticed the pale yellow of her fluttering hair, denoting her unease.

"Aye. Generosity! That be me weakness," Grash said as he turned, and space was made in the crowd as he led the way back across the bar. Onlookers had quickly all gone back to their own business like nothing had happened, Dorian's sin completely ignored when Grash's interest was known. Melia and Fable followed reluctantly, the latter giving a yearning look to the door, but as the two hulking ogres closed the gap behind them, she sighed and turned her attention forward.

Dorian followed, sensing instantly that this was not an ideal situation, at least as far his companions believed. But knowing he was too far out of his depths to do more than follow their lead, he bit his tongue and pressed on, seeing no other avenue available.

The booth in question was a big one, necessarily so, and set in the far wall. Grash heaved himself into his seat, while Dorian, Fable and Melia were easily able to sit across from him. The ogres took position a short distance away, facing outwards and discouraging anyone from getting near. In another situation, Dorian probably would have taken a moment to marvel at the unusual padded leather design of these seats and the glassy surface of the table, but now all he could think about was survival—his and the girls'.

Across the table, Grash clasped hand and claw, his head leaning down between his two immense shoulders as he grinned at the trio before him. "You're lucky I waz 'ere, in fact! I was waitin' ta meet another client 'ere, when you'z little show drew my eye. But whatcha be needin' work so badly for? With a navigator like 'im there, oi'd be thinkin' you'd be rollin' in dough."

"Just need to pay for a few upgrades for our ship," Melia said quickly, finally seeming to accept the situation. Her voice was still higher than usual, but she was less shaky. "Cannons, maybe some extra enchantments. For self defense, of course."

Grash beamed and leaned back again in his seat. "Well!" he said with a broad and welcoming swing of his arms. "Ain't that a lucky coincidence!"

"Why?" Melia said uneasily.

Even as she did, the two ogre bodyguards shifted, speaking to someone before stepping aside. Every eye at the table swung about as a woman stepped up to join them.

She was a demon, that much was clear at first glance, even though her black horns had been filed down to nubs growing from a mane of midnight hair, as soft and luxurious as an ebony pelt. Leather was the order of the day, with a jacket that hung from her shoulders, revealing the curves of firm, crimson breasts clad tight in a band of black, rubbery fabric. Tall heels lifted her up, her boots decorated with spikes, while tight black pants hugged her hips and the sultry curve of her ass.

She was sex poured in leather, and clearly knew it, radiating a lazy danger that was only compounded by the belts of ammunition bedecking her. One slung crooked on her hips, two more across her chest forming an X. The barrel of a rifle poked over her shoulder and twin revolvers were holstered at her sides. Dorian only knew them as dwarven technology on his world, but their design was smaller than he thought such things could be.

The demon stood before them, appraising, staring. Golden eyes scanned the table slowly, picking out Melia, Dorian and Fable with sharp scrutiny.

"Ah! Speak o' tha devil, I says! And 'ere she is," Grash said with a grand gesture at the demoness. "Everyone? Be pleased ta introduce you ta Emberly Brimspire! A dear associate a mine. Powdermancer, arcane artillerist, and casual golemancer. And it just so 'appens she's in th' market fer someone ta deliver some goods right quick. Say 'ello, Emberly."

"Hi. Who the fuck are these people?" Emberly said, a hiss of black smoke escaping her lips like a smoldering volcano.

"A crew come ta Sphere ta sell their services," Grash said grandly. "And they seem ta have some potential, don'tcha? Eh?" he said with another leer at the trio. "I be thinkin' they'd be right good ta have in moi back pocket."

"You think so?" Emberly said, shifting her weight to her other side, the bandolier around her hips rocking at the motion.

"'Course! I gots a fine eye for value. This navigator 'ere's got some real potential in 'im. And tha ladies 'ave all got that kinda spunk that's always useful. Why, dis skittish elf decked a pig-lookin' devil in the kisser, she did."

Melia's eyes bulged to be brought in out of nowhere.

Emberly exhaled sharply, blowing another hiss of smoke into the air. "Fuckin' kidding me, Grash?" she growled. "This job's too important for a bunch of godsdamn greenhorns. They're probably all still sick from their first star walk, flyin' around a stolen groundling ship."

"Hey," Dorian said, frowning. "How'd you know about that?"

"How do I...Look at you!" she said, gesturing at him. "You're dressed like a damn drudge from some farming world! No one who's been in the stars more'n a day wears that kinda crap, savvy?"

Dorian looked at his roughspun shirt, plucking at it uncertainly. "Huh..." he said, glancing around at the very different attire of everyone else in the room, his own crew included. "Fair point."

"Fucking hell!" Emberly snapped at Grash. "I need professionals here, Grash. Savvy? I need them rough. I need them ready! I need them hard! Hard as balls!"

"Those don't seem too hard," Fable noted. "Kinda soft, actually."

Emberly tilted her head, fixing the faun with a steely glare.

Grash bellowed with laughter and slapped the table, which left a visible crack in the surface. "Har har! You'z be surprised with dem, Emberly. Dis one," he said, jerking a golden thumb at Dorian, "just done finished breathin' fire all over a crewman from tha Nixium! Melted 'is face right off, 'e did!"

Her eyes snapped back to Grash, then to Dorian. She seemed to actually see him then, her gaze lingering on the scales that still decorated his cheeks and hands. "That pirate running down the street with his head torched? That was you?" she said.

"Well, yeah. Kinda," Dorian admitted, rubbing the back of his head uncertainly. "Well, not kinda. It was definitely me."

Emberly huffed, a plume of smoke steaming from her nose. "Hmph," she said. "Well, maybe there's some surprises here after all..."

"That's tha spirit!" Grash beamed, rising with a grand gesture. "Love me's a nice, big, happy family! Now, since we'z all 'ere now, ow'z about we takes this to a more private location, so we'z can discuss tha more...delicate aspects a this operation. Eh?"

Chapter 13

As they left the tavern, a large figure moved out of the shadows and alongside them. Dorian instantly tensed as the massive man revealed himself—skin as grey as concrete, his eyes were sallow and deep in his skull, his body clad in a thick, double-breasted coat. His skin was taut, yet the bones beneath his face seemed overly large and blocky.

Emberly saw them tense up and chuckled. "Don't mind him. That's my bodyguard when I'm on Sphere, Cook. Say hi, Cook."

"Hello," the grey man said in a flat, heavy voice.

Dorian glanced at the man's hands, noting they appeared to be five pieces of segmented metal like cables wrapped into the shape of a fist. "Hi," he said.

"Glad you lot'z are makin' friends," Grash said with a grin of his metal teeth. "Emberly? I'm 'eadin' back ta the office. Got some headcounts ta reduce. You take care a da contract 'nd the rest if ya fink we can make use a dem."

"Be a tough one, Grash," Emberly told him warily. "But I'll see what can be done."

"Love ta 'ear it. C'mon, boys. Let's go," Grash uttered with a beckoning motion to his ogres, the three bulky figures stomping off deeper into Sphere's hectic streets.

"Now then, let's go take a look at this shameful groundling ship of yours," Emberly said as she started off towards the docks, Melia soon hastening to lead the way. Fable joined her, but Dorian hung back, walking with Cook, noting that their route was far less crowded than last time, as even the drunks seemed to instinctively avoid the large man and Emberly's presence.

Dorian glanced again at Cook, who walked with the sort of steady plodding stride like not even a brick wall would divert him. "So," Dorian said. "Your name is Cook?"

"Yes," Cook said.

"Uh huh. And...do you cook?"

"No," Cook said.

"Right. Right," Dorian muttered, lapsing back into uneasy silence. He wasn't sure where he thought that line of conversation was headed.

Awkward.

He was relieved when they reached the docks once more where *The Windlass* lay at berth. This relief lasted up until he saw Emberly's expression, which had 'unimpressed' written all over it.

"That's it?" she said.

"What's wrong with it?" Melia huffed, her hair going red.

Emberly snorted and gestured at the craft. "Look at this thing! It's textbook basic. This is the *definition* of the basics. First year shipwrights would build a tub like this to show their grasp of the trade! Looks like you just stole some groundling Lord's yacht and enchanted it with a spare core, savvy?"

"Now listen here, you..." Melia began, but Fable grabbed her friend by the shoulder and gave the elf a warning look.

"That's right," Fable chirped sweetly, turning a sunny smile to the demon. "We did. Had to get off planet after our last ship crashed from a run in with some dwarves, but I think we did as well as could be expected given the circumstances."

Emberly laughed shortly. "Thought so! Well, at least you all are resourceful, I'll give you that. That'll teach you for fuckin' with dwarves, though. Let me guess—fly too close to their precious asteroids?"

Dorian listened in shock at how blatantly the theft was admitted—and celebrated no less. He had a sudden feeling that those who traveled the Black didn't have much respect for those who remained earthbound. It was a somewhat sobering thought, and he didn't know if he liked it much. After all—that had been his life not even a few days ago.

"Let's take a look aboard," Emberly said, striding towards the plank.

"Hold up," Melia stopped her, drawing out the warding stone and directing it at the ship. There was a flash, and the bubble around *The Windlass* shimmered briefly before fading. "There. Go ahead."

Emberly strode aboard, her heels clicking across the deck as she toured the vessel, her golden eyes quick, missing nothing. Melia and Fable watched the demoness closely, but both had to admit she seemed to know her business, at least. Melia crossed her arms, but Fable was quick to provide any information the powdermancer wanted, asking in sharp, clipped tones as if hoping to catch them off guard.

"Core in the wheel?" Emberly inquired, inspecting the helm closely.

"Makes the most sense with a draconic navigator," Fable said.

"Suppose so. And those oars? They steer it?"

"There's a rudder, but the oars provide initial push. You'd be surprised how fast it can go," Fable said proudly. "Though that's mostly thanks to Dorian."

"Hmph," Emberly grunted—or grumbled, perhaps. She strode to the center of the deck and stopped, her head slowly turning. Taking in the full expanse of the vessel, her hands rested on her hips. She let out a hiss of smoke and slowly, almost reluctantly, nodded.

"Hmmm. Well, it's nothing special, but if you lot are worth the investment, maybe I can make you passable. Savvy? You!"

Dorian perked up at her tone. "Me?"

"Yeah. You! How long've you been flying, pretty boy?"

Dorian shrugged. "Uh, lemme see. About...two? Almost three days? Hard to measure time up here."

Emberly raised a swooping eyebrow. She suddenly burst out with a sharp, barking laugh. "Ha! Well, you lot are entertaining if nothing else. And the definition of fuckin' underdogs at that. You're just lucky I love that sort. But I don't love losers, savvy?"

"Savvy," Fable quickly squeaked.

"Yeah, sure," Melia said sourly, crossing her arms and blowing a crimson wisp of hair out of her face.

"Good! So we're gonna try and turn you into the encyclopedia entry for fuckin' winners. And you know what winners have?"

"Trophies?" Dorian guessed. He felt kind of proud of that guess. He was definitely technically correct if nothing else.

"Hell no! Winners have firepower!" Emberly roared, her eyes lighting up and sparks crackling around her. "I'll stick some arcane cannons on this tub, some more discreet little somethings to make a big surprise. And you ever heard of ramming stones?"

"Er, no?" Dorian said.

"Well you're gonna! Because I'm gonna slap one of those bad boys right on your prow, savvy? And normally, I'd charge you all an arm, a leg, and maybe a few other appendages. But since you're working for Grash, we can work something out. Only there's gonna be another condition."

"Can't wait," Melia grumbled.

"First job you do for big green over there? I'm coming with," she said with a sharp look. "Not just for insurance for our mutual boss, but for the weapons I'm slapping on this tub. Contract'll be for a year of exclusive work for the boss, and if you take any other jobs, he gets a cut. We agree on that, I'll supe up your ship so it'll run against any other craft this side of the Spinward. Savvy?"

"And, what's the benefit for a deal like this instead of just freelancing?" Dorian asked. "I mean no offense, I'm just new."

Emberly scoffed. "You kidding me? You're getting the premier experience here under contract, navigator. You get the gear, free repairs, access to crew if you need 'em, rations, supplies, the works! Savvy?"

"And the drawbacks?" he asked.

"Well there's gonna be that, sure," she admitted with a lazy shrug, her jacket riding the roll of her shoulders with a metallic clink. "You gotta work for him, take jobs he orders, so on, so forth. But Grash knows how much privateers value freedom, hence why we're going with a one year contract, savvy? But most renew all the same once it's done."

Melia frowned, thoughtful, and Fable hung close to the elf. The pair exchanged a look, then Melia looked back to Emberly. "It sounds interesting, but we'd like a bit to think it over—and to see a draft of the contract."

Emberly rolled her eyes, as if begging the heavens for patience with fools who didn't know a good thing when it was staring them in the face. "Fine. Fine, fair enough. I'll send for the scribe. Need a bit to take a look at my arsenal and see what I've got that'll work with this ship anyway. But don't think too long, savvy?" she added with a warning finger as she strode towards the gangplank. "Offers like this don't come around often. C'mon, Cook."

"Hrrr," Cook rumbled, striding after the smoky demoness.

Dorian watched the demoness go, and only once he saw her meandering down the crooked docks did he turn to his companions. "So," he said. "Thoughts?"

"I like her aura," Fable murmured. "She has a nice one. Trustworthy and brave if a little rough around the edges."

"Really?" Dorian said skeptically. "Trustworthy?"

"Sure. I mean, yeah," Fable said with a shrug. "She's clearly out for herself, but you know. She's not lying to us at all, I think. Grash is different though." She sank into a whisper as her face scrunched in distaste like she'd tasted something foul. "He's got a nasty one. Manipulative and cunning. Not the worst aura you'll find around here by far, but definitely dangerous. He's got a long game in mind."

"You can tell that?" Dorian said with amazement.

Fable tilted her hand and gave an uncertain wiggle. "Yes. Mostly. It's more of an impression. Right? But he's got more in mind than just this contract."

"I'm sure he does," Melia said, crossing her arms and leaning against the mast, her hair flickering cold, analytical blue. "A guy doesn't get to where Grash is by not being ruthless. But he's got a reputation for playing fair with contracts, and I think he values that reputation. And seems to respect Emberly. Genuinely."

"Sounds like she could be a good ally to have around," Dorian mused.

Fable nodded. "Yeah? You think so?"

Dorian realized both were looking at him. He considered it, then shrugged. "I think we should take the deal. I mean, what's a year, right? We'll spend a chunk of that traveling, from what I understand. As long as the contract looks reasonable, I think it'd be alright. And, I know I'm still new to this whole..." He gestured vaguely at the station around him and space overhead. "But it seems to me like getting the gear he's giving us would be pretty expensive on our own...Not to mention take a long time to get. Right?"

"Well..." Fable began.

"It would," Melia agreed reluctantly. "The way Emberly's talking, it sounds like we're skipping three or four steps ahead if we sign. With our current setup, we'd probably be running livestock world to world along with other less than appealing cargo for a while before we even start equipping this ship with the gear we need."

Dorian nodded. "I thought so. And hey! If we can get Emberly on our side during the journey, she could go to bat for us with Grash. Just my thought, I suppose."

Melia threw up her hands. "Alright! I guess we have our answer, so long as the contract isn't shit."

"Where you going?" Fable asked as the elf strode off towards the hatch.

"Down to the hold. I'm starving, and since someone barbecued a pirate, I didn't get to grab food at the cantina."

"He was choking you," Dorian reminded her.

"And I appreciate the effort, navigator, really. But my stomach is still sucking up against my spine, so I'm going to go see if I can finish off that bread and some of the jerky. If anyone wants to join me, come on down!"

Saying this, Melia's head vanished into the hold, her voice echoing the last few words.

Fable snorted and gave Dorian a soft smile. "Really did appreciate you coming to bat for her in there," the cute faun said.

"Glad someone does," Dorian sighed.

"That's just Melia being Melia," Fable said as she clopped in closer, her arms clasped behind her back and a teasing smile hovering on her lips. "You heard her. She really did appreciate it. And so did I."

With that, Fable leaned up, and pressed a quick kiss to Dorian's lips. His eyes shot open in surprise and Fable eased back, touching her lips coyly. "Good things are happening thanks to you, Dorian. Really. And we're really grateful you're here, and that you trust us."

"Uh, yeah," Dorian said, resisting the urge to lick his lips to taste her. "Me too."

Fable giggled, blushing lightly. "Good. Then, let's make that the first of many." With a wink, Fable spun about, fairly skipping down the hatch and into the hold, her voice demanding Melia save her some bread echoing up in her wake.

Dorian leaned on the rail, shaking his head in amazement. It was a strange world he'd found himself in, that was for sure. Briefly, he considered going below and joining the pair, but reconsidered. It would deflate Fable's parting line.

He grinned, still tasting her lips on his. Yeah, he mused, looking up at Sphere's layered face. This trip definitely seemed to be worth it. He was eager to see what happened next.

Chapter 14

Dorian wandered about the deck, checking it just in case some of their equipment had 'wandered off' while they were ashore. Sphere didn't exactly inspire him with tremendous confidence when it came to security. The place looked like someone had created the galaxy's biggest back alley, filled it with wooden spars, and overflowed its people with booze.

As he walked around, he noticed the reptilian warder from before moving about the docks along with a few other wizards in similar garb. They passed near the pier where Dorian was docked and stopped, watching him check some barrels fastened to the rail. Under their withering stare, Dorian cleared his throat and pretended he was dusting the barrels before making his way back to the helm. He caught the warders slowly shaking their heads at him before ultimately moving on.

Dorian sighed and leaned on the wheel. Gods above, he really felt out of his element here. Well, not entirely. He felt home, finally, out here among the stars. But his ignorance was really beginning to grate on him. Sure, his instincts were sharp when it came to navigating, but his knowledge about life in the Black, in space—it was woefully lacking. An almost complete reversal from his life up to this point, where before he had knowledge galore but felt terribly uninspired by life in Clemmen.

He chuckled thinly. "It has only been a few days," he said to himself. Yet that didn't feel like a good enough excuse. He sighed and crossed his arms on the wheel, resting his chin on his wrists.

...Then lifted his head again at the clump of feet on the gangplank.

Dorian watched with puzzlement as a goblin tromped up the gangplank. But not a goblin like any he'd seen before. Though, given the recent batch of encounters he'd had so far, he really needed to stop being surprised. Come to think of it, he'd never heard of a well-dressed orc with metal teeth, and that didn't seem to bother him all that much.

The goblin was dressed in a purple waistcoat and white shirt beneath. A pair of spectacles sat on his hooked nose and an expression of learned sourness twisted his lips. In one hand he carried a leather briefcase, and a pencil was tucked behind a pointy, ragged ear.

Dorian cleared his throat. "Uh, can I help you?" he said.

The goblin looked his way. "Perhaps," he replied, his voice a wheedling, thin thing like he was doing Dorian a favour by merely acknowledging his presence. "My name is Emeritus. Is this *The Windlass?*"

"Yeah."

"Mmm. Good," Emeritus said, setting down his briefcase on some barrels and opening the latches, revealing reams of labeled folders like an overstuffed accordion. "I am here to discuss the contract you wish to sign with Mister Grash, with rather favorable terms proposed by Miss Emberly, I might add."

"Oh. Right."

"And I would thank you," he added with a pointed look and even sourer puckering of his thin lips, "not to look at me like that."

"Er—"

"I will do no business with someone with prejudiced opinions on goblins," Emeritus said, snapping shut the latches of his briefcase. "I am fully capable of doing my job."

Dorian flushed. "No, no. I didn't mean...I just, well, most goblins I've met..."

"Clearly," Emeritus squawked with another reedy, contemptuous sniff, "you have not met many goblins at all."

"Well...no, not a lot," Dorian admitted.

"What's going on up here?"

Dorian looked in relief over to the hold as Fable's antlers emerged, followed by the rest of the faun.

"Hey!" Dorian said, nodding at the goblin. "This is Emeritus. He's the scribe, I guess."

"Oh! Fantastic!" Fable beamed, clopping up, Melia poking her head out moments later. "We were just discussing the terms. My name's Fable. This is Melia."

"Excellent to meet you," Emeritus said with a dismissive eye at Dorian. "Finally, someone willing to look past their prejudicial views on other races."

Fable glanced at Dorian, who gave her a helpless gesture. She rolled her eyes. "Sorry about that," she said to the goblin. "He's been a groundling until about a day ago."

"Ignorance is hardly justification," Emeritus answered with another cutting look at Dorian. "But no matter." He returned his attention to Fable and Melia. "I have come to see the contract signed and all legal documentation put in order," he said, handing over the clipped papers to Fable. "The contract is more than fair."

Fable scanned the papers, Melia reading over the faun's shoulder as Emeritus rattled off the terms in his reedy voice. "You are paid per job completed for Mister Grash, but are guaranteed a job with a minimum payment of two hundred gold whenever requested. You are permitted to take on jobs for other employers, so long as it doesn't interfere with tasks Mister Grash has, but any payment gained through such employment shall have fifty percent of profits deducted for Boss Grash, as opposed to the twenty percent when you do jobs through him."

Melia whistled sharply. "Fifty percent?" she gasped. "That's skyway robbery!"

Emeritus peered at her over the gold rims of his spectacles. "I assure you," he said in a tone of nonplussed indifference, "it is very fair. Consider the many supplies and boons you will be provided. Mister Grash will be subsidizing all your expenses and repairs going forward. Besides," Emeritus added magnanimously as he pushed his glasses back up the curving slope of his nose, "this is highly unusual to begin with. Normally, you would work exclusively for Mister Grash. You are being given special consideration, though for what reason eludes me."

"Makes sense," Fable mused diplomatically as she reached the second grouping of documents. "And this is..."

"The specific contract for your first task," Emeritus said with a sniff of his hooked nose. "You will be delivering a crate to the *Blue Roamer* along with Miss Emberly."

"The *Blue Roamer*?" Fable said with sudden interest, shooting a look at the goblin. "Those Null Mages out in the wyrmway?"

"You are well informed," Emeritus admitted begrudgingly.

"What are the goods?" Melia asked.

"I cannot say."

"What?" Melia said with a glare. "What do you mean you can't say?"

"Hmmn. Exactly that," Emeritus told her, adjusting his spectacles peevishly. "The goods are of a sensitive nature, and I do not have permission to disclose their contents. Should you be curious, Miss Emberly knows, and may have clearance to reveal their contents, should she be inclined."

Melia grimaced. "Forget it," she grumbled. "The less we know the better."

"A most wise decision," Emeritus noted smugly.

Dorian wasn't so sure of that. It seemed obvious to him they should know what they were transporting, especially given the dangers that it could present. He'd only had a taste of the strangeness of the Black thus far, but it seemed to him that the risk was very real.

But he kept silent, noting how Fable nodded along and Melia didn't press the issue. He still knew little of how things beyond worlds worked, and it seemed a consensus was reached anyway.

He listened to Emeritus drone about deeper technicalities of the contract, Fable and Melia pressing in places, clarifying others, all of which went over Dorian's head until finally Fable sorted the papers.

"Might we have a minute in private to discuss them?" she asked.

"Mmm. Of course," Emeritus said.

"Thanks." Fable jerked her head and moved towards the rail by the helm, Melia and Dorian joining her.

"What do you think?" Fable asked, her voice dropping to a near whisper.

"Seems pretty fair to me," Melia said. "Surprisingly so. And it's our ticket to the big times. With this, we'll be somebodies."

"I dunno," Fable said, shifting uneasily, her ears flicking.

"What do you mean?" Melia asked.

Fable nibbled on her lower lip. "Well, I mean, doesn't this all seem to be happening really quickly?" she pointed out. "We're here for twenty minutes and get offered a job by one of the biggest players on Sphere? Maybe the sector? Something just doesn't feel right."

"It's not like he's doing this out of the goodness of his heart," Melia pointed out, jerking a thumb at Dorian. "He's looking to monopolize our navigator."

Dorian straightened. "Really? Me?"

Melia scoffed. "Of course! Or didn't you notice him trying to monopolize you like a pretty girl at a ball? I mean, let's face it. People like me and Fable? We're a dime a dozen in space. But you? Dragonblooded navigators are a hot commodity, and you're obviously something special. The lingering scales, the way you pick up every skill you try, that little trick you pulled in the tavern—it means you've got big potential, and Grash wants a piece of that action before a competitor snatches you up. Me and Fable? We're just bonuses."

"You're more than that," Dorian protested.

"Love to think so," Fable said sadly. "But she's kinda right. Trust me, Dorian. We've been in this game a long time, and we aren't about to oversell ourselves. You're the one he wants. If he wants us, it's only because he thinks we're a package deal with you."

Dorian frowned, but he didn't have the argument to refute that. It was true, he'd felt Grash eying him like Grouse did to a traveller when they brought out their money pouch. Grash had plans for Dorian, that much was plain.

He decided to say his piece. "The fact that he wants to control me so badly is more reason to be concerned," Dorian pointed out. "A deal as good as this sounds? There's got to be more to it we're not getting told. Aren't you worried about that?"

Melia shrugged. "Not really," she admitted. "People are going to be looking at us like Grash is anywhere we go. Honestly, if he'd cracked Dorian over the head and dragged him off in a sack, that'd still probably be the best deal we'd be getting out here. And if we're working for Grash, we can tell anyone else to fuck off, or they deal with him."

Fable squirmed uncomfortably. "I guess. Dorian?" she said with an uneasy look his way. "What do you think?"

"Honestly?" Dorian said. "I just got here. I'm making this up as I go along, just trying to keep up. I'm completely lost here and flying by the seat of my pants."

Fable chuckled, giving him the first real smile he'd seen since the goblin had come aboard. "Then use those instincts of yours here, cutie. What do you feel is the best call?"

Dorian took a deep breath, then let it out. He'd always trusted his gut when it came to big decisions, so he reluctantly nodded. "I...think we should take the deal," he finally said. "It makes a lot of sense right now, and Melia brought up some good points. If people are going to come after me like you two think, then it makes sense we team up with someone big enough to give us cover."

Fable sighed, her ears wilting a little. "I guess. I do like Emberly, but Grash scares me."

There was a sudden clank and the trio looked over to the gangplank, just in time to see the devil herself strut aboard. The demoness glanced over at Emeritus, and then to them. "So?" she called out, lazily hooking her thumbs in the loops of her ammo belt. "Make a choice?"

"Yeah," Fable said with another confirming look at Melia and Dorian. "We'll sign."

The demoness gave a lazy grin. "Beauty," she said. "Then I didn't have this crap lugged down here for nothing. Bring 'er up, boys!" she shouted, stepping aside.

With a grunt, two burly men waddled aboard under the heavy weight of a massive crate, several more coming aboard after them, dragging or hefting yet more equipment, Emberly directing them with sharp barks of commands and the occasional emphatic arm motion.

The time to work had begun.

Chapter 15

ONCE EMBERLY WAS SATISFIED the goods were being brought aboard properly, she returned to Dorian, Fable and Melia and began to go over the specifics of the mission, her voice rising over the banging of crates and materials being unloaded.

"Alright, this is gonna be a simple job, savvy? And the best way to get that done is for everyone to know what they're doing."

"Does that include knowing what's in the cargo?" Dorian asked.

"Good question, and the answer is no," Emberly emphatically replied. "The less everyone knows about what's being shipped, the better. Savvy? My job is to worry about what's in the crates. Which I don't at all, because it's nothing dangerous, toxic, or explosive. Unfortunately."

"Unfortunately?" Dorian smirked.

"It's just confidential to the client. So everyone keeps their eyes on the job, and everyone stays happy. Savvy?"

"Savvy!" Fable chirped with a wink and a thumbs up.

"See? She gets it. Your job is to escort me and the cargo to the *Blue Roamer*. Simple trip, but needs to be fast. Savvy?"

"Gotcha," Melia said. "We can do it."

"Groovy," Emberly said.

Dorian hung back, a bit more uneasy about the whole thing than at least Melia was. Though he had agreed to do the job, the details hadn't soothed his worries. He'd accepted they'd be working for Grash, but such ignorance of the cargo was sticking with him. How could they be so blase about transporting goods they didn't even know? Were they really just fine with it? Just like that? Was this really how business was done in the Black?

"Dorian? Dorian!"

"Hm?"

He looked up sharply to find all three women staring at him, their faces all telling a different story about what they thought of his distracted state. "Sorry, what? I was just ah, lost in my own thoughts a bit..."

Fable gave him a compassionate smile and patted his back. "Maybe take a break, Dorian. You've been working pretty steady for almost two days now. And we'll need you at the top of your game soon."

"She's got a point," Melia agreed, digging a hand into a pocket. "Here." She shoved some coins into Dorian's hand. "Have some fun and get some food or drink on the docks. But, uh, don't go too far. We'll need you back here come launch time."

Dorian took the coins. "I'm really okay..."

"Come on," Fable said gleefully, giving him a shove towards the gangplank. "Enjoy yourself! You earned it! We'll be flying for a while after this. May as well enjoy your shoreleave while you've got it."

Dorian slowly walked towards the gangplank, casting an uncertain glance back at the trio, who were already once more deep in conversation. He looked at the coins in his hands, then the sprawling depths of Sphere's layer with trepidation.

"Looking for a good time?"

Dorian turned towards the voice, spotting several of the loaders idling near some of the crates on the deck. The speaker—a half-orc, maybe—nodded at the coins in Dorian's hand. "I said, looking to have some fun?"

"I...guess so," Dorian replied.

The loader grinned, stepping forward and slapping Dorian on the back. "Great! We know a fantastic place not far from here. There's a gentlemen's cantina real close. Reeeeeal classy place. You're gonna love it!"

"I will?" Dorian muttered.

"Sure! We go there all the time. Don't we boys?"

"Aye!" came the boisterous chorus from the rest.

"See? And bringing in a genuine dragon blood navigator? That's gonna be worth something to the madame. Not to mention some drinks. So let's go live a little!"

Dorian wasn't so sure about that. But he was resolved to at least have some fun before returning to space, and the dock workers clearly knew their way around Sphere, so he supposed he would tag along. With a shrug, he allowed himself to be steered through the tight streets along the wharves and deeper into the planetoid, the shadows of the ceiling soon lit by red lamps that glowed from the fronts of buildings crowding the narrow avenue.

His guides turned in toward a particular building, the name *Ladies for the Lads* written in a strange tongue, swirling ink above the door, lit by two fluttering crimson lamps of brass. For some reason Dorian could read the unfamiliar script, but he didn't even question it since unexpected strangeness seemed to be the name of the game out in the Black. The doors swung open at the dockworker's push, and Dorian froze in shock at what he beheld.

Nothing in his life had prepared him for *Ladies for the Lads*. The interior was dark. Smoky. Lamps with some sort of glowing fish sat on every table in the room, illuminating the club with a cold blue light that glowed off the paint that the women within wore—they seemed to wear little else.

The floor rose in tiers like a massive staircase, the tables on each filled with men, waited on by women of a dozen races. 'Scanty' was barely adequate to describe the women's clothes. 'Nude' was evaded by a knife's edge. He saw an elf in nothing but two belt-like straps of leather swaying by a table and sliding the drinks down. At another, he saw what looked like a succubus with high, curling horns and a tail spaded like a heart slide into the lap of a grinning orc and grind herself against him with a sultry smirk. Still elsewhere he spotted two goblin women with petite figures but breasts anything but sitting on either side of a man in a naval jacket, cooing over his old scars.

Poles descended from the ceiling here and there, and on them danced yet more women in steadily less clothes. And the less they were dressed, the more money was thrown onto the table. A honkytonk bleated under the masterful touch of an alien with four arms, a master of his craft—and possibly a wizard judging by how the hues of light changed to the tune.

The sight seared itself in Dorian's eyes like staring into the sun. He'd never dreamed such debauchery was even possible. In a village where he knew everyone else by first name, it was like being punched by an ogre wearing a glove sparkling with sequins and pink feathers.

"Love it here!" Dorian's guide shouted and pulled the stunned navigator over to a large table with a pole sticking out of it, the dockworker sliding in and planting Dorian down beside him. Several other men took their places around the table. "Let's get some drinks!"

"How, uh, do we order?" Dorian asked.

"We wait. And not long! Looks like you're getting a fair bit of attention," his new friend said with a leer.

Dorian glanced around. The man was right. More than a few of the servers were eying him across the room. He was surprised, but there was an undercurrent thrill to it as well.

"Hey there," a dark elf said, sidling up beside him with eyelids low and flirty, her hair a fluttering mane of midnight laced with stars. Her skin was plum purple and her clothes nothing but a tight strap of rubbery fabric around her ample chest, while a band of silk slipped between her thighs like a loincloth. "Haven't seen you here before, big guy."

"Ah, right you are. First time here," Dorian admitted.

"Oooh," she cooed, a shift of her body setting her plush ass in his lap. "Then that means you should be getting some special treatment. Right?"

"I don't suppose I'd argue with that," Dorian said, finding some confidence.

"Attaboy," the elf giggled, and she lifted a cup of ale to her lips and took a long drink. Before Dorian knew what was happening, she'd leaned forward and kissed him.

Dorian froze, his eyes shooting wide open, especially when he felt the warm ale slip from her lips into his. He instinctively gulped it down, and though the liquor was hardly much to write home about, the taste of her lips and the kiss surely made up for it. It wasn't lost on him that this was the punishment for the dice game that Melia had originally proposed on The Windlass. The thought of the other elf doing this to him made his heart beat even harder than it probably otherwise would have.

The dark elf leaned back, exhaling warmly, her soft lips parted and a shiver coursed through her, hair fluttering with ecstasy. "Oooh," she breathed, eyes opening again. "I'm Stella, by the way."

"D-Dorian," he breathed.

"You dragonblooded?" she asked, slipping an arm around his neck.

"Yeah. How did..."

"Well, now that I look at your fingers, I can see a few scales—but elves are super sensitive to magic," she said, pulling herself against him. "Real...sensitive..."

"Almost as sensitive as demons," said another voice as a second arm slung itself around his neck from the other side, a pink skinned succubus leaning in. She had a crown of horns rising from her brow and pupils slitted like a snake's. Dorian briefly wondered what else was reptilian about her—and then wondered no more as her forked tongue flicked against his cheek.

Dorian tensed, feeling his heart quicken and body warm with desire in the presence of the two women and the shameless show being put on. But a thought lingered in his mind. This kind of treatment couldn't be free, and he cleared his throat.

"So," he said, glancing between succubus and elf. "This is probably going to be expensive, and I..."

"Don't worry, hot stuff," the elf giggled, rubbing her ass against his bulge. "We haven't done anything that'd cost you just yet. We're just getting to know a new patron, that's all."

"Emphasis on 'yet'," the succubus added, her hand teasing down his chest, playing with the laces of his shirt.

"But as handsome as you are, I don't mind spotting you a bit of fun," the elf added. "Just to make sure you come by again when your purse is a bit...heavier."

"A taste of the *Ladies for the Lads*," the succubus added, leaning in and gently kissing his neck, sending shivers racing to his toes. Her hand squeezed his inner thigh.

"O-oh. But...what about the drinks?" he gasped.

"Two silver a pop," Stella admitted.

Dorian goggled at the price. He had money for what he'd had so far, but that was pretty high for drinks.

"But we make the cost of drinking well worth it," the succubus added with a knowing look as she no doubt read his face.

"Sure do," Stella giggled.

Well, they had him there, he had to admit. And hell, why not live a bit? Everything these last few days had felt like a fever dream, so why not indulge a little? A short time ago, he was doing laundry for a peasant-run inn, wondering if his future career would be throwing out the drunks or, if he was lucky, taking care of the casks.

And yet here he was, in a tavern among the stars, being waited on by an elven beauty from the deepest dreams of any man, and a demoness from the same damn place. Had father Matland from the local temple seen this, he surely would have had a heart attack.

But he wasn't here. Only Dorian was. And it was time to have some fun.

And fun was surely had. The dockworkers joined Dorian in drinking and egging him on, and soon ale flowed freely. Though Dorian had always had a strong constitution, the sheer quantities began to tell even for him. The colours of the club swam in shimmers. The touch of deft and feminine hands tingled on his body. The lips of temptation whispered and kissed.

Dorian felt like he was floating, lifted from the world like *The Windlass* had from the docks of his former lord, but now he was carried onto the table. His shirt was lost at some point, and more women had joined the circle. They whistled and called out as he danced, moving to the music, and soon Stella and a stunning half-orc in nothing more than shimmering body paint.

"I fucking love space!" Dorian roared in delight.

Cheers came up from all around him.

And so did something else.

"What the *fuck* am I looking at, navigator!?"

Dorian knew that voice. It was like someone had thrown a bucket of cold water on him. He stopped dancing and peered blearily down, his eyes straining to adjust. Three faces resolved from the shimmering haze of drunken bacchanalia. Melia stood, hands on her hips, looking up at him in tight-lipped anger, Emberly standing by, arms folded and a lazy smirk on her lips, while Fable hung back, staring up at him with something like shocked amazement.

Dorian dropped his arms from around the two nubile women who'd been until then grinding against him. "Oh. Hey," he said, his mind fumbling for something to add. "Uh...wanna drink?"

Judging by the further angry tightening of Melia's face and the suddenly crimson flare of her hair, this was not the right answer.

"Dorian!" she barked. "You...you..."

"Hey now," Emberly drawled, slinging an arm around Melia's shoulder with a lazy leer at him. "Give the poor grounder some credit! You told him to have fun, and he managed to find the seediest club this side of Sphere, and even after two hours his pants are still on! Seems like an impressive feat to me, savvy?"

"You call *this* impressive!" Melia said with an incredulous gesture at Dorian.

Emberly looked Dorian up and down lazily, licking her lips. "Hmm. Yeah, actually. Kinda," she said with another grin of sizzling amusement.

"What's her problem?" Stella whispered from beside Dorian, then greedily licked his cheek. He didn't even react.

"Er..." Dorian grunted, "I better...yeah. Anyone see my shirt?" he said.

"Aw, looks like yer momma's callin' ya home," one of the other men at the table hooted, getting laughs and raucous cheers from the other loaders.

Laughter erupted, making Dorian flush as a helpful hand passed him his shirt. He hopped down off the table, staggering a little, though already he could feel the alcohol burning out of his system. "So," he said, tugging on the shirt hastily. "Uh, work's done, is it?"

"*You're* done, that's for damn sure," Melia growled, her hair glowing red. "Come on. We're getting back to the ship."

"Sure. Let me just...uh...how much...You know what? Just take it," Dorian said, shoving all the money he could find in his pockets into Stella's hands.

"Come again soon!" the dark elf cheered, already counting the money as Dorian sheepishly followed a seething Melia and cackling Emberly towards the doors.

Dorian found himself (somewhat unsteadily) walking next to Fable and cast her an uneasy sideways glance. She'd said nothing, and was giving him an unreadable look, so unlike her normally expressive personality. He cleared his throat, tasting again the sweetness of the booze and the lips of the women he'd shared it with. "So," he said. "Uh, listen. I guess...well, it seems like the booze here is a bit, er, stronger than I'm used to. And I uh...Well, I didn't get, you know, too crazy, I think. At least, I didn't...well..." He trailed off, waiting for an answer that failed to materialize. "Are...Are you mad?"

Fable gave him a close look. "You have a six pack," the faun finally murmured.

Dorian blinked. "Uh. Yeah? What about it?"

An impish grin stole across the faun's lips. "Nothing," she said in a singsong voice, hands clasped behind her back. "Nothing at all."

Dorian slowed in confusion as Fable clip-clopped forward, prancing after Melia and Emberly. Dorian rubbed his head, which had begun to ache.

Space was weird...But also very awesome.

Chapter 16

Dorian slept.

Or, at least, he rested.

He had a vague idea he'd gone to bed after returning to *The Windlass*, but the specifics of the how eluded him. He wasn't sure how long for either, but when he awoke, he felt more himself again—well, himself with a headache. The memories of his time in *Ladies for the Lads* was also very fresh, and he found himself groaning and rubbing his face at how much he'd embarrassed himself in there.

Vaguely, he recalled Melia being annoyed, but that nothing more was said about his...indiscretion at the club, which worked for him. He'd much rather leave it behind. Far behind. A galaxy behind, if that was an option.

Well, maybe not quite that far, he mused, recalling Stella's impressive rack, which she'd been more than happy to let him sample. He shook his head firmly and rolled himself out of the crew bunk he'd collapsed into. With a plodding step, he made his way back above deck, peering about uncertainly.

Much had changed aboard, he noticed first of all. Most pressingly a large arcane cannon worked near the prow, along with smaller ones on the sides of the ship. They had a narrow tapering barrel and seemed to have been installed on rotating platforms, which itself was interesting, but there were a number of other additions Dorian noted, like new ropes for the sails, the deck having been polished to a shine, and the swirling engravings of the enchantment looking more permanent and buffered. On the prow was also what looked like a curve of metal, which must have been the ramming stones, and it looked like the anchor had been replaced by something that looked like a buoy made of heavy metal.

"Cutie! Over here!"

Dorian looked towards the sweet voice and saw Fable waving at him near the helm. Melia and Emberly were there too, the former giving him an annoyed look and Emberly a smirk.

Cautiously, Dorian made his way over to them. "Hey," he said. "So uh...About last night..."

"Don't worry about it," Fable said, patting him on the back cheerily. "Everyone goes a little crazy on their first shore leave. Melia was just a bit surprised to see you shirtless and looking so sexy."

"I was not!" Melia huffed. "It was...I...Ugh! Forget it," she growled. "We have more important things to worry about."

"You're right about that. Good timing, by the way, navigator, because this is mainly for you," Emberly said as she unfolded what she'd been showing Melia and Fable. It looked to Dorian like a chart or a map, but when Emberly opened it, the image upon the paper glowed, projecting itself into the air, sending globes of planets, twisting ribbons of stellar winds, and the scattered masses of asteroid belts floating into the air.

Dorian leaned in, no longer astounded at such displays of everyday magic as Emberly pointed at a particular orb. "This is Sphere," she said "Nice, hm? And the wyrmgate we need to get through is here." She dragged her finger through the shimmering projection, dashes of red light following in the wake of her nail. "We'll be heading past Jarxe's Reef and the Twelve Brothers, which are these asteroid clusters. Then, we'll make a stop here at Asimova's Spire, an air station where we can refuel and then hit the wyrmgate nearby. Savvy?" she said, an X forming where she stabbed the point in the void.

Dorian nodded slowly, more than understanding the route she suggested. But something bothered him about it. A concern Melia put into words moments later. "Seems a bit convoluted," she noted. "It'd be shorter to take the wyrmgate here and come out near Apostle's Rest."

"It would," Emberly said. "But thanks to Elven Imperial interference around that area, we'll be avoiding it. The client doesn't need those gilded jackasses taking a look at the cargo, savvy?"

Melia sighed and nodded. "Fair point. Guess we have to," she said begrudgingly.

Dorian wasn't sure he agreed, but after last night, wisely chose to bite his tongue at the moment. His stock of 'stupid statements' had been all but used up. Best to wait until it refilled after a bit.

As he was considering that, he felt and heard a change around the docks and looked over the rail. He spotted Boss Grash at once, the huge orc a presence wherever he went, even without the normal bustle of the docks diverting out of his and his two ogre bodyguard's path.

"Company," Dorian said aloud, drawing the three women's attention as Grash reached their gangplank, the wooden beam bending under the orc's weight as he came aboard.

Grash grinned his metal teeth, eyes gleaming as he clapped his hands, the metal one one hissing with pistons as he did. "'Ello 'ello! And how'z moi favourite crew doin', eh? Gettin' along?"

Emberly closed the map, the projection shimmering out of existence. "Of course," she said.

"Good ta 'ear! And how'z you feelin' about dem now, hm? Tink they'll do da job?"

Emberly gave the three of *The Windlass* a mildly amused look. "I think we'll manage."

"Wonderful! And how'z about my new navigator, eh? I be expectin' great tings from you, ya know," Grash said with a beaming grin directed Dorian's way.

Dorian tried to return the smile. "I'll try not to let you down."

Grash's smile dropped abruptly. "You'll do more'n try, moi lad," the big orc said flatly. "You'll do. Ya clear, eh?"

Dorian felt the sudden steel in the orc's tone and the change in the air. He nodded. "Yeah. Got it."

Grash beamed again, all smiles a moment later, but though the air lightened, Dorian still felt the chill of the previous moment linger. "Good! All I needz ta hear. And so, I think parting gifts be in order, eh?" Grash guffawed, waving his bodyguards and their burdens forward. "You lot! Bring it aboard. And be quick about it, ya 'ear!"

The two ogres grunted as they hefted some chests up and laid them down with bangs on the deck. Grinning, Grash grabbed the lid of one chest and pulled it open, revealing piles of clothes.

"'Ere we are! New clothes for tha lot a ye. When I heard abouts you'z old ship gettin' lost, me old 'eart near broke at tha thought! And so I get ta thinkin', and I figger it'd be only fair ta give you lot some new things ta wear."

"Oooh," Fable said, clip-clopping towards the chests. "That's so nice!"

"Ain't it just?" Grash guffawed, patting the chests. "'Ere. One fer each a ya. You needin' anyfing else?" he asked Emberly and Melia, pegging them for the de facto decision makers.

"No," Melia said. "Thanks, boss. All the supplies we need are here now, thanks to your men and Emberly's coordinating everything. We'll be ready to take off soon."

"Good!" Grash said, patting the open chest. "Then I wish you'z da best, and look forward ta hearin' of your big success! C'mon boyz! Let's leave our new friends ta enjoy tha fruit a workin' for ol' Grash, eh? Ha ha ha!"

With that gravelly laugh, the orc headed off once more, followed closely by the two ogres. Dorian watched them go, feeling the tension of the moment linger. Though Grash may have claimed his purpose was dropping off the chests, Dorian felt certain that the true reason had been the not-so-subtle reminder of who they worked for.

Well, he was committed to the path now, Dorian reminded himself, and looked back towards Fable and Melia as they rooted through two of the chests.

"Not bad," Melia had to admit. "Someone was really good at eyeballing our sizes. These look like perfect fits in the making."

"Oooh! This is a nice belt," Fable giggled, putting it away before grabbing the trunk and hefting it with a grunt. "Better get these to the cabin, huh?" She swayed on her hooves for a moment before balancing.

Melia grunted an agreement, hefting her own chest as well and following the faun down the steps and below decks.

Dorian turned to the remaining chest and pushed open the lid. He examined the men's clothes inside thoughtfully. They weren't like any clothes he'd seen back home, but he kind of liked them. A long coat in particular caught his eye. Something about the tough but dark fabric was oddly appealing...

"Like that one?"

Dorian glanced back at Emberly, finding her examining the jacket as well. He shrugged. "It's not bad," he confessed. "Nicest clothes I'll ever wear, most likely."

"Yeah, it's pretty good. Much better than your current stuff, no denying," the demoness said, crossing her arms under her breasts and giving him a knowing look. "Wanna try them on?"

Dorian shrugged. "Don't see why not," he said, closing the lid and lifting the chest.

"Where're you going?" the demoness asked suddenly.

Dorian paused. "Well...below. To change in privacy."

Emberly guffawed, the ammo belts crossing her chest rattling with her amusement. "Privacy? You think anyone in the Black cares much for that? Trust me, navigator. Spend a few months in the Black on a ship this size with a crew this small, and you'll know every intimate secret of us all—including what we look like in the buff. Savvy? Go ahead," she said with a careless gesture. "Stop wasting time and change up here. I don't mind."

Dorian glanced back at the chest, then shrugged and put it back down. Well, when in the stars. Taking off his shirt, he followed it up after a moment with his pants, kicking both aside and leaving him in nothing but his small clothes. He couldn't help but notice Emberly watching him intently, looking vaguely bored, but never averting her eyes from his masculine form.

Pulling on a new silken shirt, Dorian followed it up with some sleek pants that fit comfortably. A belt went next, the pouches on it looking handy, and finally the long coat. It fit great, he had to admit, and the gold trim along the sleeves and hem made him feel quite piratical. Maybe even rakish.

"Not bad," he admitted, giving the coat's collar a tweak. "Not bad at all."

"I'll say," Emberly said with a lazy smirk. "And thanks for the free show, hot stuff."

"Free? You said it was normal," Dorian said.

"Yeah," Emberly chuckled with another snort. "I say lots of things."

"Wait, you mean that was a lie?!"

"'Course it was," Emberly said, now openly laughing. "Can't believe ya fell for it either! Ha ha ha! Gettin' naked in front of me? C'mon! But I did love it, I must admit! Ha ha ha!"

Dorian sighed and rolled his eyes, grinning along with her. "Suppose I really should have figured that one out," he said with a self-deprecating shake of his head.

"Aw, don't go feeling so bashful, handsome. I'm told I can be very persuasive, savvy?" Emberly said with a lazy sway of her hips.

Dorian watched the motion, the ammo belt riding on her shapely hips and her slim stomach flexing subtly. "Don't suppose you'll be returning the favour?" he mused.

Emberly chortled. "You got balls to ask that of a demoness, navigator. I'll give you that. In fact, pretty sure I saw them poppin' out but a minute ago. Still, you'll have to really impress me before I show you anything past what you see here. Savvy?"

"Savvy," Dorian said. "Looking forward to our bright future together." He winked. She laughed again, but her yellow eyes consumed him from head to toe once more as though she was already planning the time and place.

The familiar clopping of hooves drew his attention once more to the steps as Fable and Melia emerged. The faun was dressed much the same as before, though she'd done away with the singed parts of her old denim. Instead, she wore a pair of tight trousers and a vest over a shirt with the sleeves rolled up.

Melia by contrast seemed to have dressed in even more garish clothes. A tailed jacket hung on her shoulders, undone at the front to reveal the tight corset she wore beneath. Ruffles sprouted from her sleeves, and her belt rode her hips, holding up a pair of loose pantaloons. Her hair streamed out behind her in a flutter of blue, and belted at her waist was a sword and several daggers.

"Not bad clothes," Melia noted, tugging at the cuffs on the ends of her sleeves. "Grash has good taste." She noticed Dorian and stopped, blinking as if it were her first time seeing him.

"What do you think?" he asked, gesturing to his new ensemble.

Melia's eyes roamed up and down him, and maybe it was Dorian, but he swore he saw a flutter of pink in her hair. "...Not bad," she muttered. "Seems you clean up well. You're finally looking like a proper privateer, at least, and not some groundling turd farmer."

"Oh yeah. Looking really good," Fable said, openly ogling him, only to frown. "Wait. Where'd you get changed?"

Dorian coughed. "Er..."

"No way," Fable gasped as she spotted the pile of his old clothes nearby. "Up here?" Her eyes flicked to the demoness, who was openly grinning. "In front of her?!"

"What?!" Melia barked, her hair flaring red as she rounded on the demoness. "You horny—"

"It was my fault," Dorian quickly said. "I should have guessed it was a trick."

"What's the matter with having some fun with the community eye candy? Jealous much, dears?" Emberly asked smugly.

"Wha...of course not!" Melia barked. "But I'll not have you taking advantage of us while aboard."

"Yeah! I was supposed to get his pants off first," Fable huffed. "No fair."

"Fable!" Melia cried.

Emberly barked a laugh and leaned back against the helm. "Seems you girls are having a bit of boy trouble, hm? Well, don't mind me. I'm just along for the ride."

Melia groaned and gazed skyward. "The gods are testing me," she said. "It's the only explanation I can think of."

"It's really fine," Dorian muttered.

"I didn't ask you, star slut!"

"Ouch," Dorian laughed, clutching his chest. "Let's not keep that nickname nocked and ready to fire, please."

Emberly snickered and idly glanced over the rail at the docks. Dorian saw her stiffen suddenly, amusement dying faster than a bilge rat in the vacuum of space. He looked where she was, and in the crowd he spotted several figures in dark cloaks move out of a side street and onto the wharves.

That couldn't be good...

Straightening sharply, Emberly dashed towards the mooring rope. "Alright, fun's over. Time to sail! Navigator! Get that ass to the wheel. Now! We need to fly. Savvy?"

"What? Why?" Dorian said, even as he moved to the helm, responding reflexively to the tension in the demoness's voice.

"Because we're about to have unwelcome company!" she barked, untying the mooring rope.

As she'd claimed, the dark figures had spotted them. One pointed and they immediately started forcing their way through the crowds. In the confusion, one of their hoods was knocked off, revealing a head like an octopus, a bandana wrapped around his brow bearing a skull with squid-like tentacles over two crossed swords.

Dorian caught a glimpse of the figures as he grasped the wheel, in an instant feeling once more his close connection to the ship as the core flared gold and red. Scales grew along his arms and hands, and throughout the boat he sensed the new additions that had just been installed, but didn't have time to further explore them. He tensed, putting in an immediate pulse of will into *The Windlass*. The winged oars beat, pushing them into motion.

"Go fast. Now!" Emberly barked, throwing free the last mooring line.

"Fast?" Dorian repeated.

"Yes! Fast!" the demoness snapped.

Dorian grinned. "If you say so..."

Fable sucked in a breath. "Wait!" the faun cried. "Not—"

Too late. Dorian sent a surge of willpower into the ship, and the oars gave a mighty beat. *The Windlass* surged forward, throwing Fable and Melia off their feet to thump across the deck with startled yelps. Emberly was only saved by the rail, falling against it with a startled shriek at the ship shot into the void of space like a rocket, fairly streaming sparks in its wake.

She saw their pursuers reach their pier and stumble to a halt, gaping at the sudden flight of the ship. The demoness grinned wildly and cackled, throwing the four a mocking salute as they rapidly shrank in the distance.

"Yeah! See ya, seafood!" she cried, throwing some crass gestures at the distant dock.

Melia groaned as she found her feet again, bracing against the acceleration of the ship. "What was that about?" she demanded hotly of the demoness.

"Trouble, I bet," Dorian said.

Emberly turned back around with a dismissive gesture. "Don't worry about it," she grumbled dismissively. "Those are just some sore losers."

"They're not the only sore ones," Fable groaned from where she'd rolled to a halt. "Ouch."

"What do you mean?" Dorian asked as he steered the ship away from Sphere, instinctively starting along the route Emberly had outlined to them. "Are we in trouble?"

"Nah, nah," Emberly grunted. "It's just professional issues, savvy? They were the ones Grash originally wanted to hire to transport the goods. Until I came along. But they were a bit bitter about the whole business, so wanted to rough me up a little. Show who was boss, maybe try and take the cargo for themselves. You know, the usual crap. No big deal. That's why I had Cook around. Make 'em think twice before starting shit on the docks.

Guess with me taking off, they figured it was a good time to make their point."

"That going to be a problem when we get back?" Melia said, squinting at Sphere as the planetoid shrank behind them.

"Nah. Don't worry about it," Emberly reassured her with a shrug, bandoliers rattling. "Once I get back, I'll have money enough to make things sweet. Savvy? Money solves every problem," she said, rubbing two fingers together pointedly.

Dorian eyed her at that, but quickly turned his attention back to open space. It felt vaguely comforting to hear the admission. He'd been so long out of his depth that finding out that cocky professionals, or what passed for them among the stars, also made reckless moves. It made him feel a little better. Or at least, not quite as out of his element as before.

Or maybe it was just having his hands on the wheel again. Dorian smiled, flexing his talons. It felt good to be back at the helm. Like everything was making sense again. That he would know what to do, come what may, so long as he had a ship under him and at his command. It was soothing, really.

"Hmm..."

Dorian glanced over at Fable who was leaning over the rail, peering ahead with her eyes glowing the blue of aura reading.

"What is it?" he asked.

"Not sure," the faun said, lips pursed as she leaned on the railing. "Sensing a lot of auras up ahead."

Dorian tensed, peering ahead but not making out anything beyond the seemingly endless traffic of ships. "Danger?" he asked.

She shook her horned head. "I don't think so," she said. Then grinned. "Actually...Maybe an opportunity..."

Chapter 17

THE WINDLASS CRUISED ONWARD through the void, Dorian guiding their ship through the chaotic traffic of barges and ships that headed in and out of Sphere. As they neared the direction they needed, Dorian slowed their vessel, noticing a build up of crafts ahead, all turning carefully, crowding the space above and below a wall of what appeared to be blinking lights flowing across space.

"What's going on?" he asked.

Fable whipped out her spyglass and peered through it. She smiled smugly, ears flicking at confirmation of her theory. "Yep. Just as I thought. Swarm of space jellies," she said, lowering the glass.

"Dangerous?" Dorian asked, tensing.

"Can be," Fable admitted. "Their sting can paralyze you for a few hours. But they usually keep to themselves."

"Exactly," Melia said, tapping her chin thoughtfully. She shrugged. "Fuck it. We'll go through them. Just keep it slow."

"Should work," Fable agreed, closing her glass and tucking it back into her belt. "As long as they're not startled, jellies keep to themselves. Onward, cutie!"

"Alright," he said, wary but trusting their judgment. The oars beside *The Windlass* swept at space, ferrying their craft into the immensity of the swarm. Dorian kept it slow as they glided into the jellies.

It was a surreal experience for sure. Glowing, blinking lights filled the small, jellied creatures, their transparent caps wobbling as their tentacles wiggled and pushed them through the air. As Melia had hoped, the ship's slow passage didn't bother the jellies, who merely swam around it as their blinking lights washed over the deck and quartet in eerily beautiful waves.

"Wow," Dorian murmured in amazement, struck by the strange beauty of the scene.

"Not bad, huh?" Emberly noted with a lazy grin his way. "And a great opportunity!"

"She's right," Melia chimed back in, brightening visibly before vaulting over the rail.

"She is?" Dorian watched as Melia vanished below decks. The elf emerged moments later, hauling several large nets. "Uh..." Dorian said.

"Jellies may not be great for flavor, but they're wonderful for hydration and even sustenance in a pinch. Plus, they take forever to go bad," Fable explained.

"Sure do," Melia said, looking more delighted than ever before, her hair a dancing mane of purple flames. "And a perfect chance to make things a bit...interesting."

"Oh?" Emberly giggled, turning fully towards the elf. "Got a little contest in mind, elf?"

"Just an idea." Melia dumped the nets amidship. "Whoever catches the most jellies in two minutes, wins!"

"Wins what?" Dorian asked, his brows raising.

"Good question. Let's wait until the end to think of something," Fable said with an impish smile.

Dorian gave the faun a hard look, which she shrugged off with a flirty lip bite. He gave up and shrugged. "Fine by me," he said.

"It was my idea, so I'm game," Melia said.

"Yahoo! Let's do it!" the faun cried.

Emberly cackled. "Why not?! Let's play!"

"I'll go first, then Fable, Emberly, and finally, Dorian," Melia said, and though Dorian could see she was trying to hide her excitement, he was hardly fooled as her hair soared through the entire rainbow in a matter of seconds.

Emberly counted every name off on her fingers as Melia spoke them. "Sounds good to me."

"I got the stop watch!" Fable shouted, pulling a timepiece from one of her pouches, holding it at the ready.

Grabbing one of the nets, Melia tensed.

"Reeeeady?" Fable raised her arm. "Go!" she cried, arm dropping and thumb clicking on the watch.

Melia bounded forward and leaped onto the rigging, climbing up the mast as deftly as a squirrel. She halted along the spar, balancing as she looked down at the deck, her hair crackling like purple flame as she watched the jellies flow below, waiting for her moment.

"Thirty seconds!" Fable called.

"Now!" Melia barked, leaping from the mast, the net unfurling behind her, the heavy ropes falling over a dense bulk of jellies as they passed.

The net came down, dragging the jellies to the deck, and Melia quickly dragged the net along, avoiding the stinging tentacles stabbing from the gaps. She tied off the end and held the large net triumphantly. "There!" she said. "Beat that!"

"You got it," Fable giggled, tossing the stopwatch to Melia, who caught it easily. Grabbing another net, Fable stood like a sprinter waiting for the starting shout, one hoof forward, the other behind, body angled and braced for movement.

"Aaaaand go!" Melia cried.

Fable sprang into motion, quite literally. She took two steps and leaped into the air, the net fanning out and sweeping up a group of jellies. No sooner did she land, than did she start over again, every bound capturing more of the humming swarm, and though she often lost some as she opened the net, she invariably captured more.

"Time!" Melia shouted as Fable landed, huffing with exertion, but beaming with triumph as she held out her bulging net.

"Mine's biggest!" she crowed.

"So far," Emberly said as she strode forward and grabbed another net while the other women stored the captured jellies in empty crates on the deck. "Time me, elf!"

Melia rolled her eyes but prepped the watch as she finished up with Fable's load. "Alright. Let's...go!"

The watch clicked and Emberly burst into motion. She swung the net about, building momentum before letting it fly. The net soared through the air and opened wide, falling upon the jellies swimming through the air. However, either through instinct or another sense, the jellies broke from their path, the net falling on some, but hardly as many as had been hoped.

Emberly cursed beneath her breath, reeling in the net and its sufficient, but mediocre catch.

"Nice one," Melia said with a smirk. "Guess you're no good without a cannon to back you up."

Emberly scoffed. "If you told me cannons were allowed, this would have been a very different result. Anyway, we'll see who gets the least yet, eh, navigator?" she said with a sidelong look at Dorian.

"We'll see," Dorian sighed, leaving the helm and making his way down the deck. He grabbed the net and looked up at the jellies swimming through the air. They'd thinned out somewhat, perhaps sensing what had happened to their fellows. How was he going to do this?

"Ready?" Melia asked.

"What? Wait, I—"

"Go!" Melia called, starting Fable's watch again with a click.

Dorian cursed and turned to the jellies. He flung the net up, but it fluttered, tangling around itself and flopping through several groups of them.

Emberly burst out laughing and Dorian growled, reeling the net back in.

"A minute thirty left!" Melia said gleefully.

"Oooh! Better do better than that!" Fable chimed teasingly.

Better, eh? Fine! He'd do better. He knew he could! He just had to...had to...

He noticed a glow suffusing his skin. The laughter from the trio had abruptly stopped, and Dorian looked back, seeing a pair of ethereal wings sprout from his back, bound like constellations with globes of light. He looked down and saw his fingers had grown talons again, as had his feet.

Yeah, he thought, grinning and baring fangs. That'd work.

He crouched, wings tightening in, then he propelled himself into the air with a mighty leap. He soared above the deck, his wings fanning out again, hanging him midair near the edge of the oxygen bubble, the flow of jellies and deck far below.

Folding his wings, hurling the net outward, Dorian came down like a meteor, gold light flashing in his wake. He swung the net, sweeping up jellies with ease. Moments before he hit the deck his wings fanned out again, slowing him sharply so he landed lightly, his hands pulling the night tightly closed.

The mass of jellies flopped onto the deck, buzzing with shock, several squeezed out as Dorian tightened the neck of the net and tied it off, fit bursting with the blinking aliens. He turned to the trio of women, grinning his fangs, horns glowing bright where they grew from his brow.

"Looks like I win," he noted.

Fable, Melia, and Emberly stared at him with jaws hanging open. Reflexively, Melia's thumb clicked the stopwatch, halting it. She stared at the sound, recovering and glancing at the watch, then at the net.

"Uh. Yeah," she said as she stared at the bulging net. "Looks—um...like it."

"Hooooly shit," Fable breathed, her face breaking out in a broad grin. "Dorian! That was *amazing*, cutie!"

"Thanks," Dorian said as his horns shrank and the wings dissolved like gossamer. "I thought it wasn't half bad."

"I'll say!" Fable said, admiring his catch. Then, a greedy smile lit her lips and she gave a sly glance over at Emberly. "And for your reward, how about some turnabout? You get to watch Emberly change."

Emberly's mouth snapped shut and she drew herself up with surprise. "What?!" she gasped.

"Yeah," Fable cackled, grinning even more deviously. "Since you took advantage of our navigator's innocence and trust in you, it only seems fair. Or...are you backing out?" She made a mock gasp. "Surely not, right?!"

"I don't know if I'd describe it as fair," Dorian chuckled, trying to give the demoness an out...which was resolutely ignored.

"You think I wouldn't?" Emberly demanded hotly, gnashing her teeth and making fists. "I've got some sense of honor, y'know! I know fair is fair!"

"I'm not saying you don't," Fable gasped, swaying with a look of angelic innocence. "Just noticing those hot pants are still on."

"Ha! I don't care a whit if he sees. Fine! Bring me my leathers to change into."

"Er—" Dorian began.

"I'll get them!" Fable chirped gleefully, prancing down the steps into the hold.

Dorian watched her go, then glanced back at the fuming demoness. "Listen," he said. "You really don't have to—"

"What? You think I won't?" Emberly demanded. "You think I haven't the powder to do it? Well I do! Savvy? I could strip down to my skin and bounce in your lap for an hour and it wouldn't even faze me."

He felt his new slacks tighten at the interesting visual. "Oh. Well..." Dorian grunted.

"Got it!" Fable chimed, springing up from the hold with a clop of hooves as she returned bearing a bundle of clothes clutched in her arms. She skipped up towards Emberly and pushed them into the demon's hands. "Let's see the goods, hot stuff," the faun said with a teasing smile.

"If you can handle it," Emberly scoffed, tossing the garments onto the rail and turning around, head tilted back, her eyes glaring down at Dorian.

He straightened under that challenging stare, feeling more like he was starting a duel than spectating a strip show, if that's what this was. And as Emberly began to pull off her clothes, Dorian was certainly leaning towards it.

Emberly's hands moved slowly, shoulders rolling as she shrugged off her jacket. Her hands then brushed over the straps of her ammunition belts. She lifted them over her shoulders, tossing them onto the rail with a clatter. With a swing of her hips, she turned about, her thumbs finding their way to her belt and unbuckling it with a click. Dorian's eyebrows rose with interest as she bent forward, tugging her pants down, the globes of her glorious ass pushed out towards him as she stepped free, panties a lacy dark thread framing them.

Emberly straightened, turning back around, her smoldering glare more than just poetic license as she grabbed the hem of the black band about her chest and pulled it up and over, her breasts bouncing a little as the fabric came free, revealing the crimson orbs cradled in a lacy black bra, her arms toned and muscled in a most appealing way.

Dorian felt his face heating at the intimate display. He cleared his throat and hastily looked away.

"What are you doing?" the demoness demanded, audibly angered.

"Uh, giving you some privacy?" he said.

"You think I care if you watch me change? Eyes up front, navigator. I'm more offended if you act like my body's not worth your time."

Well, if she insisted...Dorian turned back towards her, watching as she pulled on a vest, clipping it shut.

"So you've got some dragon powers?" she said as she grabbed a pair of tight leggings and started pulling them on.

"Hm? Oh, uh, seems so."

"What can you do?" she asked, looping her belt back in and snapping it shut.

He shrugged, finding it easier to talk the less skin Emberly was showing off. "I'm pretty much playing it by ear, honestly," he said. "Sometimes, my instincts just tell me to act and, well, I do it."

"Huh," the demoness said as she pushed her foot back into a boot, bending over to tie the buckle, and giving Dorian a sudden gander down her vest, a sight almost more interesting than when she wore just a bra.

"Yeah," Fable said. "He's grown horns. Wings. Got buffer. Cooked a guy's head in a bar fight."

"He glows sometimes when he gets all draconic," Melia says. "Skin turns a kind of gold."

"Really brings out the complexion," Fable added with a note of teasing, elbowing him.

Melia cleared her throat, her hair fluttering a light pink. "Well, I don't know about that…"

"What? You mean you weren't staring at his arms as they filled out that shirt? Hey Dorian," Fable continued with a look his way. "Maybe you should go sleeveless so Melia can see better."

"That's not necessary," Melia said.

"Oh yeah! It'd be much more apparent if he let you *feel* his arm. Maybe hang off him a bit while he's flying, like the covers of those books you totally didn't used to have hidden under your bed."

"Fable!"

Emberly scoffed as she straightened, tugging the ammo belts into an X across her chest once more. "Honestly, if you two are so desperate to make a sandwich with Dorian filling, you should just get on with it."

"Wh-what!" Melia barked. "I'd never—"

"I would," Fable giggled. "I'm *gonna*."

Dorian wished there was a little bit more room in the crotch of his pants as he felt the attention shift to him again. Though he certainly found the idea appealing, he kind of doubted it was the right time to suggest a threesome. He was still reeling from the fact that he half-transformed into a dragon a minute ago. He hastily cleared his throat. "I think the jellies are starting to thin. I should probably get back to the wheel..."

Melia seemed to sag in relief. "Yeah, that's good," she said. "Do *that*."

With a private groan, Dorian returned to the helm and grasped the wheel once more. He felt again the subtle thrum of the ship's energies radiate through him as the jellies grew thinner in their swarms, and moments later the prow of *The Windlass* broke through the mass and cut into open space once more.

"There we go," Fable said, admiring the twinkle of stars and ribbons of galaxies spreading out before them. "Now," she said, turning back towards Emberly. "Maybe we should get a breakdown of what weapons you hooked onto this thing."

"Now that," Emberly said, her eyes lighting up like pilot lights, "sounds like my idea of fun!"

Chapter 18

Dorian's head spun as Emberly took them through the ship, describing the new equipment she'd had installed. Much was of a more practical nature, such as reinforcing the enchantment magics on the ship, giving the hull a bit more protection against magic attacks, and the drift anchor that would keep them in position in normal space short of a black hole sucking at their craft.

"Of course, this was just what I could install in the time I had," Emberly said as she brought them above deck once more. "But the real beauty is *this* puppy!" she declared, gesturing at the long cannon on the prow.

"Oooh," Fable cooed, admiring the weapon as she worked her way around it. She touched the barrel, stroking the dark metal. "Nice. Is this a Flenning Mark 1?"

"Pft! No way. We're working well past the Mark 1, savvy? This baby's the Mark 3!" Emberly cried, gesturing grandly at the weapon. "Gaze upon the smooth barrel. Marvel at the pivoting platform! And the range. The range, dammit! With this baby, you'll never need to worry about pursuing your enemies. You can shoot off their rudder with ease! Then, hammer them with the twin pairs of arcane cannons on either side of the deck without mercy!"

"Maybe a little mercy?" Dorian suggested.

"Hell no! They wouldn't show you any. You gotta make them know they fucked with the wrong ship, savvy?" Emberly shouted with a flash of fang and fire in her mouth.

"Oh. Alright then," Dorian muttered, unable to stop himself from smirking at the passionate, if a bit bloodthirsty, display.

"And now, shall we test it?" Emberly said, pulling a disc out from a canister set in its brace.

Melia groaned with exasperation. "Another contest?"

"Ha!" Emberly scoffed. "I wouldn't do that to you lot. It'd just be cruel! Like kicking a crippled puppy. No, this is just to see what you all can do!" Emberly declared, cranking her arm around and hurling the disc into the void.

The disc buzzed out beyond the field, spinning whitely in the starlit black. Emberly grabbed the cannon and swung it about by some handles, spinning a wheel on the side to depress it. She sighted down the barrel, one eye closed, tongue poking from her mouth.

Dorian jumped as he sensed a sudden build up of magic in the demoness, the etchings carved in the cannon beginning to glow. "Aaaaand...Boom!" Emberly cried.

With a thunderous boom indeed the cannon fired a missile of sparkling magic. Dorian stared in awe as it arced through the oxygen barrier and then smashed the target with a flash of crimson sparks.

"And there you have it," Emberly declared, grinning at the others and patting the barrel like a dog who'd performed a trick. "Range and adjustable firing! Channeling the power of your own magic, it unloads a blast of pure arcane power. Lacks a bit of punch like the side cannons, sure, but for precision shots, you won't need anything else."

"Not bad," Melia confessed, nodding with her arms crossed in front of her. "Lucky we all have magical capabilities, I guess."

"My turn!" Fable cheered, bounding forward and grabbing the cannon, swiveling it around with some effort.

"Great," Emberly said, pulling another disc from the canister, drawing it back. "Ready?"

"Give 'er!" Fable cheered.

Emberly flung the disc, sending it whizzing out into the void. Fable grunted, hastily shoving the barrel to a new position, then adjusting the barrel with a frantic turn of the wheel. The marks along the cannon began to glow, filling up to the brim.

With a blast of magic, the cannon fired, sending a purple blast of power soaring through the void, but missing the disc wide.

"Aw," Fable moaned. "Shoot!"

"Tough luck, faun," Emberly cackled. "You weren't entirely off, though. Elf! You're up!"

Melia smirked and sauntered up to the cannon. She grabbed the barrel and glanced at the demoness. "Throw it."

"Gladly," Emberly said, picking up another disc and drawing it back. She threw hard, sending the disc whirling out before the ship.

Instantly Melia swung about the cannon, the barrel dropping sharply as the runes began to glow, filling quickly. Her hair flared cold blue of concentration as she aimed down the barrel.

"Gotcha," she murmured, and fired.

The cannon roared, a blast of blue magic screaming through the void before hitting the disc, bursting with a crash of blazing blue magic.

Melia straightened, smirking with satisfaction. Emberly let out a low whistle. "Not bad, elf," the demoness muttered. "Not bad at all. I confess I might have underestimated you."

"As if there was any doubt," Melia laughed coldly, brushing some of her blazing blue hair from before her eyes.

"You're up, navigator," Emberly said.

Dorian looked at the cannon uncertainly, but moved forward all the same. He ran his hand along the black metal, and as he did, the markings along it began to glow like molten gold was being poured into it.

"Ready?" Emberly asked, pulling out another disc.

Dorian crouched down, aligning the barrel with care. "As I'll ever be," he admitted with a growl of focus.

"Good!" Emberly declared, and whipped the disc into the void.

Instantly Dorian swung the cannon about, turning the handle to adjust the barrel to keep the target in sight. He grit his teeth, aligning the cannon as best he could, and willed it to fire.

The barrel blazed with light, and with a scream of golden power the cannon shot seared through the void, tearing through it for the target, but just missing.

Dorian banged a fist on the barrel with a sigh.

"Not bad for a first try," Emberly reassured him. "Nearly perfect form. But keep practicing. As for me," Emberly said as she stretched. "Mmm, after all the work, I think I deserve a nap. If anyone needs me, I'll be below deck, enjoying the new bed. Savvy?"

"We got it," Melia said.

"Damn right you do," Emberly chuckled, sauntering towards the steps. She scooped up her cast off clothes, tossing them over her shoulder before vanishing down the steps below decks.

Dorian sighted down the cannon once more, wondering if he should try again. It seemed like a skill he'd need. Although he would be at the helm most of the time, it would be a useful trick to have in his back pocket in case...

Fable patted his back. "Hey, cutie! Come on. No need to keep working on that now. You should take a breather. We're on a set course and should be fine for a while."

"Well..." Dorian said.

"C'mon," Fable said, giving his arm a tug. "I don't care how much your dragon blood can keep you going, you're gonna collapse eventually if you don't take a breather now and then."

"Suppose you're not wrong on that front," Dorian agreed.

"Damn straight! Now get over here."

With a shrug, Dorian allowed himself to be tugged away from the gun and back across the deck. He sat down on the steps leading up to the helm with a sigh. Fable plopped down beside him, beaming at him and pressing close against his side.

"See?" Fable cooed. "Isn't this nice?"

"It is peaceful," Dorian said.

"For now," Melia corrected him, striding up to stand before him.

Dorian lifted his head, glancing at the two women, sensing something in the air. "So..."

"So—Dorian?" Fable began slyly. "Me and Melia were talking about this and that. And we got to thinking..."

"What about?" Dorian asked innocently.

Melia's eyes widened and she gave the faun an alarmed look. "Fable? Are you really going there right the fuck *now*?"

Fable nibbled on her lower lip, scooting in closer to Dorian, pressing herself against his arm and side, antlered head tilted his way and lashes low over her eyes.

"See," Fable said softly. "Dorian. Cutie...We need you."

"Well, don't sell yourselves short," he told her with a grin. "We're a team."

"No. Well, yes. Not like that. I mean, we need you in *another* way. Specifically without clothes on, bending me over a bed or a guardrail or something and pounding away at my wet little pussy while I scream your name. That kind of need, y'know?"

Dorian's eyes popped open. "O-oh," he murmured, momentarily dumbfounded by the very explicit image conjured through the faun's linguistic talents. "I see."

"Fable!" hissed Melia, her hair making the quickest transition to apple red Dorian had yet seen.

"Oh, right," the faun giggled. "Sorry, that might not have been very clear, right Melia? What I mean is, we want you naked on the bed while I bounce on your dick and you eat Melia's sweet nectar straight from the source while she waits for her turn."

"Fable!" Melia cried, her face as beet red as her fizzing hair. She covered her eyes in horror.

"Am I wrong?" Fable asked with a sideways look at the elf.

Dorian looked at Melia and the elf bit her lip, her fingers lowering to nervously play with the puffy lace coming from her sleeves. "That's not...I mean, no, you aren't, but..."

"Exactly," Fable giggled triumphantly, touching Dorian's chest and leaning in a little, looking up at his face. "And the reason we were so shocked and testy about finding you in that club was because we were worried some other woman was going to get to you first and, you know, steal you away from us. And we really like you. Honestly. So that would break our hearts."

Melia took a deep breath, let it out in a heavy sigh, her hair lightening from embarrassed red to a more suggestive pink. "It's true," she said, moving forward. "But let me be clear. We're not suggesting we want to do this just to keep you with us. If you do decide to stay, well, I won't lie. That would be wonderful. But that isn't our aim here. Single women out in the Black, all alone, almost always on the run? It's been...tough. Really tough. And we've gotta be careful out here. But you make it feel like we can, you know, take a little time. Relax a bit. Have some fun..."

"Lots of fun," Fable murmured, scooting into his lap.

Dorian's eyes narrowed. "And...well, you're both into this idea? Sharing me with each other, I mean?"

Fable and Melia made eye contact and nodded, then looked back at him.

Dorian glanced between them and gave a laugh of contented surprise. "How could I in my right mind say no?" he said happily.

Fable giggled. "Damn straight. Now pucker up, lover boy," she squealed, throwing her arms around his neck and pressing an adoring kiss to his lips.

Dorian shivered with delight as he felt the faun's curves press against him, her lips working with his. His arms almost instantly wrapped around her, pulling her closer as he deepened the kiss.

"Mmm," Fable moaned.

"Always have to be first," Melia sighed as she moved up behind the faun, but her playful smile belied her tone as she knelt down behind her friend, reaching around Fable and undoing the buttons of the deer girl's top.

Fable moaned into Dorian's mouth, rolling her shoulders and allowing Melia to tug the deer girl's top and shirt off, baring the pale softness of her breasts. Melia cast aside the fabric and shrugged off her sailor's jacket, tugging off her own shirt soon after.

Dorian broke the kiss with a gasp, admiring the two topless beauties before him with awe and amazement, marveling that such a thing could be happening to him.

Oh yeah. Space was so much better than potatoes.

"Maybe we should...should head below decks," he suggested.

"Fuck that," Fable breathed, shoving off his coat. "Next time. I can't wait another second."

"Agreed," Melia said, somewhat shyly. "I've been thinking about doing this under the stars with you since we hit the Black."

"Well, far be it for me to deny you that experience," Dorian chuckled.

"Damn straight." Fable grabbed Dorian's shirt and yanked it up.

Willingly, Dorian raised his arms, allowing her to peel the shirt off him revealing his bare chest. Fable's eyes sparkled on beholding his naked flesh, her tongue teasing along her lips greedily.

"Mmm. Now that's what I like to see," she said, resting her hands on his abs. "All for me."

"For *us*," Melia corrected sharply as she moved around behind Dorian and sat down.

"Then get in here," Fable giggled and kissed Dorian again.

Dorian groaned as her lips met his, his hands tracing Fable's body until his hands met her pants.

His fingers hooked into the band of her trousers and panties and Fable cooed, lifting her hips and allowing him to tug the fabric down. She rocked, kicking her pants off, leaving her naked.

Dorian sucked in a breath as he felt Melia lean against his back, her hands stroking his chest and her lips kissing his neck. "I want this," she breathed in his ear. "*We* want you so bad."

"Sooo bad," Fable gasped between kisses. Then she sank into a quiet whisper pressed directly against his ear, inaudible even to the elf. "She even masturbated while I whispered a horny fantasy about you into her ear."

Her hands wandered down to his pants, easing them open, his cock springing out. Dorian grunted, resting his hands on her hips once more, easing her back down. Fable quickly got into position in his lap and whimpered as she felt the thickness of his manhood against her entrance. She groaned in delight as he parted her, filling her slowly—but quicker than expected due to the size disparity. She was just so fucking wet.

"Oh f-fuck!" Fable gasped as he pushed in deeper, her arms reaching behind Dorian to hold Melia's hand.

"Is it good?" Melia whispered.

"Super, but...he's big," Fable warned her. "It's going in, but—be careful."

Dorian couldn't suppress a chuckle at that as he gently eased into the faun, Fable's ears and tail quivering with pleasure as she felt the heat of his manhood inside of her. With a low moan he filled her totally, and with a lazy motion of his hips and hands, began to bounce the faun on his lap.

Fable gasped, panting with her tongue out, her eyelids quivering with pleasure as his cock pumped into her. It started slowly, then progressed more urgently as her own hips began to rock against him in turn, riding him in desperate search of more of that pleasure he was giving her.

"Oh...oh f-fuck!" Fable panted. "Oh stars, yes! Dorian...Oh god-fucking-dammit y-yes—ahhhh-hh!"

"Fable," he grunted. It's all he could manage.

"Is *she* good?" Melia asked, gently kissing his ear, her hands stroking his chest admiringly, her thighs rubbing with arousal as he felt his muscles tense with the thrusting into her crewmate. "How's my best friend's pussy for you, navigator? Nice and tight?"

"So good," Dorian gasped.

Fable beamed, blushing, relinquishing Melia's hand to put her hands on his shoulders, bracing herself as she rode his cock with growing urgency. Her breasts bounced with the motions, her inner walls tightening around his manhood. She was leaking down the length of him, juicy, lewd noises coming from her squelching cunt.

"Oh...Oh stars. Dorian," she gasped, biting her lower lip at the swelling pleasure rising within her. "I'm...I'm close. I'm so...so c-close. Oh. Oh fuck! Dorian. Dorian! I...I...mnnnn!"

Fable cried out, antlered head thrown back, her body tightening deliciously around him as she came with a shudder of pure ecstasy. The sudden tightness pushed Dorian over the edge. He groaned, hands tightening on her hips as he came with her, body flexing with every burst of his pleasure and the pump of his seed.

Fable moaned, collapsing against him and breathing hard. "That...that was good," she said dreamily.

Dorian chuckled, gently easing out of her. Fable practically flopped over, draping herself on the steps and breathing in slow, heavy pants.

No sooner had she slid out than Melia pulled Dorian around. He found himself crouching over the elf, who had lain herself out on the steps, her cheeks flaming, her hair a fluttering mane of needy pink arousal as she looked up at him. Her slender figure was bare, the last of her clothes abandoned, leaving her naked beneath him.

"Let's...let's go slow," Melia murmured, reaching up and moving her arms around his neck.

"Gladly," Dorian said, leaning down and capturing her lips.

Melia moaned softly, her lashes fluttering as she tasted his tongue, her body tensing as his hand cupped her breast, gently kneading the soft flesh. She shifted beneath him, her hips shyly rocking, rubbing her mound against him, his cock stirring and stiffening anew against her body.

Melia's arms twined around Dorian, pulling him closer as he felt his arousal grow along with his cock, stiffening him to full mast in short order. The pink glow of her hair lit his face as he looked down into her eyes, dim and smoky with desire for him.

Dorian growled softly, and he felt Melia shiver at the feral sound. Her hips rose, feeling his tip nudge against her slick lower lips.

"Please," she breathed, licking her lips.

A request Dorian was happy to oblige.

He pushed forward, filling her with a stroke. Melia cried out, her voice smothered by another hungry kiss as he began to thrust into her, feeling her tightness flex against his cock, but soon relax, her body welcoming his thrusts. Her breath hitched as he plowed the gorgeous elf beneath him, her hair flaring as he pumped into her like flickers of pink need.

Dorian began to move faster—rutting into the elf, fucking her on the steps as she groaned, her normally fierce demeanour melting in the face of her burning desire and the sensations rocking her slender form. His cock claimed her. Took her. Bore her to new heights of ecstasy as she gave herself willingly over to the sensations. Gave in without reservation.

"D-Dorian," she panted between hot lips. "Navigator. I...I'm close. Oh fuck. P-please. Please. Don't...don't s-stop."

"Wouldn't dream of it," Dorian said.

He kissed her again, but she was too out of her mind to kiss him back. She just stuck out her tongue and let him suck on it, moaning all the while.

Seeing how fallen-apart she'd become, Dorian felt a thrum of exhilaration take him in a bestial frenzy. He laid into her with a sudden rush of his hips.

Melia cried out at the sudden assault. Her core throbbing with need, her pussy tightening with greedy contractions. Her body rode his thrusts, meeting them with rockings of her hips. Her cheeks flamed. Her body gave in. Tensed. Electrified.

And came.

Her hair blazed with pinkish red light, her lashes fluttering as her inner walls greedily milked his cock as her orgasm swelled through her like a wave. Dorian groaned as he felt her high meld with his, his cock burying in her tightening folds as he came with her, manhood pulsing as he filled her like he had Fable.

The elf whimpered at the heat that spread through her body, soothing her on clouds of pleasure. She relaxed atop the steps as she panted hot and fast, relishing every tingling moment of her orgasm and the bliss that followed.

Dorian inhaled deeply, sweat gleaming across his naked form as he leaned over the elf, admiring her flushed and panting face. He couldn't suppress a grin.

"Enjoy that?" he asked.

"As...as if you need to ask," Melia said with a bit of the old fire.

He chuckled and kissed her again, laying down beside her, feeling suddenly weary. He heard a rustle and looked aside as Fable swung a tarp over the three of them, the faun snuggling against his body, looking up at his face with impish delight.

"That was great," the faun cooed, leaning up and kissing his cheek. "Gonna have to do that again some time."

"Any time you want," Dorian offered magnanimously.

Giggling cheekily, Fable nuzzled into Dorian's side, Melia soon rolling over and doing the same to his other.

Dorian shook his head, marvelling at his luck. Here he was, laid out beneath the stars, two gorgeous, naked, otherworldly women pulled tight against him as he gazed up into the starlit heavens of the void.

All in all? Pretty good career choice.

Chapter 19

Dorian groaned as wakefulness imposed itself on him with merciless insistence. He opened his eyes, sitting up and looking around.

And found himself not on deck anymore.

His brow knit with puzzlement as he looked about the familiar trappings of the captain's cabin. That...wasn't quite right. Let's see...he'd been with the girls on deck and—had some fun. A lot of fun, now that more of the tantalizing details made themselves known. And then he'd fallen asleep.

He tugged off the blankets and noted he was wearing his pants again. Alright. Good first sign. And this was hardly the worst place he could have woken up, true. With a grunt Dorian got up, locating the rest of his new clothes folded neatly on a nearby chest. One problem solved, he mused as he tugged them on, but the next one was how Melia and Fable would react when he showed himself. After what happened last night (or day? Whatever, time seemed to have little meaning out in the Black) he wondered how they'd act. Ideally well. He sighed, mussing his hair with a sharp motion. No matter. Time to face the music either way, he supposed, and then made his way out of the cabin and onto the deck.

As he emerged he spotted Fable leaning against the helm, watching the horizon with the glowing eyes of her auramancy. She blinked it away as she spotted him and beamed, bouncing down from the helm and towards him with a clopping of hooves.

"Hey there, cutie!" she cried, throwing her arms around him in a crushing hug, leaning up and meeting his lips with a needy kiss.

Automatically, Dorian's arms moved around her, pulling her close, much to her delight to judge by the affectionate moan that escaped the faun. Dorian broke the kiss as he grinned down at her. "Hello yourself."

Fable giggled. "Last night was amazing," she said earnestly. "Most fun I've had since we evaded that star kraken a decade ago. Honestly, even more fun!"

"Star kraken?" he said.

"Huge squid monsters. Lots of tentacles. Once they get big enough, they try and eat ships they can catch, but I've heard of ones so big they eat moons!"

Dorian tried to picture such a thing, but the scope of it defied his imagination. "Sounds...impressive," he said.

"Almost as impressive as you last night," Fable teased, her eyes heavy lidded all of a sudden.

"Right. Speaking of—"

"Happily," Fable said.

"Yeah. This...well, obviously changes things," Dorian noted. "Maybe we should sit down with Melia and talk things through."

"While naked?" Fable proposed.

He chuckled "We'll see where things go," Based on this, he at least had a pretty good idea where Fable stood on the matter. Or, rather, where she'd like to sit, judging by the way her leg was rubbing against his.

The tap of footsteps from the hold drew his attention, and Fable quickly slipped from Dorian's arms as Emberly emerged from below, looking groggy and tired—and dressed, Dorian couldn't help but notice, in little more than frilly pajamas. Melia followed moments later, looking far more awake and dressed than the demoness, her hair fluttering with neon blue like cold flame. The colour lasted until she looked Dorian's way, when it gravitated towards something more pink.

With the awkward gait of someone trying to walk with natural nonchalance, Melia came towards them. "How are you feeling?" she asked Dorian.

"Better," he said. "I think. And a bit confused…"

"Ah. That," Melia said with a sideways glance at Fable. "Probably nothing to worry about. Space sickness hits most grounders sooner or later. Usually sooner, but you have a few things going for you that probably helped you ignore the symptoms for a while."

"Symptoms?" he said. "Anything serious?"

"Some wooziness. Lightheadedness. Nothing that should impair you for long," Fable informed him casually. "But it should be pretty debilitating for most greenhorns."

"Ha! Too true," Emberly said with a wry grin as she leaned against the rail, shoulders propped up on it as she took a sip of coffee. "Mmm. I remember my first time netherborne. Down for almost three days feeling sicker than a dog! Always hits you when you're doing something strenuous too. So," she said, taking another lazy sip, eyeing Dorian through the steam. "What were you doing when the sickness hit you?"

Dorian glanced at Melia and Fable. Melia met his eyes and quickly turned hers away, blushing, but Fable merely grinned and wiggled her eyebrows suggestively. Dorian cleared his throat. "Oh," he said. "This and that."

Emberly glanced between the three and guffawed. "Ha!" she barked. "I bet you were! Assuming now that this adorable faun is 'this' and the testy elf is 'that'. Where did it go down? Right out here on the deck? Hope one of you swabbed it afterwards. Don't want any stains."

Dorian flushed and Fable patted his arm. "She's just kidding," Fable quickly said. "No one expects us to swab it. That spot is too special to clean now."

"Watch your mouth, demon" Melia hissed sharply, stepping towards the demoness with a snap of her boot, the elf drawing herself up with a flutter of her jacket and red flare of her hair. "Keep your nose out of crew business."

"Is that what it is?" Emberly said with a laugh into her coffee. "And here I thought we were just throwing around some scuttlebutt. Emphasis on butt. Which, I might add, is quite impressive," she said with a wink at Dorian.

"Er..." Dorian grunted, watching Melia as the elf seethed in an anger that seemed like it could explode into violence at any moment. "Thanks."

Fable patted his arm. "It is a fine ass," she assured him. "Well toned. Very squeezable."

Dorian blinked, not sure what to say. "Umm...Appreciated."

Melia stormed forward and grabbed the demoness by the front of her lacy pajamas, hauling Emberly upright, the elf's eyes blazing with anger. "I'll just warn you now. Watch yourself, bitch," Melia growled. "You're little better than cargo we have to suffer here, not crew, and if it comes to it, I'll gladly stick you in your cannon and fire you into the Black if you poke your nose in affairs that have nothing to do with you!"

Emberly laughed, seemingly utterly unperturbed at Melia's fury. "Think so? I'm here to supervise the shipment. If you really don't like my presence, might I suggest you take it up with Grash?"

"I don't need to run to your boss when I have a problem with you," Melia barked, shoving the demoness back against the rail. Stepping back, Melia drew her sword, the steel gleaming. "I demand satisfaction!"

"H-hey now," Dorian stammered quickly, stepping forward. "No need for that! She was just lightly teasing, that's all."

"She was judging us!"

Emberly rolled her eyes. "Typical hot headed elf," she said. "You can leave the Imperium, but you carry it with you, thinking every argument can be solved with some ceremony and fisticuffs."

"What did you say?!"

Emberly raised her hands and lazily tilted her head. "Hey now, I'm not saying I don't like it. If you lot want to fuck on every inch of this ship, I'm not one to tell you no. Besides, if you get the job done, what do I care? And it seems like you three can manage it. Probably better than most I've seen with twice your numbers and ten times your years in the Black, savvy?"

"If you think you're getting out of this just by tossing around some compliments, you're very mistaken," Melia snapped. "This is our ship, and you don't get to come aboard and disrespect our relationship like that!"

"Your ship, my guns," Emberly said with a shrug. "In fact, it's probably mostly *my* ship, since my guns are much more valuable than this tub you call a boat. But if you really want to, should we fight to the death?" Emberly asked sweetly.

Melia grimaced. "Of course not! To first blood."

"Well, if it'll give you any satisfaction," Emberly chuckled, turning her head. "Here. A cut along the cheek, and then we can all be friends again."

Melia hesitated, gripping her sword, but looking suddenly uncertain about the whole affair. Dorian felt immediate sympathy. The elf was indeed hotheaded, that much he certainly knew, and now it had backed her into a corner where she looked like a fool no matter what she did.

"No need for that," Dorian said firmly, stepping between them. "If we're going to travel together, we shouldn't be carving each other up. Or butting into the business of others," he added with a hard look at Emberly.

The demoness shrugged. "Fair enough. I apologize."

Melia growled and shoved her sword into its sheath. "Fine," she muttered.

"But next time you three have some fun together, do let me know," Emberly said with a lewd grin. "I'd love to watch some unique mating. Two on one isn't that odd, but a dragon blood, an elf, and a faun? That sounds like a real good time."

"Deal!" Fable chirped, springing forward and hanging off Dorian's arm, giving him a full blast of her gorgeous eyes. "As long as you're okay with it, Dorian."

The cuteness radiating from the faun's face quickly overwhelmed the, admittedly scanty, reluctance he had for such a scenario. "Er, sure. Melia?"

The elf scoffed, arms folded as she turned her back on Emberly. "Fine. Maybe the hellspawn will learn something."

"Absolutely," Emberly laughed, throwing her arms wide, bed robe flapping around her. "Teach me!"

Dorian sighed, suddenly feeling very weary. "Good. Then, if everyone's fine, I'm going to man the helm. We are still on a journey."

Turning, he made his way towards the wheel. His departure seemed to spur the others, who hastily made their way to their respective posts, all looking a little embarrassed at the exchange.

Emberly began to check the forward cannon and Fable clambered onto the rigging, pulling out her telescope and peering through it at the stars around them. Dorian nodded as he took the wheel in claw again, adjusting their bearing minutely along the path of gold only he could see. Finally—a bit of sanity aboard *The Windlass*.

As he adjusted the wheel, he felt a stare on him and glanced up, spotting Fable looking his way. The faun's jaw was slack, her eye peering at him through her enchanted spyglass.

Dorian glanced behind him, but saw nothing in their wake save the pinpricks of stars and the ribbons of galaxies. "Uh," he said, looking to the faun again. "See something?"

"Yeah. I think I do," Fable said, flicking a dial on the glass, lenses clicking before her eye. "I think I really do..."

Chapter 20

ONE OF THE BARRELS on deck had been dragged up to serve as an impromptu table, and the spyglass now rested on it like a piece of evidence at a crime scene. The four members of *The Windlass's* crew stood around it uncertainly, Dorian especially so.

"I'd been tweaking with the arcane filters and lenses on the mast," Fable began. "And I'd switched it to wyrmgate location. It tracks draconic magic, and displays it like it would with aura vision—just more specialized. Navigators, as a result, always glow a bit, as you'd expect, but Doria n...Anyway, look at Dorian with it," she muttered, her voice fading away.

Melia glanced at the faun, then at Dorian. She picked up the spyglass and turned it on him thoughtfully, only to suck in a startled breath.

"Yeah," Fable said. "I know. See the size of his draconic aura? And the purity?"

"What?" Dorian said.

"Quit hogging it! Let me see," Emberly demanded.

Testament to Melia's shock, she said nothing as she passed over the spyglass. Emberly took it up and peered at Dorian through it. She let out a sudden low whistle. "Well, well!" she said, lowering it with a grin. "Will you look at that…"

"Can someone please fill me in?" Dorian mumbled in exasperation. "What's going on?"

"I'll tell you what's going on," Emberly said, her golden eyes shining like polished coins. "You're gonna make me rich!"

Melia snatched the telescope from the demon. "The hell he is!"

"What?" Dorian protested. "Don't hold back on me."

"You don't have a dragon in your family tree at all, Dorian," Fable said, fairly vibrating with excitement, her teeth biting her lower lip as she hopped from one hoof to the other again and again.

"Then how can I do all the...navigator things?" he said. "Did I eat some crystals and not notice?"

"No no! You got me all wrong, cutie," Fable giggled, eyes shining. "You don't have a dragon in your family tree. You *are* a dragon!"

Dorian stared at her in bafflement. "What...what?" he protested. "That's ridiculous! I'm not...I mean, I can grow scales and everything, but I'm not, you know, a giant lizard. I think I'd have noticed by now."

"Not necessarily," Fable quickly said, raising one dainty little finger to her cheek.

"No, I think I'd have noticed that," Dorian interrupted.

"Nope! Because, see, dragons can take on human forms if they want to."

"Yeah. Or did you think those giant lizards were getting it on with normal sized women when they made half-dragons?" Emberly asked with a chuckle. "Not that I'd rule it out, mind you."

Fable wagged her finger, staring at Dorian with mounting interest. "I don't even think our cutie's a half-dragon, though."

"This is...I can't..." Melia muttered, shaking her head. She suddenly fixed Dorian with a steely eye. "What do you know about your parents?" she demanded. "Don't hold back."

"My parents? I...well, not much, honestly," Dorian said. "I never knew my father, and my mother passed away when I was an infant. At least, that's what I was told," he added, sudden uncertainty creeping in on him.

"What about childhood?" Melia continued. "Anything special happen? Unusual?"

Dorian shrugged helplessly. "Uh, not much. Clemmen wasn't exactly known for the unexpected happening. Though, I have always been really good at picking up things."

"What things?" Fable said, a notepad suddenly in her hand, pen poised and her attention so fixated on him even her deer-like ears seemed to be pointing his way.

"Most anything, really," Dorian offered with a shrug. "I've always been quick to get a knack for something. Smithing. Weaving. Carving. Fishing. It only takes me a little bit to do well at them.

Actually," he added as something flashed across his mind. "There was one thing…"

"Spill!" Fable gasped, already scratching notes.

"Well, it happened when I was a baby," he went on. "I was in my crib in the home of my wet nurse when there was a storm. Some lightning lit the cottage's thatch on fire. My nurse grabbed her kids and got out of there, and I was left in the crib."

Fable gasped. "How horrible!" she said.

Dorian shrugged. "Can't really blame her. If it was me, I'd probably have gone for my own flesh and blood too instead of a random orphan. Anyway, by the next day the fire was done and the house burned to the foundations. But they found me in the ashes, perfectly fine, if sooty. People called it a miracle."

Fable nodded along, finishing her writing with a flourish. "Got it!" she declared, beaming.

"You do?" Dorian asked.

"Yep," Fable said. "See, dragons have been known to mate with each other in both human and dragon form. But if the mother is in human form when she gets pregnant and has her child, then the child will be born looking human."

"I have heard of that," Emberly said. "Old lore, though. I always assumed that was speculation."

Fable grinned with pride. "Nope! It's rare, but has been recorded. Seems most children figure out how to shift into their true form at some point in the first few years, but if there wasn't a parent dragon around to show them how, who could say? I think that Dorian here is a dragon, likely some lesser astral dragon, and he just never figured out how to turn all big, bad, and scaly."

Melia said nothing, staring at Dorian in awe. He could understand why. The elf likely was coming to grips with the fact that, if she was right, she had literally fucked a dragon—one of those fabled creatures. She suddenly blushed but hastily shook it off.

Emberly just grinned, a trickle of smoke escaping the corner of her mouth. "Beeeautiful," she purred.

Melia heard it and suddenly rounded on the demoness, jabbing a finger at her, hair flaring dangerously red. "You will not be telling Grash anything about this!"

Emberly guffawed and held up her hands. "Hey now," she crooned. "No need for that. I'm no snitch, savvy? Besides, the last thing we want is for Grash to know what he's got his green mitts on. A true dragon? Hah!" Emberly scoffed. "Odds are he'd try and sell Dorian off for parts after he was bored with enslaving him."

"Parts!" Dorian yelped.

"Oh yeah," Emberly said, blowing a smoke ring in the air. "Sure as shooting. Real dragon parts are prized all over. Scales, limbs, heart, and there are those who'd even be able to bottle up your soul and make you a navigational aid. And folks would pay a tidy sum—but even more for you whole."

Fable shuddered. "You mean...dragonwood ships?"

Emberly aimed a fingerpistol at the faun. "Bingo."

"A what?" Dorian muttered darkly.

"Dragonwood," Melia said grimly, her face ashen and one hand holding tight the hilt of her sword. "A forsaken practice across the galaxy. A dragon is bound into a ship, blood bled into the vessel, soul chained, and body molded into a monstrous flesh craft. An abomination, not seen in centuries, but unspeakably dangerous. The last one to make such a thing was the necromancer, Mordhem, turning it into his flagship, *The Star Reaver*. He tore whole fleets apart before he was stopped."

Just the thought of such a thing made Dorian shiver, his very soul shrinking instinctively from the idea. Somehow, he felt like he could fathom such a fate, and dreaded even the notion. "Sounds monstrous," he said. "But that Mordhem was the last one who could do it?"

"That we know of," Fable said grimly. "And after he was killed, all of his notes were destroyed ...So they say. But that'd hardly stop someone new from trying all the same."

Dorian gulped. "Yeah. Okay. I vote for...not letting that happen to me."

"They'll have to go through us first," Melia promised.

"Damn straight!" Fable said, grabbing his hand and squeezing it. "No one's cutting up my dragon boyfriend."

"I'm here too," Emberly said. "But agreed. It'd be a damn waste to let some greasy necromancer waste that perfect body on something as uninspiring as crafting a legendary ship."

Dorian couldn't suppress a smile, giving Fable's hand a squeeze and the other women a grateful look. "Thanks," he said. "Even if I'm probably not actually a literal dragon. It's just...it's too ridiculous." He shook his head. "Fable's lens is probably just broken or something. I can't do much dragon stuff aside from...briefly transforming and breathing fire. And surviving housefires, I guess."

"Do you hear how absurd you sound?" Emberly scoffed.

"Actually," Fable said, looking back at the demoness. "That's probably the problem. Dorian? You *think* you're human. I doubt you'd be able to fully explore your potential unless you really did believe you could."

"Think so?" he said skeptically. "Then...how do we test that? Aside from shooting me into space to see if I grow wings?"

"Well..." Fable muttered, scratching her chin.

Melia had been silent, peering into the Black behind them, apparently lost in thought. Her eyes narrowed and she strode past the pair, snatching up the spyglass and putting it to her eye once more, peering through. A glint again caught her attention, and she thought she could just make out something blocking out the stars.

"...Fable?" the elf said, her hair crackling cold blue. "Can you sense anything behind us?"

Fable glanced at the elf, then moved past Dorian. She blinked, her eyes glowing a bright blue as she peered into the void, feeling and faintly seeing the auras that filled the vast emptiness.

"...I'm sensing a cluster of small hostile idiots behind us," she said. "Probably a goblin or kobold ship. Raiders, or maybe wannabe pirates." She blinked the aura away. "We can probably just outrun them."

"Yeah, we could do that," Emberly agreed. "We surely could. Or, and hear me out, we could blow them to pieces, steal their damned cargo, and test out my weapons and our navigator in an actual battle, savvy?"

Fable and Melia exchanged a glance, then looked at Dorian, who considered the idea. It was true that it might be good to try his hand at piloting during a proper battle. And though he wasn't looking for a fight, one had evidently been looking for him. He shrugged. "I'm ready for some destruction," he admitted. "Let's do it."

Emberly grinned, baring her fangs. "Beauty," she said. "Then let's show some pirates a bad fuckin' time."

Chapter 21

Dorian cruised the ship slowly, keeping an eye at their back as the enemy boat neared. Emberly was beside him, a hand on his shoulder as she watched the goblin ship closely, scrutinizing, searching for weaknesses, no doubt.

"That's right," Emberly whispered softly. "Nice and slow, darlin', Nice and sluggish. No reason to let them think we're better than we are, savvy? We'd spook 'em. These fucking scavengers," she scoffed, narrowing her golden eyes at the enemy ship. "They're only coming after us because we look like some aristo's pleasure yacht. They hope they can just cut us off and grab what they want. More guns than sense, and that's gonna be their downfall. Savvy?"

"Understood," Dorian said, watching the enemy ship closely. He could well believe they were scavengers. Their ship was a ramshackle thing of mismatched wood and bolted metal, like someone had slapped a junkyard into the shape of a boat and stuck some sails on the top. The whole hull seemed to have been worked around a massive cannon, and he could make out small figures scrambling over teetering rigging.

As the other ship closed in, Dorian maneuvered their own craft carefully forward, keeping a safe distance between them. The goblin ship awkwardly turned its bulk, gliding with them, and Dorian spotted a figure climb onto the prow of the other ship.

The goblin captain (and it surely was a captain. His silk sash, too-large captain's coat and ratty oversized hat marked him as such among his ragged crew) brought up a speaking horn, and from the crude craft his reedy voice boomed out.

"Hello thar!" snapped the goblin. "This is Cap'n Gabrino of the *Mean'n Green*! Stow your sails and oars, and prepare to be boarded if'n you know what's good for yas!"

Emberly rolled her eyes and gave Dorian a reassuring slap on the backside. She sauntered over to the rail, smiling genially as she lifted her own speaking horn. "Hello Captain!" she shouted back. "By that, are we to assume you intend to sack our ship, enslave our crew, and steal our goods?"

"Surrender peaceably, and we'll leave you and your crew alive and unharmed," the goblin said, though by the leer of his eye as he looked Emberly up and down, Dorian rather suspected he intended anything but. Dorian shook his head. Honestly, they only fed the stereotypes…

"Understood!" Emberly said, smiling with mock cordiality. "Just wanted to make sure, savvy?" She lowered the horn.

And swung up her rifle.

In a single motion she had braced the stock against her shoulder, her other hand rising and grasping the barrel. Her eye narrowed around the sight, and she fired.

The crack of the shot sounded across the deck, the arcane bullet shrieking as it tore through the void in a hail of crimson sparks. It slammed into the startled goblin's chest, throwing the short creature off his perch in a spray of blood.

"Now!" Emberly shouted—unnecessarily, for Dorian had already fed a surge of force into *The Windlass*. The oars boomed as they swept the air, lurching their ship into sudden motion even as the goblins shouted about the *Mean'n Green*. The tub's cannons went off one after the other in a chaotic assault—a cannon shot thundered in the wake of *The Windlass*, the ship's sudden acceleration throwing them forward and past the goblin's frantic assault.

"Fire!" Emberly snapped out.

Melia and Fable popped up behind their guns along the deck and quickly manned them. The arcane cannons glowed as Dorian brought their ship around, tilting their course to keep them out from in front of the goblin's menacing prow artillery. With a shriek of magic, the two cannons on *The Windlass* fired, sending bolts of crackling blue and green projectiles raining down on the deck of the goblin craft like comets.

Green bodies went flying as the arcane blasts detonated, blasting holes in the deck. Goblins scurried this way and that, shouting and harrying each other into action, but with their captain dead, discipline was quickly breaking down, even as Fable and Melia fired the second set of cannons facing the goblin craft.

"That's it," Emberly cooed, almost erotically, moving back up behind Dorian and teasing him as she pressed her ample chest into his back. She exhaled a hot breath onto his nape and uttered some more praise before turning away.

The demoness kept an eye on the battle as Dorian maneuvered their quick ship around the floundering goblin craft as it tried to turn with their sleek vessel. "Keep circling like a sky shark, you magnificent beast. Stay out of range of their smaller weapons if possible. First and foremost, just watch out for their cannons."

Dorian nodded, his grip on the wheel tense as he watched the goblin ship try and maneuver. As they passed near, the cannon on the prow suddenly fired, the shot blasting through space with such force the recoil sent the *Mean'n Green* rocking on its keel. The mere passage of the shot near them sent *The Windlass* rocking, but Dorian quickly righted their craft, avoiding the hit.

"Assholes!" Fable shouted from her post and fired her own cannon again.

This latest shot blasted through the helm, sending several goblins flying and obliterating the wheel and whatever they used as the navigator. Fires burned all over the ship, and goblins broke from the attack, their meager courage giving way. Practically fighting each other to be first, the goblins scrambled through the cargo hold and below decks, away from the punishing fire of the cannons and some hopeful safety.

"Good job, navigator," Emberly crowed, slapping Dorian on the ass once more. "We'll make a proper starfarer of you yet!"

"Thanks," Dorian said, eying the burning craft as he resisted his urge to massage his buttcheek.

"Damn right. Now bring us down! It's lootin' time!"

"Ah, yes. Looting," Dorian chuckled.

"Of course! They'd have done worse to us," Emberly said. "Now, let's go grab anything worth taking from that tub."

"You're sure it's safe?" Dorian asked.

Emberly cackled. "Nothing is safe out here. Assume everything's out to kill you and be pleasantly surprised when you're wrong. Which just means you need to be deadlier than anything else! Savvy?"

"Savvy enough," he grunted, cracking his knuckles.

Emberly nodded towards Melia and Fable, who were already arming themselves with swords and pistols, evidently anticipating the imminent boarding action.

Though still unsure, Dorian nevertheless steered *The Windlass* towards the goblin ship, making sure he didn't put their ship in range of the guns below deck. Though the crew may have looked beaten, Dorian had no intention of letting that lull him into overconfidence.

"Alright, elf," the demoness said as she strolled down amidship as *The Windlass* cruised in alongside the *Mean'n Green*. "Let's see what we got."

"My name is Melia, *demon*," Melia said hotly, her hair still fluttering red with bloodlust and excitement.

"Is it? Fantastic. Good for you. Now, let's go!" Emberly said, drawing her pistols and kicking a plank between the rails of the two ships.

Melia growled like a rabid dog and followed the red-skinned woman aboard the burning ship, their weapons panning the deck for any sign of attack. Dorian kept his eye on the other vessel, but not a single pointy green ear was seen, and soon Emberly was scouring the deck for anything of value.

There didn't seem to be much. The damage done to the goblin ship had obliterated most of what they possessed, and that which it hadn't was little more than scrap or rubbish. He saw Emberly curse, kicking away a green arm still clutching a dagger. "Fuckin' bollocks!" she growled. "Bunch of losers, this lot."

"Shame," Dorian said, turning his attention to Melia, who barely glanced back at the other woman. Her sword glittered in the light of the flames as she scoured what remained of the helm. The cannon shot had been aimed well. Little save chunks of kindling remained, and Dorian saw the elf deftly pick her way through the ruins. She suddenly stopped, bounded up the ruins of the steps and crouched down.

"Find something?" Dorian shouted across the ships.

Melia straightened, one arm held over her head, something flashing in her grasp. "Found their core!"

"Hey, that's not bad," the demoness barked, hefting a sack she'd shoved what little booty she found that was worth finding. "Better than the scraps I found. Want to chance going below?" she asked, glancing at the entrance below decks.

Melia seemed to consider it, then shook her head. "Just us? Not worth it. Goblins backed into a corner are always more dangerous."

"True enough. Probably nothing down there anyway," the demoness said as she sauntered back to the gangplank, Melia close behind.

The sight relieved Dorian a fair bit. The fight had gone well. No need to imperil themselves further.

...Was what he thought, when a voice suddenly boomed in his head.

"Attention vessels!" the aristocratic voice said, layered with all the dry menace of the dutiful powerful. "You are to cease all conflict immediately and wait to be boarded by the Imperial Fleet!"

Everyone's head whipped around, quickly spotting the vessel in question. Like a swan layered with gold, wood, and cannonade, a warship of the Elven Imperium glided out of the darkness of space like in a spectacle of white and gold, sails snapping in the astral winds, propelling it towards the two locked ships.

"Shit!" Melia cursed, quickly crossing the springing board and dragging it over after her.

"Oh fuck. Oh fuck!" Fable stared at the approaching vessel, on the verge of panic.

Dorian glanced at the pair, then back at the warship as Emberly sauntered up behind him. "If they board us," he asked. "What are the odds they'll be happy about our cargo?"

"Mmm," Emberly mused, tapping her chin. "I'd say about...zero percent. Savvy?"

"Uh huh," Dorian grunted, flexing his claws on the wheel. "And, what are the odds they can catch me?"

Emberly flashed her fangs in an excited smile. "Hmm. Well, since they won't dare leave the goblin ship for long, and assuming you being an actual dragon aren't all talk, I think we'd be sitting at...eighty percent."

"Only?" Dorian said as he widened his stance, bracing himself at the wheel. "Tsh. Give me some more credit than that!"

"Gimme a good show, and I'll give you a proper sorry. Savvy?"

Dorian grinned. "Hold on to something!" he shouted.

Fable and Melia looked at him in shock, quickly realizing what he was going to do. Fable immediately bounded to the mast and grabbed hold for dear life, Melia doing the same to the rail.

Excitement bubbling in him, Dorian pushed his will into *The Windlass* in a sudden surge of power. He felt the energy within him feed the vessel, the golden designs that swirled across the hull and deck glowing with swirls of crimson hues, like veins of power infused across the hull. The oars on either side gave a sudden beat, hurtling *The Windlass* forward and deeper into space.

Emberly barely managed to brace herself before the sudden acceleration, far stronger than the last time she encountered it. She laughed wildly, hair streaming out behind her as she looked back at the Elven Imperial warship rapidly shrinking in their wake. "So long!" she cheered, waving farewell.

The massive ship tried to give chase, sailing after them under full sail. A few desultory shots from arcane cannons spat from the immense vessel's forward guns, but the shots went wide, losing power as they chased the fleeing ship, reduced to sputtering embers of gold—and then nothing.

Dorian laughed, exuberant as he spurred their ship onward and away, draconic wings of starlight and magic stretching out behind him as natural as his own arms. He could get used to this.

Fable bounded past him with a clip clop of hooves. She leaned against the rail of the stern, her spyglass at her eye as she watched the elven ship recede. A laugh broke from her. "They're turning around and heading back to the goblin's ship," she said triumphantly.

"Good," Melia said, coming up beside them. "That'll keep them busy for a while, and probably get them off our tails. They'll have better things to do than chase us once they find out those little green bastards are pirates."

"Then we're in the clear?" Dorian asked.

"For now," Emberly sighed, slapping Dorian on the back, mindful of his ethereal wings. "But keep it up for a while longer!"

"Gladly." Dorian smirked as he poured more power into the ship, relishing the freedom of open space as *The Windlass* soared on into the endless black.

Chapter 22

As the miles vanished in their wake, Fable turned from the stern and bounced over to Dorian. Planting a hand on the wheel, she vaulted it, straddling the pedestal it was attached to.

Dorian glanced down at her, hardly able to ignore the beautiful faun shooting him the lovey-doviest gaze he'd ever seen levied at him. "Um..."

"That was some nice flying back there, cutie," she giggled, reaching up and brushing a hand along his cheek.

"Think so?" Dorian said, feigning humility. "Thanks."

"Sure do," Fable giggled, leaning in over the wheel and pressing her lips to Dorian's.

Dorian stiffened as their lips met, his ethereal wings fluttering behind him as the kiss zinged through him like a bolt of pure adrenaline. Fable moaned softly, her lips tingling from the sheer amount of magic Dorian was filled with.

"Fable," Melia groaned. "He's trying to steer! Save it for later when we both can have a go, for the sake of the Void."

Fable broke the kiss, licking her lips. "Mmm. He can steer fine. There's nothing in our way. Besides, Melia, you've got to try this! When he's got the wings out, it's like kissing raw mana."

"Fable," Melia growled, but it must have sounded half-hearted even to her.

"I uh, can still steer," Dorian said. "Good view between Fable's antlers."

"Is that so?" Melia said, sauntering closer.

"Yeah. I—"

Melia suddenly grabbed his face, turned it around, and kissed him hard. Dorian's eyebrows shot up, particularly when Melia's hair flared like someone poured some gas on a pink bonfire. The elf broke the kiss with a gasp, panting quickly.

"Damn," the elf breathed. "That was…"

"Now he really can't see," Fable giggled, leaning forward and touching Dorian's chin, turning his head back around and kissing him anew.

Dorian offered no complaint, one hand rising off the wheel, his more clawed hand touching Fable's face as the faun moaned, nestling her cheek in his scaly palm as he gave her the affection she came to him in search of.

Emberly licked her lips where she lingered near the rail, one of her hands lazily cupping her own breast and fondling herself through her top. "Mmm. Nice," she said. "Am I about to get my show already?"

Dorian broke the kiss with Fable, chuckling. "Not today," he said. "I've still got to settle our course again. We're pretty off after that run. After that—well, when I finally am in the mood for some voyeurism, I'll give you a shout."

"Fair enough. It's quite a journey for me already—but don't back down on me, navigator." Emberly warned him with a wolfish grin. "Now I'm real curious. Savvy?"

Dorian laughed aloud that time, giving Melia another quick kiss before focusing on his work.

It was some hours before he managed to leave the wheel, for a meteor shower crossed their trajectory soon after, requiring some deft flying from him while the girls hastened to charge up an atmospheric barrier to slow the rain of stones, then sweeping them off the deck.

And so they journeyed on. The miles melted behind them, the days passing in a blur to Dorian. New sights assailed them each day. Asteroids drifting past. Gas giants seething with chemical storms the size of continents. Moons aglow, some showing signs of civilization, others barren, and one bearing the ruins of what had once been a fortress, now no more than rubble preserved in the airless void for eternity.

And then, they reached Asimova's Spire.

Dorian had thought that he'd been growing accustomed to shocking sights among the stars, but he had been wrong. Fable was the first to spot the air station through her telescope, guiding him towards the location by the sheer size of its aura, and the reason for that soon became plain.

Asimova's Spire had once been a large meteor tethered to the gravity pull of a small planetoid like a miniature moon, but then the sylvans had chosen it to make their home. Now, the immense rock had been reformed, shaping great bowls in the stone surface, all of it overgrown with vast forests of immense trees. Like a chunk of fertile earth cast into the void, vast root systems pointed down towards the planetoid below, while huge trees sprouted from the body of the asteroid, reaching out towards a distant sun.

Ships whizzed about the place, tethering themselves to spindly roots stretching forth from the great trunks of the mighty star trees. A system so different from Sphere with its cold, artificial beauty, yet somehow no less impressive.

Dorian couldn't help but gape at the sight, words escaping him from the shock of it all.

"Pretty nice, eh?" Fable said, elbowing him in the side.

Dorian recovered belatedly. "Y-yeah. It is."

"And just in time too," Fable noted, waving her hand. "The air's getting a little stale around here. About time we refreshed it, huh?"

"No argument here," he said, and tilted the wheel, skimming *The Windlass* in towards one of the root formations.

As they came nearer, Dorian could sense the moment they entered the field around the air station. He inhaled deeply, feeling the air of the ship suddenly refreshed, scented now of summer warmth and a forest growing in its prime season. He sighed happily, beaming as he guided them towards one of the vast roots, the oars of *The Windlass* beating slower as he brought them towards an empty berth.

The ship slid along one of the natural docks, its surface flat as any pier, yet made from a single continuous branch. As they came in, Fable bounded off *The Windlass* with a mooring rope, making it fast as Dorian brought their ship to a full halt.

He sighed in relief, releasing his hold on the wheel and stepping away from it. "So what's the plan?" he asked.

"First of all, don't make any trouble," Melia told him sternly. "Air stations are true neutral zones. No one makes a problem here, not pirates, slavers, or anyone. Even Elven Imperials watch their shit when they stop at air stations."

Dorian nodded, but he was curious. "Why?"

"Because if you cause problems, you're gone," Fable said with a flip of her hand as she came back aboard. "And not just the air station you fucked around in. But any ones connected. Sylvans who keep the stations are very serious about that stuff. And they take no shit!"

Dorian winced, recalling the last time he went ashore. "Right," he said uncertainly. "Then, maybe we should just stay aboard while we refresh the oxygen…"

"And where's the fun in that?" Emberly asked as she sauntered back up from below, dressed once more in her leather boots and jacket, her hair fluttering around the stumps of her horns. "If you get trigger shy just from a day spent on Sphere, then you'll never be ready for big space. Besides, we need to stock up on some supplies. Always fill up when you've got the chance! That's my motto. Especially when Grash is paying for it. So keep those receipts, savvy?"

"Well..." Melia began.

"Besides," Emberly pressed on, swinging an arm around Dorian's shoulders and tugging him down to her level, grinning up at him with her fanged teeth, "I'll be looking out for him while we get shopping, and I promise to keep him out of trouble."

"Uh—"

"Or were you planning on letting poor little me go ashore all alone?" Emberly whined with a teasing pout and flutter of her dark lashes.

Dorian reddened slightly, strongly suspecting if anyone would need saving, it would be whoever tried to start something with Emberly.

"We could use a top up of the water," Fable noted. "And booze. Not to mention some different food. Getting kinda sick of jerky, if I'm being honest, and we've been out of bread for days."

"See?" Emberly said with a smile at the pair. "You two can watch the ship while we're gone. C'mon, Dorian. Let's go do some trading!"

Slapping him on the back again, Emberly let him go and sauntered down the ramp and onto the dock. Dorian rubbed the back of his head, glancing at Melia and Fable, then shrugged and headed off after her. He'd have been lying if he said he didn't want to see Asimova's Spire. He'd seen a number of alien places since leaving Clemmen and hitting the stars—and yet, the familiarity of the air station's wooden construction, when expanded to truly expansive proportions, made it seem even more alien than the more unfamiliar things he had seen.

He followed Emberly down the root and towards an entrance into the tree proper. Two elves stood guard, though they were far from the gilded Elven Imperials he had seen before. Instead, they looked to be armoured in something like tree bark conforming to their figures, the whorls of the wood swirling in dizzying designs. Helmets swooped back on their heads, and they both carried spears whose metal tips looked more like natural extensions of the bark than anything else.

They said nothing as Dorian and Emberly passed, moving up some stairs that then opened up in a vast plaza, built under the roots of another great tree as if from natural pillars. Marble stone spun outwards from the plaza, where shops and stalls filled the space, many carved into the roots like homes built into the very tree. Motes of golden light hung in the air overhead, drifting like fairy lights, washing the whole scene in a glow like perpetual noon.

Dorian gaped at the sight, unable to hide his amazement, until Emberly nudged him, pulling him back to the present.

"Best close that jaw, Dorian, or everyone's going to know you're a groundling on his first trip netherborne," she said teasingly.

Dorian hastily complied with a rueful grin. "Sorry," he said. "This is just...incredible."

"Too true," Emberly agreed as she walked him down some marble steps and into the plaza, heading straight to the shops. "These places are run by sylvans, and they're very protective of their trees. Some might say too much so. But more than a few would love to take over these places. There's been some attempts, but few successful. Only sylvans can tend the trees properly. Anyone else tries, and the whole thing soon withers and dies."

"That's terrible," Dorian said.

"You're telling me! Fortunately, few are dumb enough to try—and those who are tend not to last long. Every ship on a station like this would swarm them if they did, even if the sylvans themselves didn't take care of it. So don't try anything, savvy? Especially since that's not why we're here. We're here to make some perfectly legal, wholesome, and moral trades!"

Dorian agreed and resolved not to try anything while about the station—particularly as he spotted several more of the elven guardians in their wooden armour standing here and there, watching the crowds and shops with intent vigilance.

"Love these places," Emberly sighed admiringly as they moved through the stalls. "You can find damn near anything you could want from across known space! And sometimes even from unknown space. Not as good a collection as Sphere, sure, but some things you can only see around here. Why once, in my early days I saw a dragon like you wandering around."

Dorian's attention swung from a near naked catgirl selling glittering jewelry off her own body and back to Emberly. "A dragon like me?"

"Well, not quite like you. He was in his dragon form. But yes. It was incredible," she breathed. "Unlike anything I'd ever seen. Majestic. Powerful. Beyond my comprehension. It was the first time I realized I was far, far from home."

Recalling his own encounter with the gargantuan dragon in the wyrmway, Dorian had to agree. The sense of awe he'd felt at that moment hadn't been matched by any of the amazing sights he'd seen since. But something else she'd said drew his attention and curiosity. "What was your home like?"

Emberly's smirk grew wry and bitter. "Ha! Want to know about that, hm? Well, sure. Why not? It's not a big secret," she said, tossing a coin at a shopkeeper and snatching up a strange, purple fruit from his stall. "You've been in the wyrmway, yeah? Well, guess what? Hell is a lot like that, in that it's a sort of...in between places—existing sandwiched between this one and another."

"Oh?" Dorian said.

"Mhmm," Emberly said as she examined the skin of the fruit. "Just as how we call Prime Space 'The Black', we call Inferal Space, 'The Red'—and it fucking sucks, savvy?"

"Does it?"

Emberly tore a chunk from the fruit, chewing before swallowing. "Mm. Not bad. And yes, it does. Which is why demons are always happy to get the *Hell* out of there. But it's hard. Usually, it takes some poor sod working up a ritual to summon one of us, and then we're bound to him in a compromised form. But there's other ways. There's tears in reality here and there through space, sort of like the wyrmgates. Rips in reality through which formless chaos bleeds like wounds in existence ...And sometimes, there's whole worlds that get caught in them."

"Worlds?" Dorian said, feeling a shiver in his soul.

Emberly nodded, taking another bite from the fruit. "Mm. You better believe it. Sometimes, it's because a sorcerer or civilization made a big ritual to summon a demon. Sometimes, it was just bad luck. But demons have a hard time existing in reality as you know it. We've gotta make ourselves a physical form that can withstand it, and let me tell you, the galaxy is lucky more powerful demons can't find anything that can hold the immensity of their forms."

Dorian nodded, looking her over at the mention of 'form'. "Noted," he said.

"Anyway, I'm pretty small potatoes, so I managed to make myself a humanoid body on one of those hellworlds. Not bad workmanship, eh?" she said with a scandalous swing of her hips.

"Impressive," Dorian agreed with a grin. "I'm an admirer of your craft."

"Damn straight!" Emberly crooned with a flutter of her long lashes. "Anyway, some hellworlds welcome mortals. Warlocks and slavers and so forth. Pay a pretty penny for that shit. One time, a sorcerer came to buy some stuff from my family. His stories were pretty interesting, and I figured hey, that sounds like fun! More fun than endlessly tormenting captured souls at any rate, so I hopped aboard his ship, and here I am!"

"Feels like you left out a fair bit of detail there," Dorian observed.

"Ha! I bet it does," Emberly said with a cocky grin. "And maybe I'll tell you about those missing details some day. But that's all you get for now, savvy? Now come on! We got some goods to buy!"

With a wink back at him, Emberly sauntered off among the stalls, and for a moment Dorian just watched her go, marveling not just at the sight, but at the story behind the demoness's arrival on his ship. He shook his head. The universe truly was a strange place, he mused before hastening after her, and among the stalls of the tree.

Chapter 23

Trade aboard Asimova's Spire was an interesting thing for Dorian to experience. It was about as far removed from the Clemmen Marketplace as he could imagine, but it bore its superficial similarities. He mostly kept his mouth shut as Emberly wheeled and dealed. She spoke in tongues that shocked most merchants as they suddenly found themselves trying to barter in their own language. She started each encounter off with syrupy sweetness, then hammered in the details with ruthless expertise.

They extracted some supplies from aliens who were wrapped totally in bandages, and whose essence beneath crackled like static. A robed alien with a face like a spider clicked and whined, buying a crate of the ship's jerky and sending a man to retrieve it and deliver several crates of goods in trade. Ropes, water—even some clothes were gained by Emberly's silver tongue and impressive skills, shocking Dorian at the sorts of battles traders engaged in.

When they stopped for lunch, eating some meat skewers from a stall, Dorian could only shake his head in wonder.

"You're incredible," he said.

Emberly laughed. "Ha! You think this was good? You should have seen the performance I put on to get Grash's contract. And once, I bargained an impadan merchant prince down to the clothes he was wearing, all for a shiny rock that may or may not have been a diamond. Now that was a good day," she said.

Dorian shrugged the pack of supplies he was carrying. Not much. Most had been ordered to be delivered at once to the ship by porters employed by the merchants, but a few things had been small enough the fee for delivery hadn't been worth it. "Still," he said. "I can see why Grash trusts you to get the job done."

Emberly wagged her now barren skewer at him. "Ha! Grash doesn't trust anyone. And he's smart not to. I suggest you remember that if you're gonna be working with him."

"I suppose. But—"

"Upon my oath! If it isn't Emberly Brimspire."

The brash, booming voice froze Emberly where she stood, her crimson face greying like tombstone. Dorian quickly turned towards the source and forced himself not to take a startled step back.

A huge man bore down on them, if man could describe the creature. A thick, black coat with golden buckles draped his broad shoulders. Six eyes peered from folds of grey skin, his face sloughing into a mass of wriggling tentacles. A tricorn hat sat on his head, and the mark of a squid-like skull with crossed blades immediately caught Dorian's attention, a similar design decorating a golden amulet dangling from the pirate's neck. Dorian had seen that sign before, and it took him a moment to recall the men who'd tried to pursue them on Sphere's dock.

"C-Captain Scarro," Emberly said. "What...what are you..."

"Doing here? Why, where else should I be, my girl? Har har har!" the captain bellowed as he came up, towering over the pair of them. "Needed a breath o' fresh air, ya see, and upon my oath, who should I espy? Why, it's my favorite little demon wench struttin' around without a care in the world. Which means, of course, you took my offer."

Emberly swallowed hard. "I...I don't know what..."

"What?" Scarro interrupted her, the tentacles of his maw parting, revealing a saw-toothed smile. "Well, upon my oath! Didn't those elves on Sphere I sent deliver my message? That it was their job to take Grash's cargo? But I heard you wheeled a deal underneath them, which meant they must have told you you'd be delivering it to me instead. Surely they let you know?"

Emberly tightened her lips, drawing herself up. "I never agreed to any deal. I got that contract fair and square."

"Of course!" Scarro cried, his stomach wobbling with laughter. "Well, good for you! Unfortunately, the whole o' the Black has an extra little contract with me, and the fine print says you give me what I want and no less. After all, everyone knows when Scarro makes you an offer, you take it! Otherwise, some truly unfortunate things'll happen. And I know you're too smart for that, aren't you?"

Emberly drew back as if the pirate's bulk was pressing down on her. "I...I didn't..."

"So tell me where you're docking, and I can send my boys to grab the goods all pleasant-like—no fuss, no drama. We can all stay friends after that! For upon my oath, I," Scarro declared, hand pressed over his heart, his eyes looking radiantly skyward into the eaves of the roots above them, "Yes, I! Captain Scarro, am a man who values his friends. And everyone wants to be the bosom buddy of Captain Scarro, eh? Because after all, me lads," he said, his head tilting as he hunched over Emberly, the tentacles of his face tilting up her chin so she was looking into his six eyes. "If yer not my friend, that only leaves one thing for you to be. Wouldn't it?"

Emberly drew back until her back hit the wooden wall of a root pillar. Dorian looked between her and the pirate, and then stepped between them, staring straight into the captain's monstrous face.

Scarro's six eyes switched to him, the pirate's tentacles twitching. "Well well!" he bellowed, straightening, rocking back on his heels and looking down on Dorian amiably. "What have we here! Please ta meet ya, boy. Captain Scarro! Master and commander of the *Sky Kraken*! Perhaps you've heard of me?"

"Not really," Dorian grunted, though now that he thought back, he recalled the face from the wanted posters he'd seen on Sphere. Even among all those mugs, it wasn't one easy to forget. "You seem to think you're pretty important, but I'm afraid our orders are to deliver our cargo on behalf of Boss Grash."

Scarro belted out a laugh. "Boyo, I do admire yer gall. Think you're brave, don't you, standing between the greatest pirate in all the Black and your busty demon strumpet?" Scarro asked jovially. "Let me ask one more time: Are you sure the person you're deliverin' to isn't little ol' me?"

"Sorry, but I don't believe it is," Dorian said, not backing down even as Emberly cringed beside him and squeezed his arm. "You looking to start something in an air station?"

Scarro continued to smile, but a narrowness came to his six eyes. "No, sir, no! That would be a problem. Yes it would. Not as big a problem, of course, as you not coughin' up the goods. And upon my oath, that'd be a *real* problem—and much bigger for you than me, I dare say." He turned his head, looking down at Emberly. "Does this cocky human speak for you, dearest Emberly?"

Emberly rallied, straightening and looking Scarro in his eye, which was somewhat difficult as there were six of them. "The cargo is already getting delivered properly," she said. "I won't break a signed contract, savvy?"

Scarro's tentacles writhed around his grin. "Is that so? Well! Upon my oath, the gods know I am not a violent man, but if someone tries to cheat ol' Scarro from what's his, well, what other solution have we?" he said with a lazy shrug of his broad shoulders.

"You wouldn't dare," Emberly growled. "Not even you'd try anything here of all places!"

"Me?" Scarro said, looking shocked. "Here? Of course not! Upon my oath, I am a man who respects the noble rules of the sylvans and their great mother tree. I would never break the Pax Flora. But of course," he said, stroking one of his face tentacles as if it were a flowing mustache, "when one *leaves* the station, the Pax no longer applies. Does it?"

Dorian gently took Emberly by the shoulder, then gave Scarro a harsh look. "We're leaving," he said.

"Of course! I'd hate to keep you," Scarro said, tipping his hat affably. "Until we meet again. And I do hope it's under much better circumstances. Har har har!"

"Go fuck a plate of calamari," Dorian hissed, just loud enough to be heard as he made a rude gesture over his shoulder at the pirate captain as he steered Emberly away and walked her quickly across the marketplace. "Are you okay?" he asked softly.

Emberly shuddered, gritting her teeth. "We have to go," she said.

"Go?" Dorian asked. "Did we get everything—"

"Now. We have to get back to the ship. We have to take off before the *Sky Kraken*!"

Dorian listened to the tension in her voice, feeling the alarm that quivered in her. He'd never seen Emberly afraid, and that the man they'd met could inspire it in her made Dorian grimly nod.

Without another word, they both burst into motion, sprinting across the marketplace and back towards the stairs leading to the docks. He just hoped they made it out in time...

Chapter 24

DORIAN AND EMBERLY WERE running full pelt by the time they reached the stairs, cannoning up them and past a number of merchants and sailors going to and fro. Some paused to watch them pass, but most ignored them—which Dorian was grateful for.

They reached their dock fast, a couple of crates of their less essential purchases still waiting to be loaded aboard. Fable looked up from them as the pair came running, and her delighted smile dropped to alarm at their expressions.

"What happened?" she asked.

"Aboard. Now!" Emberly barked, grabbing the faun and shoving her towards the gangplank. Fable stumbled forward, but quickly regained her balance, her hooves clopping across the plank and back aboard their ship.

Melia turned from inspecting a vase she'd pulled from one of the crates at the thunder of their boots. She tossed them a baffled look. "What's going on?" she demanded.

"Captain Scarro saw us," Emberly gasped as she hastily undid the mooring ropes. "He wants the cargo!"

The vase shattered, dropped from Melia's suddenly nerveless hands. Fable tripped on her own hooves from the shock of that name, nearly tumbling to the deck as she sharply straightened. "Wh-what?!" she yelped.

"No time!" Emberly snapped as the mooring line at last came free. "We have to go. Now!"

Fable and Melia exchanged a look, then burst into motion. By the time Dorian grabbed the wheel, scales rippling up his arms, both women had unfurled every stitch of sail, which snapped taut, catching the astral winds as Dorian willed the winged oars into motion, spurring their craft forward.

Some shouts came from the loaders on the dock, but were ignored as Dorian swung their ship out and towards open space. Spurred forward, it swept about the blossoming bulk of the air station.

"Look!" Melia shouted, pointing overboard.

Dorian swung his head that way and felt his body go numb with fear and horror. As they swung about the station, they came into view of a massive branch of the tree.

And something was rising from it.

Dorian had seen many squids in his time. Living by the sea, a number of fishermen had pulled them in from the lines. So too had he heard tales of immense monsters lurking beneath the waves—tentacled horrors who could drag down ships and their crew with ease in a maelstrom of violence and hunger.

And yet, those myths paled in the face of the *Sky Kraken*.

Its head bulged like that of an octopus the size of a castle, its limbs titanic tentacles big enough to grapple a house. Huge, malevolent eyes glowed on either side of its head. Bony growths swelled across its rubbery frame like jagged armor, and atop its head, seeming to have been built into the very mass of its flesh, was what looked like the closed helm of a ship, cannon turrets riddling its frame, the whole thing resembling a helmet of black wood and iron girding the monstrous kraken's scalp.

Even from a distance, Dorian could tell the monster dwarfed their vessel as a shark did a minnow. The tentacles of the monstrous kraken fanned out, then swung in, propelling itself through space in a shocking burst of speed.

And right after them.

"Oh fuck," Fable whimpered.

Dorian gripped the wheel, throwing a sudden burst of power into the ship. With a sudden beat of the oars, The Windlass surged forward, trailing a wake of arcane flows behind them. Dorian risked a look back as the *Sky Kraken* pursued, shooting through the void with every pulse of the monster's tentacles. As he watched, a flash lit up one of the cannons on the creature's crown, a streak of crackling red magic screaming through the void after them.

"Incoming!" Emberly shouted.

Dorian jerked the wheel, *The Windlass* tilting sharply, the shot howling past, so near that Dorian could feel the hairs on his arms stand up from the crackle of magic. He gasped at the shot, amazed, the range and aim leagues apart from when they'd faced the goblins.

Melia cursed. "They're good!"

"Too good," Emberly growled as she watched the monstrous craft continue after them. "Scarro's a master of the chase. Only a matter of time until he cripples us with a shot."

"Then what do we do?" Melia demanded.

Dorian looked about frantically, wincing as another shot of screaming magic roared past them, even closer than the last one despite his skill at the wheel. The rings of debris rotating around a nearby gas giant caught his eye and he nodded. "Can we lose him in there?"

Fable ducked reflexively as another shot of crimson magic shot past the bow. "Better than waiting out here," she cried.

"But what about golems?" Dorian shouted. "Are we going to run into them again?"

"Rather face a golem or a rock worm than those pirates," Melia shot back.

Well, she had him there. Grimly, Dorian agreed. He hauled on the wheel, the sails creaking as their little ship swooped away on a new course, another shot of magic fire whistling past them, thrown off by the sudden change in direction.

Dorian braced himself, throwing in another burst of power, his wings of draconic magic flapping from his back and horns leaving thin streams of light in his wake as he pushed the ship to new surges of speed. He didn't stop to think if he was good enough to manage the hurtling rocks below. He didn't dare to hesitate. To doubt. He had to trust his skill. Because if he was wrong, their ship would be battered to splinters in an instant. It was their one chance.

He just wished it wasn't so slim.

The Windlass soared into the asteroid field, two huge rocks smashing into each other just behind them. Dorian grit his teeth, rattling the wheel as he maneuvered, every sense straining for any warning of an incoming boulder.

"Man the cannons!" Emberly shouted. "Blast anything coming too close!"

"Think that'll help?" Dorian asked tensely.

"S'all we can do," Emberly said as she moved up behind him, grabbing his shoulders. "The air field around the ship will slow them down a bit, but not enough to save us. It's up to you mainly. Now, pull back some of that power from speed. Push it into maneuverability. That's what we're going to need here."

Dorian did as she said, the sense of speed thinning as he concentrated more on the oars and rudder of *The Windlass*. The ship slowed as he moved it through the boulders tossing around them. The largest didn't concern him overly. They were easy to avoid. But the smaller ones were another matter, considering 'smaller' in this case meant merely the size of a house instead of a castle. He eased the wheel, nipping around an asteroid tumbling towards them, then skimmed over another, setting them ever deeper into the field.

"Good. You're doing great," Emberly said soothingly. "Keep at it."

"Right," Dorian grunted. "Uh, you said something about...rock worms? What are those?"

"Huge, worm-like monsters," Fable shouted from across the deck as she adjusted a cannon, tracking an asteroid that came dangerously near before a flap of *The Windlass's* winged oars sent them swinging out of its path. "They make their homes in asteroid fields like these and eat the mineral deposits. But they're very territorial, and are big enough to really threaten a ship."

"Right. I'll...keep an eye out for that," Dorian said.

"Plus the asteroids. And the *Sky Kraken*. And maybe Roid Hoppers, which are low rent raiders who hide in fields like this. But, you know. No pressure, savvy?" Emberly said.

"Yeah. None at all," Dorian said in a tight voice.

Emberly patted his shoulder as she peered about the asteroid field. Silence hung heavy around them. There was only the soft moan of air and creak of oars as the immense rocks tumbled around them, whirling in their eternal dance around the planet below.

Dorian's eyes scanned the rocks, careful to keep their ship moving through them, keeping close but never too close to the stones.

Melia eyed their surroundings from the forward cannon, carefully maneuvering the mass of black metal to and fro. "I think...I think we lost them," she dared to say.

"Ahhh! Jinx!" Fable cried.

"Oh come on," Melia said. "It's not—"

With a thunderous boom the asteroid beside them split apart, and out of the smoke writhed eight massive rubbery tentacles. Fable screamed as one of the massive limbs grabbed their ship, wrapping around the forecastle.

"Upon my oath!" Scarro's voice thundered, amplified by something magical as the *Sky Kraken* poured through the gap in the asteroid's shards like a nightmare, the squid's eyes fixed on the ship, its beaked mouth clacking as more of its limbs reached for their tangled craft. "I am not a cruel man, my friends. But I will see what's mine be mine!"

"Shoot it!" Emberly shrieked as she vaulted past Dorian and over the helm, drawing an axe from her belt. "Shoot it now!"

Melia swung the fore cannon about on its platform, unable to completely turn to face the tentacle grasping their ship, but as the kraken dragged the ship towards its waiting mouth, a part of the tentacle holding them came into range. Melia didn't waste a second, the cannon glowing as she fired.

The shot of violet magic screamed through the void before exploding against the kraken's limb. A shriek of pain came from the monster, its tentacle loosening.

"Punch it!" Emberly roared as she swung her axe into the rubbery limb clinging to the ship, hacking a slice in the quivering red flesh.

Dorian threw himself against the wheel, a flash of power radiating from his expanding wings as the oars gave a frantic beat. *The Windlass* strained, stretching the kraken's limb, the ship swinging about at the sudden torque. Melia fired again, the second blast and the sudden awkwardness of its limb breaking the kraken's hold. With a tearing sound several spars were ripped free from the hull, but *The Windlass* tore from the monster's grip.

Dorian grimaced, tensing as he found himself racing alongside the kraken's bulk. The immense monster turned with them, limbs swinging, smashing asteroids around them to rubble, fragments tumbling about them in ruins.

"Shit! Shit! Shitty shit shit!" Dorian swore as boulders and flailing tentacles swung around them. He spun the wheel, *The Windlass* turning upside down to evade a spinning boulder. He hauled on the wheel, skimming their ship over a flailing tentacle, their keel scraping on the rubbery limb, bouncing them up and over.

"Why isn't he shooting us?" Fable gasped.

"Too close! He won't risk the cargo!" Emberly shouted back.

Dorian ignored them, focusing all his efforts on piloting. Their ship soared past the *Sky Kraken*, but already the monster was turning to follow them, malevolent eyes fixed on their boat. Another echoing screech came from the creature as its many tentacles reached for them, the monster shooting after them as it pulled itself in their wake via asteroids in their path.

Dorian cursed, dodging the bulks of asteroids as they flew past them. Every iota of his focus narrowed to the immediate as he frantically dodged and weaved, survival hinging on a heartbeat's decision and a hair's breadth between them and tumbling asteroids. Escape was all that mattered. All that concerned him. The core in the helm throbbed and pulsed with power as if to the beating of his heart.

He wasn't this good, Dorian knew. No one could be this good at flying. But every instinct seemed honed to perfection, a razor's edge of skill balancing his life. He swung around another asteroid. Another.

"Ahead!" Fable screamed, her eyes glowing blue with aura reading.

Dorian snapped from his near hypnotic trance and looked ahead. A breach awaited between asteroids. Open space lay beyond.

But something was in their way.

It slithered out of the holes pockmarking a massive asteroid. Pink flesh writhed in coils like some serpent of nightmares. The head was plated with calciferous natural armor, and its maw opened revealing a maw of teeth in sinking rings, made to bore and tear through solid rock. Nearly as big as the *Sky Kraken*, its blind head shrieked, a sound that stabbed Dorian's ear drums like needles.

He stared in horror at the rock worm blocking their path, his mind blanking in shock and scrambling for some purchase. Some way out. Some hope.

The core in the helm flashed, turning from gold to crimson.

Dorian stiffened—trembled like a bolt of lightning raced through his veins. Gold and red light glowed in his skin and tinted his wings. He let go of the wheel and moved across the deck.

"Dorian?" Fable asked, her head turning, her mouth agape.

"Grab the wheel," he told her as he stopped amidship, his ghostly wings fanning out. "Keep going forward. Whatever happens."

"What the..." Melia breathed, turning from the cannon.

"Now!" Dorian barked as scales gradually covered his body.

Fable jumped and ran to obey, practically falling against the wheel. Once he was sure she was there, Dorian bunched his legs beneath him.

And jumped.

His wings fanned out behind him, beat, carrying him in a single burst into the air and off the deck. He glowed, hot as the sun, his veins burning with energy, his wings expanding. His body changing.

He could feel it. Feel his teeth grow to fangs. His arms expand. His back stretch as his body tore through his clothes and claws grew larger. Stronger. He swelled in size, scales rippling across his body, glowing gold and red in swirling hues, his wings sweeping with power.

Freedom sang in his veins. Might. Strength! The galaxy seemed a part of him. A home he could traverse at will. Within moments he was as large as *The Windlass*, the rock worm shrieking again, lunging for him.

Dorian instantly tucked his wings, his draconic form rolling, dodging the lunging fangs. He looped around the monster's neck, swung about. The rock worm screamed in frustration, twisting in the void, teeth snapping as the blind horror chased him.

Dorian longed to relish his freedom. To soar. To leave the petty world and cares behind him, but as he banked, he caught a glance of *The Windlass* shooting through space below, and the *Sky Kraken* chasing it down through the maze of boulders like the horror the monstrous ship was.

Rage surged in Dorian, and he turned, shooting towards the horrific vessel. He could sense the life of the gargantuan squid and the others aboard. The magic of its core and the cannons as they fired for him. He banked, dodged the screaming missiles, the rock worm ignoring the few that hit its armored head.

Dorian flew at the *Sky Kraken* and suddenly twisted off course, speeding past the kraken's bulging head so near he could have reached out and clawed it.

And the rock worm behind him did far more than that.

The snaking monstrosity collided with the *Sky Kraken*, the two monsters screaming in pain and surprise as they were suddenly entangled with one another, limbs and coils battling in a vicious and bloody contest to the death. Dorian spun about, taking in the sight of the writhing horrors with grim satisfaction.

And yet, as he hung there, he felt a sudden weariness. An aching as if someone had punched a hole in his chest from which his energy was leaking out in a tumult. His body shuddered, his glow fading as he turned, putting a sudden burst of effort into his wings as he soared after the fleeing *Windlass*.

Where before he'd outdistanced the ship in moments, now he struggled to catch the craft under full sail. He could feel his body shrinking again. The arcane essence that animated his wings was crumbling away as if growing stale like week-old bread. He laboured, heaving as his face shrank back to human guise.

The helm of the ship rose up before him, and Dorian tumbled to the deck, the last of the glow evaporating from him like steam from boiling water thrown into the heart of deepest winter's cold.

"Dorian!"

He flopped over onto his back, finding Fable, Melia and Emberly's terrified and shocked faces all around him.

"Look...look at that," he said dazedly. "Looks like...like I really am a dragon."

Then his eyes rolled back, and he knew no more.

Chapter 25

Fable had watched Dorian transform with a shock even greater than the other two.

As she clung to the wheel, her eyes still attuned to the aura of the universe, she'd seen Dorian change, his form expanding as if the aura within him was spreading its wings—quite literally. How it had filled him, changing him into a form more true to the nature of his essence than his human one had ever been.

Then, when he'd clashed with the rock worm, it had taken every ounce of self-control she had to follow his instructions, speeding *The Windlass* past the snaking monstrosity as it chased the young dragon and clashed with the kraken.

And no sooner had their ship broken from the asteroid field, than Dorian had returned, naked, and collapsed on dock.

All in all, one hell of a five minutes.

"Gods. Oh gods! Is he okay?" Melia gasped, frantically checking Dorian's pulse.

Fable peered at Dorian, and let out a relieved sigh as she saw the glow cease dimming in him, though far weaker than it had been before. "I...I think he's just tired," she said. "He used up a ton of energy there."

"By the nine pits of Rath!" Emberly breathed, looking down in amazement at the man stretched on the deck. "I never saw the like!"

Melia shook her head, seeming to throw off, or at least put aside her amazement for the moment. "Right!" she said. "Fable! Take the wheel. Plot us a course towards the wyrmgate as best you can. The helm should still respond for the time being. Emberly? Help me lift him down below and put him to bed. That rock worm'll buy us time."

"Maybe they'll kill each other," Fable said hopefully.

Emberly scoffed as she crouched down, grabbing Dorian's legs. "Keep dreaming. Scarro wouldn't have the reputation he has if he let something as small as that stop him. Mark me, he'll be on our ass in a day at most, once he's gotten his beast healed up and ship repaired, savvy? Our best bet is that Dorian is faster than him. Now, let's move this great lump!"

Fable bit her lip, fearing the demoness was right. She'd heard stories about the dread Scarro from other merchants like he was a boogeyman of the nether stars—a thing birthed from the blackest pits of the void to stalk the spaceways. She hurried to the wheel, blinking her aura vision back into existence. She was fortunate, for they were near enough to the wyrmgate she could dimly make out how the auras of the astral winds shifted around the gap in the stars. She worked the wheel, watching with one eye as Emberly and Melia carried the unconscious Dorian below.

The faun tapped her hoof on the deck, continuously glancing behind them to try and read the aura of the *Sky Kraken*. She could still sense it, gleaming like a malevolent red star in the asteroid field, but it was fading with every minute.

She turned back around sharply at the sound of footsteps as Melia and Emberly emerged again.

"How's he doing?" Fable asked.

"Asleep, at least," Melia replied with a faint smile. "And not dead, which is certainly a bonus."

"Too true." Fable sighed, leaning on the wheel and staring into the starry void dreamily. "And this will mean so much. Think of it! Our handsome boy is a real dragon." She shivered in excitement. "We're set, Melia! With Dorian, every job will be a breeze once he gets the hang of things. We can run a few bigger jobs and be totally set for life. Imagine retiring on the ship, and anchored to the docks of a cozy air station. Or even buying a place on the upper tiers of Sphere! Nothing is beyond us anymore."

"Yeah," Melia said, her hair fluttering a dreamy purple. She shook her head. "But regardless, we shouldn't think too far ahead."

"But it's nice to dream," Fable breathed.

Emberly roared with laughter, head thrown back as she lounged against the rail. Both Melia and Fable started and looked at the demoness in surprise.

"What's so funny?" Melia demanded, hair fluttering a reddish tint.

"Oh, nothing," the demoness said, wiping away a tear of mirth. "Nothing at all. Just here you two are, thinking up these grand dreams, when your biggest worry should be him realizing he doesn't need any of us, savvy?"

"What?" Fable said, straightening.

"Yeah," Emberly went on with a wry grin. "Look. He's a dragon. Right? That means he can fly through space on his own once he has a handle on it. He doesn't need to breathe, and can probably rip open gates into the wyrmway on his own—think of that! A dragon with the heart, mind, and sympathies of a man? He's gonna be the hottest fuckin' commodity this side of the Angel Stars. Not even Grash could do much if he decided to break the contract. Let's face it, ladies. He's so far beyond our league he's playing the champions!"

Melia and Fable exchanged a worried look. Fable bit her lower lip, hands tensing on the wheel uneasily. Melia cleared her throat.

"Well," the elf said, her hair dulling in its blue. "If that is how it goes, well...That's how it'll go."

"But...But I don't want it to go like that," Fable sniffled. "I really like him. Not just the life he can provide—I like *Dorian*."

"Fable..." Melia began, moving up behind her friend and rubbing the faun's back. "Me too, but be realistic."

"I mean it, Melia," Fable huffed with puffed cheeks, trying to hold back the tears. "Really. He's nice, handsome, strong, and doesn't mind working hard or listening to our opinions. We can trust him, and he's adaptable and...and I don't want to lose him. I really don't. I finally feel like...like we got something good going on, and I don't want to..."

"I know," Melia said gently. "I know, little doe..."

Emberly looked between the pair, then snapped her fingers. "Ah," the demoness said with a lazy grin. "I get it. You're smitten!"

Fable lifted her head in shock, and even Melia looked at the demoness, stunned.

"H-hey now," she said, her hair tinting pinkish. "That's not...Look, we only met the guy a little over a week ago. And there's been...Yeah, sure, fun. It's just not—"

"Oh come on," Emberly laughed, pushing off of the rail and hunching forward, grinning at the faun and elf. "Look at you two. You're an absolute mess at just the thought of him heading off on his own! Fable there's ready to cry her heart out, and your hair's exploring every color in the system just thinking about it."

Fable bit her lip. "Well," she said, nervously clopping from one foot to the next. "Well, so what? Maybe we do like him, right? I do, at least. So...so all we need is him to like us back, and maybe he'll stay."

"Fable," Melia said gently. "That's not right. We can't...trick him into falling for us just so he sticks around. I mean, it'd be nice if he decided not to leave on his own, but still."

Fable jerked out from under Melia's hand, backing up so she could look at both the elf and demoness. "You don't get it. You're both...I can't do this with you two!" she cried. "I don't care! I'm going to see Dorian."

"Fable, he's out cold," Melia said.

"I don't care. I don't care right now, okay? I just...I want to see him!" Fable cried, turning her back on the pair and racing down into the hold, her hooves clopping on the steps.

She swung around at the bottom and made straight for the captain's cabin. Pushing the door open, she spotted Dorian in the main bed, rolled onto his side and sleeping soundly.

The sight of him seemed to recall Fable to herself. More cautiously, she shut the door behind her, careful not to make a sound. She slowly approached the bed, looking down at Dorian's face. At the sight of him. She couldn't suppress a sad smile, all of the tension bleeding out of her as she remembered their first meeting. The flight from Clemmen aboard *The Windlass*, the golem, and his awe at the Black, of space itself as he discovered it for the first time beside her and Melia.

Fable swallowed, feeling a lump form in her throat at the memory of him coming to Melia's defense in Sphere, how they'd found him dancing in the club. She shuddered with terror at Scarro's attack, and then her awe when he'd taken on his true form to save them from the *Sky Kraken* and the rock worm. She reached down, brushing her hand against his cheek.

"I really am crazy," she murmured, sniffling, several teardrops dripping onto the blankets. "But maybe that's not such a terrible thing."

Dorian muttered in his sleep, and Fable choked back a laugh. Unable to resist the temptation, she lifted the blanket and slipped under it, pushing up behind him. Wrapping her arms around his naked body, she pressed herself against his back, feeling the warmth of him radiate against her. She hugged him tight, as if unwilling to let him go, and felt the tears flow freely.

It wasn't fair. It wasn't fair.

"Why'd I have to fall in love with a big goof like you?" she muttered into his back. "The one guy with no reason to ever stick around."

"...Fable?"

She glanced up quickly and saw Dorian looking blearily over his shoulder at her.

"Fable?" he said groggily again as he rolled over. "What...are you okay?"

Fable drew back, sniffing and trying to belatedly dry her eyes. "M-me? Yeah, sorry. Just...didn't mean to wake you," she laughed. "Just um..."

"You're crying," Dorian noted.

Fable laughed wretchedly. "A-am I? Sorry. Sorry. I didn't mean to. I just got a little overwhelmed and, you know. Things. How are you? Feeling okay? I mean, duh, you're looking good. But I—"

Dorian listened to her rambling, then reached out, silencing her at once. Reflexively, he gathered her in his arms and pulled her against his powerful form. Fable stiffened as she found her head nestled against his chest, the low thump of his heart just audible. Then she relaxed, burying her face against his strong body, her arms looping around him in a tight hug.

"Please," she murmured. "Please don't leave..."

Dorian laughed gently. "Where is this coming from?" he asked.

Fable blushed hotly, but the words spilled from her like water from a broken dam. "I'm sorry. I'm sorry. It's just...you're so special and strong and smart and skilled and nice and...and everything good, and I just...I don't wanna lose you, but you could do so much better. You're a dragon, and so much bigger than us and our dinky little ship, and I'm so...I've never been so scared to lose someone besides maybe Melia. You could do anything. Have anything you want. And we're just..."

Dorian stroked her hair, gently hushing her until Fable trailed off miserably. "Is that what this is about?" Dorian said.

"Kinda. I guess," Fable whimpered. "I'm sorry. I shouldn't be dropping all this on you. I know. But I just...well...I don't want you to lower yourself to stay with us either. And I shouldn't be trying to guilt you. I'm pathetic..."

Dorian chuckled again. "Fable," he said. "Without exaggeration, you and Melia are quite literally the best thing to ever happen in my life."

Fable snorted. "Yeah, after almost dropping a ship on you and cutting your throat."

"Well, that part was less fun, I admit it," he said. "But everything else? This ship. The stars. The craziness of this adventure? All of this? It's been amazing, Fable. Even the parts where I almost died. I wouldn't give up a second of it. And especially not you and Melia."

Fable sniffled, then raised her head, looking at Dorian with her yearning eyes. "R-really?"

"Absolutely," Dorian reassured her, smiling down at her as he pulled her closer. "I wouldn't trade a second of it. I've known a lot of people, Fable. Good people. But none who've cared about me like you and Melia and, yeah, maybe even Emberly do. That's just how things were.

"But it's different now," he told her, continuing to gently stroke her hair, brushing past her antlers and down near her back. "Because I have both of you. So let me just say that I can't imagine going around, seeing the stars without the two of you with me."

"R-really?" Fable said, sniffling. "And...and you're not just saying that?"

"Nope," Dorian chuckled, cupping her chin, lifting her head up. "Promise."

Fable smiled, then closed her eyes as Dorian leaned in and captured her lips with a kiss. She shivered, melting as a tingle of pure delight raced from her antlers to her hooves, a soft moan escaping her at that tender moment.

He broke the kiss, and Fable breathed his name. "Dorian..."

"And if you're worried about me leaving for a better ship and crew," he continued with a chuckle. "Then that just means we have to make this one the best in the Black."

Fable giggled. "Now you're being ridiculous."

"You're right," Dorian said, pulling Fable close once more. "Because it already is."

Fable sighed, nuzzling Dorian's chest, feeling the last of the tension and despair fade from her as his hand continued to gently stroke her hair, soon stopping as his breathing evened, and he slipped again into an exhausted sleep. And though Fable did want to slip away and leave him to rest, she found her own eyes sliding shut as she drifted away into the most relaxing slumber she'd ever known...

Chapter 26

For two days Dorian slept, recovering gradually after the strain of his transformation. And when he finally woke, it was time to take stock.

After he confirmed their course to the wyrmway, making minor adjustments, he joined the three girls amidship, sitting down cross-legged across from Emberly and Melia. Fable took the opportunity to plop into his lap, snuggling against him affectionately, her confidence no doubt buoyed by their last conversation. Dorian offered no complaint, as aside from the fact he enjoyed having Fable's fantastic ass pressed against him, the faun had taken every opportunity to be close to him since he woke. Her wiggling doe tail tickling his stomach was a bit distracting, though.

Melia looked annoyed at her friend, but offered no comment, instead clearing her throat.

"So," she said grimly as she sat on a squat barrel, glancing at Emberly who leaned casually against the mast. "Bit of an explainer is in order, I think."

"About the dragon thing?"

"Sure, let's start there," Melia said, unable to restrain a smirk.

Dorian shrugged. "I probably know less than you all. You were the ones who said I was a dragon, and I didn't even really believe it myself until that happened. Guess that's the truth after all."

"Fair enough. You think you can do that again?" the elf asked, her sculpted eyebrow arching.

"Honestly? No idea," Dorian said with a shake of his head. "It was almost a moment of panic, but it drained me pretty bad."

"I think it's like...stretching a muscle," Fable proposed, squeezing Dorian's bicep appreciatively. "Ooh, nice. I think you're buffer than before."

"Focus, please," Melia sighed.

"Right, right," the faun giggled, leaning up and kissing Dorian on the cheek. "But I think it's like he never lifted anything heavier than a feather all his life, and then suddenly did a set with a sixty pound dumbbell. That kinda muscle work is gonna leave him pretty damn strained afterwards."

"But he's recovering?" Melia said. "Maybe getting stronger?"

"I feel better," Dorian confirmed. He squeezed his bicep as well. "And honestly, yeah, I might be a bit stronger after that."

"I bet you are, cutie," Fable said. "But your aura is still filling back up. I can see it recharging in real time when I look at you through the spyglass, so maybe go a little easy on that transformation stuff or you might burn yourself out next time."

Dorian winced at the thought, recalling the draining sensation after a mere few minutes in dragon form. "Noted."

"Good," Melia said. "So that's resolved for the time being. Now, to the real problem. What the fuck is Captain Scarro, Scourge of Seven Systems, doing on our ass? Hm?" Melia said with a pointed look at Emberly, who looked utterly uninterested in answering.

Dorian's brows furrowed. "He said something about wanting the cargo we're carrying. It must be whatever Grash is having us deliver to the *Blue Roamer*. Sounds like he was set to nab the contract before Emberly got under it."

"Uh huh. So what the hell are we carting?" Melia said with a glare so hard at the demoness it might have been capable of driving nails into her.

Emberly blew out a gust of air and shrugged in surrender. "Some special weapons and over two dozen experimental cores of battleship tier, all heading to the researchers there. But if anyone asks, I didn't say anything. Savvy?"

"Whoa," Fable said, staring at the demoness. "No wonder Scarro wants them! That many cores could outfit a freaking fleet."

"Aye," Emberly said, uncrossing her arms and giving them a steely glare. "Definitely not something meant to fall into the wrong hands. And if you're thinking about just forking it all over to him, forget it. Even if Scarro let us live after what we did to his ship with that rock worm, Grash'd have our hides."

"Doesn't much make things better," Melia growled. "Scarro has a reputation too. Even if we do deliver the cargo to the *Blue Roamer*, he's not going to let bygones be bygones. He's going to come after us. And we don't have the firepower to even make a dent in his ship. Even with Dorian."

Recalling the monstrous space kraken, Dorian shuddered, and was forced to agree. "That's true," he said. "Not at my current level of power, anyway."

"True," Emberly agreed with a lazy grin. "But lucky for you lot, I have a plan."

"Oh good," Melia groaned with oozing sarcasm. "I can't wait to hear it."

"Think you're gonna love this, actually," Emberly said as she spread her hands. "But look. There's another reason I took this job heading out near *Blue Roamer*, savvy? Those mages are positioned right over a wyrmway graveyard."

Fable and Melia instantly perked up. "You're serious?" Melia said.

"Of course!"

"Sorry, a what?" Dorian asked.

"Starship graveyard," Fable explained. "The wyrmway has some strange eddies, and when a ship is wrecked or crew killed in the wyrmway, they're often swept along until they're spit out at specific places in space. There could be hundreds of ships there from every age of space-faring."

"Bingo," Emberly said, firing a finger pistol at the faun. "And if we can find a decent one, fit it up with a proper core and weapons scavenged from those wrecks, then we may actually stand a chance against Scarro."

Melia grimaced, but looked to Dorian. "It...might work," she admitted.

Dorian realized all three women were looking at him. He considered it, recalling the firepower of the Elven Imperial warship bearing down on them. If anything would stand a chance against the *Sky Kraken*, it would be a ship that could bring that many guns to bear.

And though he had grown fond of *The Windlass*, he also realized that the ship would not be up to the sort of battle that awaited them here, or in the future. Something a bit better than their current setup would be necessary to protect the three women aboard.

Dorian reflected on the emergence of that protective instinct, realizing it was true. He did consider himself responsible for keeping the three safe, and there were surely ample numbers of enemies that would seek to do them harm. So a stronger ship was what was needed. He nodded at last. "Alright," he said. "Let's do it. But," he continued with an uncertain look in his eye, "will *The Windlass's* core be enough?"

"Not in the least," Emberly cheerfully stated. "Which is why we'll have to 'borrow,'" she said, fingers making air quotes, "one of the cores from the cargo."

"Will that be alright?" Dorian asked dubiously.

"Sure," the demoness muttered dismissively. "Don't worry about it! We can just sneak in the core you nabbed from the goblin ship and if anyone asks, say it was an oversight when the shipment was getting assembled. I'll explain everything if it comes to that. Besides, better to ask forgiveness than permission, savvy?"

"I guess so," Dorian said, having a sinking feeling Grash wouldn't be quite so understanding, but also realizing that facing Grash's wrath would still be preferable to living their lives looking over their shoulders for an oversized piece of gun-toting calamari wanting their heads. "Then it sounds like we have a plan."

"Damn straight," Emberly grinned. "Next stop, *Blue Roamer!*"

Naturally, it wasn't as simple as that. Though the miles vanished in their wake, Dorian pushing their little ship as much as he dared, it was still some time before they would reach the wyrmgate. Where his first voyage into the wyrmway and to Sphere had taken only a few days from beginning to end, this trip was scheduled to take weeks when all was said and done. It was on this journey that he would get to understand the expansiveness of space, he realized.

But Dorian found life aboard *The Windlass* oddly comforting. Even more so than his old life on his adopted homeworld. The addition of three gorgeous women certainly helped with that—especially Fable. The faun showed no signs of her desire to be near him weakening with each passing day. When she wasn't running maintenance on the ship or keeping an eye out for Scarro's aura, she was glued to Dorian's side.

Especially at night.

Dorian had never exactly been unpopular with women around his village. It had actually become a problem from time to time. He was handsome, gifted with a strong physicality, and certainly marked out as a better marriage prospect than most among peasants. Yet, he quickly found that Fable's long life had allowed her to pick up a number of interesting tricks that peasant girls back home never knew...Ones she was delighted to show him when he went below to rest, or what little rest he got.

"Once had a job in the library of the Unified Bodies Sect on Trandia," Fable whispered in his ear one night before sliding down his naked chest, her tongue teasing the grooves of his abs. "And their books were very...instructive. For example..."

Dorian learned a lot those nights.

A whole lot.

Which wasn't to say there was much time to enjoy such activities, despite Fable's best efforts to steal him away at any opportunity. There was always plenty to be done aboard. Be it scraping the hull from strange barnacle creatures, checking the rigging, examining the stores, or mopping the deck, there was ample work to do around the ship for a crew of only four.

And of course one important part of that job was always, always, watching the heavens for the *Sky Kraken*.

Yet fun was had. Dorian found himself often whittling when the work was through, Fable joining him and truly impressing him with her knife work.

"Here," she said, pressing one to him. "A deer!"

Dorian examined the sculpture with amazement. "Amazing job," he said earnestly.

"You really think so?" she asked. "It's my mother!"

Dorian shot her a dubious look. "Uhhh..."

The impish faun let out a hoot of laughter and even went so far as to snort as she tried to control it. "I'm just kidding, cutie," she laughed, "my mother was a faun, too."

Dorian grinned and nodded, running his thumb along the smooth wood and the delicate work on the antlers. The whorls carved into it gave it a form unlike anything he'd seen before, but was tactful enough not to ask if it was a design from her homeworld. In his time with the faun, Dorian had noticed how careful she was never to mention where she'd come from. And he knew better than to press such a thing.

Dorian and the girls bonded more with each passing hour, it seemed. Fable, of course, tried to hog his attention the most. At meals, she would even try to feed Dorian, which greatly annoyed Melia.

"Do you want to?" Fable asked teasingly.

"Of course not," Melia huffed, but her eyes lingered on the fork as Fable popped another chunk of seared meat into Dorian's mouth. "Perverts."

After meals they often played dice or cards together, the latter of which Melia showed herself particularly bad at with her hair often betraying her, while Emberly proved she had a devil's luck with the dice. Several times, Dorian found himself playing in nothing but his boxers, the demoness smirking as she rattled the dice in her hands.

"Never bet against the fel, Dorian," she'd cackle to much eye rolling from him.

And in the quiet moments, Fable would read.

Dorian knew how to, which had surprised more than a few at the village, where literacy was as uncommon as being free of lice (another thing he managed, and which made him quite popular among the women). And though the letters in the book were clearly alien to him, he'd been able to decipher them with disturbing ease.

"I bet it's because of your dragonhood!" Fable had declared proudly as she nestled in his lap, her own filled with the tome in question. "Dragons have a gift for tongues. Many claim every written language save the demon's tongues descend from draconic languages."

"Not sure how much I buy that," Dorian had confessed, but had been more than happy to let Fable do the reading. The sound of her gentle voice had eased his worries as easily as Melia's frequent massages did. Almost like listening to a song, and he was more than happy to fall asleep to it, hugging the lovely faun against his chest and feeling her hair tickle his chin as she curled up, nuzzling against him.

But the true surprise was one night when Fable didn't share his bed, and Melia made herself known and comfortable beside him instead. This happened more and more often after that first time.

Dorian still wasn't sure what to make of the elf and his relationship with her. It was now clear she liked him, and the feeling was certainly mutual, though to what degree he couldn't quite say. The nights they spent together never lacked for expressions of attraction or interest, but Melia never seemed comfortable lingering long in the morning. After their passions were spent, she would often rest against him, panting and vulnerable as his arms wrapped around the elf until sleep claimed her, but she'd invariably be gone by the time he awoke.

The one time she always seemed comfortable around him on deck was when they sparred. Dorian had long considered himself competent with the blade, but Melia showed him what it meant to master it. Countless times, he had suffered stinging blows from the flat of her sword as they contested the deck, the clang of arms ringing while Emberly and Fable watched, cheering him or Melia on, whoever seemed to be winning. Usually, that was Melia.

But before long, Dorian began to give as good as he got. And when he finally disarmed the elf with a well placed twist of his blade, sending her sword spinning from her startled hand, Melia had given him a look of such shock that he hadn't been able to hide his grin.

"Not bad," Melia had said, retrieving her blade and falling into a ready stance. "Again!"

And again it was. Every day, as the red wound of the wyrmgate grew larger in the dark of space like a bloodshot eye.

When they finally drew near, Dorian could feel the now familiar pull towards it that he'd come to know so well. The day before they'd reach it, Melia and Fable were below, storing everything they could in preparation for the passage through the wyrmway. Dorian was at the helm, guiding the ship as the pulls of astral wind threatened to tug them off course in the face of the rift in the world.

"Thinking you can handle it?"

Dorian glanced back to find Emberly sauntering towards him, her heels clicking on the deck. He smiled. "I seem to have a knack for it."

"I bet you do," the demoness said, leaning against the rail, her head cocked and staring at the shimmering crimson and black void in the horizon. "Permit me to ask you something?"

"Shoot," he said.

"What would it take for you to take me on your crew permanently?"

Dorian glanced sharply at her but saw only a measured seriousness in her lidded golden eyes. He measured her thoughtfully as he continued to guide their ship.

"Would that be a problem with Grash?" he said slowly.

"No problem with him," Emberly said with a lazy shrug. "He won't care. In fact, he'd be delighted. Put a better clamp on both me and you as far as he's concerned. But that doesn't mean I'm not trouble."

"So I gathered," Dorian noted.

"But nothing you can't handle, huh, hot stuff?"

"Maybe," Dorian agreed, conceding some of her point. He wasn't an egotist and knew too well he was still green out among the stars, but the more he understood what he was and could do, the more confident he came to be with his skills. More importantly, he'd used the travel time well, asking hundreds of questions about life out in the Black, and he felt he had a far better command of how things were than before.

"Damn straight," Emberly said with a cocky grin, a trickle of smoke seeping from between her fangs. "Way I see it, you might be on the road to becoming a major power in this galaxy of ours. And I'd love to get on the ground floor of that, savvy? So, what's a girl gotta do to get brought aboard?"

Dorian shrugged, his coat flapping at the motion. "I don't see why I shouldn't let you. Fable signed off on your aura when we first met you. You know your way around a ship, especially the guns. Can clearly upgrade or repair it if we need it—and you're handy in a fight. But I doubt I'll be what you think. I'm not planning on becoming some gang boss. Seems like a good way to make enemies."

"Ha!" Emberly laughed. "You're a dragon walking around in human skin, Dorian. You're going to have a target on your back sooner or later. Most likely sooner."

Dorian had to concede that point. "Maybe so," he admitted. "So why would you want to join up with me?"

"Working for Grash ain't exactly sunshine and flowers," Emberly said. "Besides," she added, pushing off the rail and sauntering towards him. "I don't mind a bit of danger. Makes things a little...exciting."

Dorian watched her approach from the corner of his eye. "Think so?"

"I know so," she said, pressing against him, tilting her head towards him with a lazy smirk. "So, you wanna seal this deal with a handshake? Or," she said, leaning in closer, "...something else?"

Dorian could taste the invitation, but knew better than to indulge in it without consulting Fable and Melia, as interesting as it was. "A shake," he said, holding out his hand. "For now. Until I check with the rest of the crew."

"Ooooh, so proper," Emberly cackled, but took his hand firmly. "And I wouldn't worry. You're already captain here in all but name, Dorian. Those two will follow you into a hellgate without a second thought."

"I'll try and avoid going that far," he said.

"You can try," Emberly chuckled, releasing his hand and looking towards the rippling distortion of the wyrmgate ahead, its glow making her golden eyes gleam and her face seem ruddy in the light. "But you never know what the Black will throw at you one day to the next..."

Chapter 27

It was strange for Dorian to travel through the wyrmgate once more. As the prow broke through the eerie haze that surrounded the entrance, he felt his body tingle, shivering with exhilaration as if he were absorbing the unreal essence in the strange realm. It was a reaction apparently at complete odds with the others' experiences, who despite bracing themselves, looked like they'd been socked with a knuckleduster and were barely keeping their feet.

"Everyone alright?" he called out as he piloted their ship through the void, no longer surprised just how easily he took to it.

"Never hrp!...better," Fable groaned, gamely keeping her lunch down as she leaned against the rail.

Emberly just responded with a thumbs up, and Melia said and did nothing at all, though she shook like the deck had slipped under her feet and her hair fluttered an unpleasant puce hue.

Dorian tried to hide his smirk and turned the wheel, guiding their ship through the wavering expanse of the wyrmway. It was an appreciatively uneventful journey, if one could call any trip through the strange expanse between space realms as such. They saw few vessels, and then none at all when Dorian followed the golden threads that guided him to a narrower tunnel within the wyrmway. A strange feeling settled on him then. A feeling of abandonment, perhaps—of disuse. Dorian had a sense that few used these paths for a very long time indeed. So how did he, a certified greenhorn, find them so easily? He grinned to himself a private grin. He knew the answer by now.

Soon enough, though, Dorian made out a dark shape hovering against the wyrmway's rippling crimson walls. It was a strange vessel, even compared to others Dorian had encountered in his adventure thus far—if vessel it even was.

It resembled a stone temple that had been built in the void around an immense blue pearl, flawless in its facets. Tiered stones climbed up and around it, cradling the orb in its confines, while a tapering bottom descended in columns from the base, rigged with ropes and cables. Iridescent light glowing from the sphere atop it like a beacon in the void. Dorian shivered as he felt the eldritch thrum of strange energy about the stone. Something unfamiliar. Bizarre. Truly alien.

"There it is, the *Blue Roamer*," Emberly said, patting Dorian on the shoulder and pointing at a stone pier jutting from the temple of the stars. "Bring us in there."

Not entirely convinced, Dorian nevertheless did so, guiding *The Windlass* down towards the odd temple. As they drew nearer, Dorian noted columns surrounding the dock, all bearing smaller blue stone orbs on their peaks, and all glowing fitfully with a humming energy that seemed to crawl over Dorian's skin like slimy fingers.

As they came down to the pier, several figures appeared from the entrance of the temple and made their way forward. They stopped a short distance away as Fable made them fast to a mooring post, and Dorian took the opportunity to study them.

They were very strange, in his opinion, though that might not be saying much these days. In fact, at this point it might have been even stranger if they turned out to be normal looking people. The leaders were tall and thin, dressed in long flowing robes that floated off the ground. Sweeps of pale metal lifted their shoulderpads, and their faces were hidden beneath black domed helmets which betrayed not the faintest flicker of light. Both were armed with tall staffs tipped with rings of bronze metal, and as he watched them come near, Dorian was pretty sure they were floating rather than walking.

Behind them were a number of wasted looking individuals. They looked like men sucked down to the dregs of life, with hollow eyes and skin stretched over bone, dressed in little more than rags. The sight of them filled Dorian with a reflexive revulsion.

As the plank came down, Emberly descended, smiling cockily and delivering a bow to the white pair.

"Greetings, masters of the stone. A pleasure to meet again the Wizards of Null."

"One shared," one of the figures said with a voice scratchy as a nail on a metal sheet. It lifted a hand ending in delicate fingers wrapped in white cloth. "You have the shipment?"

"Of course. And you have the pay?"

"The shipment first."

"Fair enough. Dorian? Would you mind?" Emberly called back.

Dorian wasn't sure he felt comfortable leaving the girls alone with the pair, but even less did he want the two figures coming aboard. "Sure," he said.

One of the figures rattled his staff, and several of the wasted men stepped forward and climbed aboard. Dorian kept an eye on them as he led them into the hold and to the crates they'd gone through so much trouble for. Showing surprising strength, the wasted men grasped the crates and hefted them, carrying them aloft once again.

Dorian followed, descending with them onto the strange temple. Emberly was deep in amiable conversation with the ghostly pair as the crates were unloaded nearby, one of the figures drifting from the conversation and to the crates. One of the wasted men pulled off the lid, and the figure began rooting through the contents.

Vaguely curious, Dorian leaned over a bit, looking inside and seeing it for the first time. Strange weapons filled one crate, while another was loaded with delicately packaged navigational cores that glowed softly in his presence, nestled like eggs in compartments stuffed with straw.

"And Grash is looking forward to doing business with you both again," Emberly said.

"One is missing," the wizard at the crates said. "One of the experimental cores, that is."

Emberly turned his way with a look of utter confusion. "What?"

The domed figure turned, his bandaged hand grasping the core from the goblin's ship. "This is a substandard core. It is not what was agreed upon."

"Huh," Emberly muttered, frowning. "That's odd. Must have been an oversight at the packers. We'll be sure to make it right in our next shipment."

"Acceptable," the Wizard of Null whispered with a nod. "There is no immediate need. We shall inform Grash through the usual channels when we require additional supplies. For now, we believe your reward is in order."

"I believe you're right," Emberly answered with a sharp and greedy grin.

The Wizard of Null reached into his robe, Dorian tensing a little as the strange figure drew out a bag of pale white cloth and dropped it into Emberly's waiting hand. She overturned it in her palm, eyes flashing in delight at the sight of the gems that rolled in her grasp.

"Lovely," she purred. "Nothing like star gems to make a girl smile."

"You are satisfied?" one of the wizards asked softly as a curtain rustling in the wind.

"Very," Emberly assured him, spilling the gems back into the bag and tucking it away in her pocket. "Now," she added with a glance between the two. "About that other reward"

"You wished to investigate the graveyard and take what you find use for," a wizard said.

"Exactly. Is that going to be a problem?"

"No," the first wizard said, turning to look at the shimmering walls of the wyrmway around them. "Not at all. Considering what we've been given, it is acceptable."

The wizard lifted his staff and waved it towards the distance. Dorian jumped as the air crackled with arcane potency, the stones topping the pillars around them glowing hotter. The great blue orb that formed the center of the distant temple fluttered like cerulean flame licked across its curve.

High above them, Dorian watched in awe as a part of the wyrmway seemed to slough away, peeling back to reveal the rift of a wyrmgate, and beyond something dark and sullen, like a mouth waiting to devour them whole.

"Gods," he breathed, sensing instinctively that it was no dragon which had made that rend in the wyrmway's fabric.

"Your payment," the wizard said, lowering his staff. "Make good use of it."

"We intend to," Emberly replied, bowing slightly to the strange figures.

She turned, grabbing Dorian's sleeve and tugging him back towards the ship. Dorian stumbled after her, but quickly recovered his footing, following at a pace. He stole a glance back at the two wizards as they directed their thralls to carry the crates back towards the temple.

"What...kind of weapons were those?" he asked Emberly in an undertone.

"Remember what I said?" Emberly muttered as the plank creaked under their feet. "Some questions are better left unanswered. That's one of them. In fact, the less we know about the Wizards of Null, the better. Weirdos, even by my standards."

Dorian stole a glance back at the ghostly figures, feeling again that strange unease he'd sensed in their presence. He shook his head as he gladly boarded *The Windlass* once more.

"Any issues?" Melia asked, watching the wizards intently, one hand gripping the hilt of her sheathed sword, her hair fluttering with wary purple.

"Not in the least," Emberly replied as she dragged the plank back aboard. "Now then," the demoness spun around to face the faun and elf. "With that done, on to stage two of my brilliant plan. Onward, Dorian, my charming navigator!" she declared, pointing at the rift in space before them. "To survival!"

"Whatever you say," Dorian said through gritted teeth as he manned the helm once more. A thrust of his will had *The Windlass* push away from the grim temple, and Dorian was glad to quit it, putting on a slight extra burst of power into the winged oars, skimming them through the void until they passed through the rift in the wyrmway.

Chapter 28

AND INTO THE GRAVEYARD of the stars.

With barely a shudder, *The Windlass* passed through the gap in reality, skimming into a dark realm where no sun shone, and in the distance only a vast, gloomy planetoid lurked, gathering the forsaken of space onto itself with the gentle pull of its gravity.

Dorian stared in awe at the derelict warships drifting in the black void. Only the fitful red light bleeding from the wyrmgate lit the scene, fluttering through the ribs of ancient vessels, many scourged with battle damage, others looking almost pristine—yet as dead as a corpse laid out on display.

The graveyard stretched for miles, consuming the horizon, trapped in the gravity well of a planetoid below. He spotted an Elven Imperial warship floating near the bones of what had once been an immense turtle, the shell melding with a ship built atop it. A pirate ship in pieces drifted by, the bolted metal not enough to have kept something from tearing the vessel in two. It was like an asteroid field of intelligent design. Of spars and beams and hulls and rigging, silent and forlorn. Abandoned to the whims and eddies of the void of space.

"Geeze," Dorian said, the only word that came to mind in the face of such grim grandeur. "That's insane."

"And just what we need," Emberly said, rubbing her hands together so enthusiastically it was a wonder they didn't spark a fire. "We're bound to find something in this mess. Keep your eyes peeled! We'll want something only in need of minor repairs, and capable of taking on the *Sky Kraken*!"

A tall order, Dorian thought to himself even as he guided their ship among the silent wrecks.

It was slow going. The light that bled from the wyrmgate illuminated only parts of their route, the ruddy glow splitting itself on the ragged ruins of ships and drifting wrecks, blocked out more and more the deeper they went. Soon, Fable needed to kindle an arcane lantern, but its ghostly light only seemed to make the journey more foreboding.

Emberly and Melia scanned the ships they passed around, their eyes sharp for some wreck that would do. Dorian did the same, though he had a feeling the others had a better grasp on what they'd need. Still, it couldn't hurt…

"What about that one?" Emberly said, pointing at a hulk drifting past.

Fable scrutinized it and shook her horned head. "Mmm. Nope. See the keel? It's cracked. It'd split in half within a week."

"What about that one?" Melia suggested.

Emberly shook her head. "No way. Too narrow. It'd roll like a barrel every time you fired the guns."

Dorian only half listened to them converse. As he scanned the wrecks, he felt…something. It was like a tug on his soul that saw him slowly turn the wheel, guiding their ship deeper into the ruins of the graveyard.

The Windlass slipped through the wrecks, Fable's lantern fluttering its light through holes smashed in hulls and ruined vessels. Dorian continued to scan the ruins until one caught his eye, and he knew somehow that this was what his senses had called to.

"What about that?" he said.

Melia, Fable and Emberly turned and looked where he'd indicated, silence filling the air.

A ship slid through the dark void like a silent blade. The hull was long and sleek, the figurehead that of a dragon roaring, the barrel of a cannon pushing from the open maw. Cannon ports ran along either side, while more silvery metal plated the hull. The masts were furled, and on either side were winged oars plated in more silver. It reminded Dorian strongly of the sleek deadliness of a fine sword, crossed with the more subdued grandeur of an Elven Imperial warship.

"Gods," Fable breathed as she turned her lamp fully on the ship. "Is that..."

"A High Empire cutter," Melia murmured.

"No way," Emberly gaped.

"Is that good?" Dorian asked.

Fable shook herself, coming to her senses. "Hell yeah! Those sorts of ships carved out the High Empire millennia ago, so they say, but the way to build them is lost. It's said they were made by dragons themselves. But I've never heard of one in such good condition…"

"Sounds like a winner," Dorian observed.

"*If* it's in good condition," Melia added.

"Sure sounds like we should find out," Emberly said.

Dorian agreed, and with a flap of *The Windlass's* oars sped along towards the ship. As they came nearer, he noted it was quite a bit larger than their own ship, but looked to lack no maneuverability for that. Sliding in close, he slowed to a halt beside the wreck, easing their oxygen bubble around the ancient craft.

A plank rattled onto the other ships deck, and the quartet warily made their way aboard, weapons ready.

"What do you think happened?" Dorian muttered as he peered about the abandoned deck.

"Likely as not their oxygen bubble ran out," Fable said as she peered at the masts. "Or the navigator died while they were in the wyrmway. Terrible way for a whole crew to go out."

"Some battle damage," Emberly observed, brushing a hand along a scorch mark on the deck. "Magic burns. Wouldn't be surprised if it was maybe a mutiny or something."

Dorian moved about the ship, ducking past the shrouds and heading for the captain's cabin. The door was open and he eased it wide.

The light fell upon the interior, flashing among the sort of grandeur that only an empire at its height could afford. Gold filigree decorated the walls and trim. An immense banner or a golden dragon dominated one wall, a bank of windows the rear, while an astrolabe sat in the middle of the room, rings of brass holding nothing in its middle. A large bed sat in the corner, shrouded by tapestries, while chests, bookcases and other accouterments of navigation filled out the rest of the room.

"Whoa," Fable breathed as she flashed her light around. "Look at all that!"

Dorian said nothing, his eyes arrested by the desk, where a figure lay slumped. It was dressed in an ancient golden armor, wearing a helmet with a tailing plume and pauldrons engraved with designs so delicate it was more a work of art than armor. The bones had the delicate build that suggested an elf, and before the corpse, laid on the desk, was a book.

Dorian picked up the book, turning it over. A thick clasp held it shut, the lock strangely elaborate. He looked again at the desk, and noted that the skeleton clutched what looked like a pocket watch in his hand.

"What's he got?" Fable said, coming up beside him with a clopping of hooves.

Dorian shrugged and passed her the book. "Ship's log, I think. Plus a watch."

Fable plucked the item from the bony grasp of the corpse, dangling it from the chain. "Huh," she mused, turning it this way and that. "Interesting. Might be something useful."

"Planning on tinkering with it?" Dorian asked, brows raised.

"Sure! I mean, why not? Provided we're not, you know, dead in the next few days."

"There is that," Dorian agreed.

"You two done in there?" Melia shouted from outside.

"Coming!" Fable said, giving Dorian a tug on his sleeve.

Dorian followed her, but his eye lingered on the dead man, wondering at the mystery of the ship. He shook it off, however, focusing ahead once more. There were bigger things to worry about for now.

They met at the helm, gathering around and sharing their discoveries. Melia jerked a thumb back at the hatch. "Cannons are old, but workable. Not many goods that aren't spoiled though. This thing's been floating around for a few thousand years, so none of that's surprising. Structure seems sound at any rate. Whatever happened to the crew, it wasn't fighting another ship."

"Unless they boarded real quick," Emberly said and shrugged. "Either way, I can hook it all back up with the stuff from *The Windlass*. Bring over the supplies and all that. The only question though is if this thing will run with the core."

All eyes went to Dorian, who held out his hand. "One way to find out," he said.

"That's the spirit," Emberly grinned, dropping the experimental core into his hand.

Dorian's fingers reflexively closed on it, and as he did the stone glowed gold and red. He felt a surge of energy race through him, even stronger than what he had known when he first activated *The Windlass*. Scales grew across his arms with a snicking sound, his fingers elongating into draconic claws.

"Ooooh," Fable breathed as the glow came from between his fingers.

"Ready?" Emberly asked.

"As I'll ever be," Dorian said, and made his way towards the wheel.

It awaited him, the frame made to resemble a dragon with wings sweeping back, the wheel set into the back. The hole where the core would fit was dark and empty, with angular lines radiating outwards from it. Taking a deep breath, Dorian reached out and pressed the core into the slot.

At once he stiffened, gasping as the glow flared even hotter. The light filled the dark lines in a rush like liquid gold had been poured into the grooves. It spread across the wheelhouse, racing through the veins of power that threaded the entire ship in a flash. The winged oars creaked and groaned as they stretched forth once more, the ethereal membranes filling with crimson light. The eyes of the silver dragon arching from the prow lit up like twin lanterns, glowing hot.

The glow spilled across the dark dereliction of the ruined ships around them, like a star igniting in the void of space.

"Whoa," Fable breathed, looking around the ship as the glow began to die, simmering in the grooves of the ship and wheel.

"Ha ha! Now that's what I'm talking about!" Emberly joyfully shouted.

Dorian lifted his hand from the core and grasped the spoke of the wheel. He grinned, feeling the ship through his heightened senses. As if the wood and spar and rigging were a part of him as surely as his own arms and legs were. And like that, he knew with utter certainty that the craft at his hands was made for him. Built to be piloted by one such as him, and that it would do things he'd only dared dream *The Windlass* could. As if the ship he held longed to sail again, and strained to do so.

"How's it feel?" Fable asked.

"Good," Dorian said, tightening his grip on the wheel. "Damn good."

"Then sounds like we have our new ship," Melia said, beaming in satisfaction. "Now come on! Let's get this thing rigged up."

With a bit of reluctance, Dorian released the wheel, the glow about the craft fading, but never dying as he joined the three women at the plank, crossing over to *The Windlass* once more. Rolling up his sleeves, Dorian set himself to the task.

Time to get to work.

And work it was. Not only did they need to drag over the entire cargo and supplies from ship to ship, but also detach and install the guns, upgrades, and anything else that could be salvaged from *The Windlass*.

It made Dorian curiously depressed to see the ship that had first brought him to the stars be slowly stripped down over the course of several days. He did agree that it was necessary, and the ship was far from the quality they would need going forward in both armaments and capability, and their new craft was far superior. Much would survive of the little ship that he'd first taken from his pastoral home and into the sky, integrated into the bones of the new one. Even so, it still weighed on him, and he was far from alone, though Melia tried to hide it.

Fable merely patted his back when she found him watching Emberly strip the cannon from the prow. "It's always tough leaving your first ship," she said sympathetically. "But it did a good job, and that's all you can ask of it."

"I suppose," he sighed.

"Hey! Anyone gonna help me lug this crap across or am I all on my lonesome here?" the demoness shouted.

With a sigh, Dorian rose, and lugged across another key piece of his former ship and worked with the demoness to install it into the new one.

Not to say the former Imperial vessel was in mint condition. Much needed to be done to bring it to sailing state, and Dorian threw himself into the work, and there always seemed to be something to do. He found it curiously reminiscent of his time in Clemmen, filling in for odd jobs here and there, though naturally he much preferred his new employers. Whether it was helping Fable hook up the astral engines, rig up the cannons, or even trim the sails, he threw himself into the work gladly.

Yet every day, after their work was done, the four of them would gather on the deck and toast to their hard work, eating in the funereal silence of the graveyard of ships and simply enjoying each other's company.

"One more day," Emberly said confidently as they lounged on the deck, a bottle of rum lifted in salute. "One more day and we'll be shipshape and ready!"

"Not soon enough, in my view," Melia said, grimacing at the hulks hovering around them like corpses of wood and steel. "Place gives me the creeps."

"Amen," Fable grunted from Dorian's lap, giggling as she took a swig from her bottle. "Mmm. But so worth it."

"No argument there," Emberly cackled. "But we still need a name for this baby," she chuckled, patting the deck beneath her. "What are we thinking? How about...*Emberly's Pride*!"

"Not nearly big enough for that," Melia scoffed.

Emberly shrugged. "Ah, fair enough. What do you suggest?"

Melia took a thoughtful drink from her bottle. "Hmm." She smacked her lips. "How about...the *Skyward Sword*?"

"Bleh. Not punchy enough," Emberly said.

"How about...*The Dragon's Wing?*" Fable mused.

Emberly cocked her head, and Melia looked thoughtful. The demoness nodded slowly. "Hmm. Yeah. Yeah, not bad. I like it. I like it a lot."

"Suits us, I think," Melia conceded with a sidelong look at Dorian.

"Does it?" Dorian said.

"I think it's perfect," Fable said, stroking his cheek lovingly. "Really gets the...point across."

Dorian chuckled and groped her breast, stealing a quick kiss from the giggly faun. "Alright then," he said. "The *Dragon's Wing* it is."

"*The Dragon's Wing!*" Fable cried happily, throwing one arm around Dorian's neck, the other lifting her drink in salute.

Emberly cackled with mirth. "Why not!" she said and lifted her drink. "To *The Dragon's Wing*, and her illustrious crew!" she called out to the darkness.

"To us!" cried Fable, and even Melia couldn't hide a smile as she tapped her bottle with the rest, the clink echoing around them.

And followed by a groan.

The sound started low. Shuddering in the air, then growing like a cry of pain from the very stars themselves. Dorian exchanged shocked glances with the rest, and when it came to Fable, he saw her eyes glowing blue, and a horrified expression on her face.

"Oh no," she whispered, staring to the east.

Dorian turned his head, and through the ruins of the fleets, he saw the wound of the wyrmgate. The thing bulged as if straining, crimson lightning crackling from it and spitting among the ships. A shockwave rippled through space, sending ships drifting anew.

Tentacles reached through the wyrmgate, and following it came the livid red bulk of the *Sky Kraken*, hauling itself into reality like a horror from beyond sanity.

Scarro had come.

Chapter 29

For a moment the four of them could only stare as the *Sky Kraken* pulled itself into the graveyard, but then Dorian bolted to his feet, pulling Fable upright with him..

"We have to go. Now!" he said, looking sharply to Fable. "Can *The Dragon's Wing* fly yet?"

The faun shook her horned head, the light blinking from her eyes. "N-no! The engines aren't hooked up yet, and some of the cannons need to still be calibrated."

"How long?" Dorian demanded.

"Uh…"

"How long?!"

"A-an hour! Maybe less," Fable gasped.

"We don't have that long," Melia said grimly, watching as the *Sky Kraken* seeped into the graveyard, hulks shoved out of its path as the tentacles made great sweeps of its limbs. "They're coming this way!"

"Must have an auramancer tracking us," Emberly cursed. "It'll find our navigator here in no time."

Dorian clenched his teeth. He had to do something. They couldn't have come this far just to be killed like this!

Unless...

Dorian glanced back at *The Windlass*, then to Fable. "Fable," he said, grabbing her shoulder. "Can you pilot *The Dragon's Wing*?"

"H-huh?" she said, looking at him in bafflement. "I uh...I can fly it a little, yeah, but it'll be wobbly—and not through the wyrmgate. Only a navigator can do that..."

"And you need an hour to get it flying?"

"Give or take."

Dorian nodded, feeling strangely calm. He knew what he had to do.

"I'll buy you that time," he said, starting towards the plank.

"Wh-what!" Fable gasped, grabbing his arm and holding him back. "Dorian! You can't mean..."

"They're tracking me, so I'll let them," he said. "I'll take *The Windlass* and lead them on a wild goose chase through the graveyard while you three rig up *The Dragon's Wing*. Then, when it's ready, I'll jump ship, and we'll head back through the wyrmgate before he can catch us."

"Dorian, that's crazy! He'll rip you apart!"

"He'll need to catch me first."

"You can't!" Fable cried, then looked at Emberly and Melia. "He can't!"

Melia grimaced, but shook her head. "It's the only way," she admitted grimly.

Fable looked pleadingly to Emberly, but the demoness just frowned with defeated resolve. Fable turned back to him, but his expression silenced her protests.

"But..." Fable whispered, tears pricking her eyes. "Dorian, I..."

"I have to," he said gently.

Fable sniffled, then pulled herself against him, her face pressed to his chest, tears staining his shirt. "Please," she whispered. "Just...just come back alive..."

Dorian rested his hand on her head. "I will," he said gently. "I will."

A thunderous cracking sound echoed through the graveyard as the *Sky Kraken* tore apart an ancient battleship in its path. The sound forced Dorian into motion, easing Fable back before he turned and raced across the deck. He vaulted onto *The Windlass* and leaped behind the helm, grabbing the wheel.

Scales instantly covered his arms as he willed the vessel into motion, the oars on either side of the ship spurring forth, throwing the slender craft away from *The Dragon's Wing* and into space. Arcane power flowed from the oars and whorls like a comet in flight.

Instantly, the *Sky Kraken* turned, tracking his movement. Dorian sped past a derelict hull and into the open, and from the crown atop the immense monster, a voice boomed into the deathly void.

"Well well! We meet again, boyo!" Scarro's voice thundered with vicious jocularity. "Upon my oath, you are a wily one. But I've been meaning to repay you for your thoughtful gift of that rock worm, and no man eludes Scarro for long!"

"Then come and get me," Dorian growled under his breath, seeing the cannons on the *Sky Kraken's* crown glow with gathering power. He braced himself, and threw a sudden burst of pure power into the ship. The oars beat with sudden vigour, throwing *The Windlass* into a burst of motion as the cannons lit up. Bolts of crimson energy seared through the space where Dorian had been but moments ago, but Dorian knew that trick wouldn't work long.

Instead, he dove into the ruins of the graveyard, the slender ship flashing among the ragged hulls of ships, a streak of light left in its wake like a path remembered.

But the *Sky Kraken* needed no aid in following him.

With careless violence the *Sky Kraken* plowed after Dorian, its rubbery tentacles smashing aside wrecks with ease, plowing through the path Dorian had taken, heedless of the danger. The great monster of the seas of stars shrieked, a sound like the end of days as its eight rubbery limbs clawed for him, the cannons that crowned it firing whenever there was an opportunity.

Dorian flew for his life and more, for he knew that if Scarro caught him, the captain would waste no time scouring the graveyard for Emberly, Fable and Melia. And likewise, it would take the monstrous pirate little time to find them. Dorian grit his teeth, the thought of the three falling prey to Scarro spurring him to put on even more speed.

Wrecks tumbled around him. A sudden opening between him and the *Sky Kraken* was cut short as Dorian dove through the skeletal maw of an ancient star whale. The bones behind him exploded under a blast of cannon fire, Dorian skimming between ribs the size of mountains even as the *Sky Kraken* poured in after him, the monster tearing through the bones of its fellow titan without care, rubbery appendages swinging, lunging, grabbing.

Dorian was floating. He didn't think. Didn't dare. His teeth were grit, every fiber tensed. Horns blazed from his brow and wings of starlight and fire trembled on his back as he let his instincts guide him, every sense keyed to the max. He spun the ship, eluding a grasping tentacle. He looped around a rib as the kraken lunged after him. A sharp turn yanked him from the path of a screaming comet of cannon fire.

Clarity. Fixation. Survival. His hands worked even without thought. A millisecond of hesitation would have seen him crushed a dozen times. He skimmed over the tailbone of the whale, letting it shield him from another blast of cannon fire, the *Sky Kraken* bursting from the bones a second later with a flailing mass of tentacles and another deafening screech.

"You're mine, boyo!" Scarro roared through the void. "Upon my oath, I will see your bloody bones strapped to my yard arm and your flayed skin run up my mast!"

Don't listen. Don't think. No hesitation. No seconds wasted. Dorian sensed the shadow of the *Sky Kraken* behind him. He suddenly dipped, forcing *The Windlass* down. He felt the groan as the spars of the hull objected to the sudden force of motion and speed, but he dove, avoiding another flailing tentacle seeking to grab him.

But there was no eluding the cannon shot that followed.

A lucky shot. A desperate roll. It was all that saved Dorian as he swerved *The Windlass* reflexively, but the explosion still blasted through the keel, ripping out the belly of his ship and nearly tearing the entire thing asunder. Dorian frantically sawed on the wheel, trying to right his ship, but it spun out, the wheel spinning all but uselessly.

Gone.

The rudder was gone.

Dorian channeled all the power he could into the oar wings, and at last he managed to right his craft. Fires burned everywhere, scouring the paint and blackening the wood. The heat beat at his back, but he paid it no attention, for he found himself in an open space surrounded by the dredges of ancient ships. Flotsam of the stars spat out by an uncaring universe.

And before him was the *Sky Kraken*.

The monster's tentacles fanned out from its gaping maw and blocked off every retreat, looking like it was preparing to pounce on him and rip him to shreds. Its baleful eyes were fixed on his wounded ship, and the echoing laugh of its master boomed through the void.

"Upon my oath that was a good shot, boyo! And a fine chase. But the time for running is over. Now, you're *mine*!"

Dorian's mind raced, trying to think of a way out. But there was none. He could feel *The Windlass* breaking apart under his feet to flame and damage, parts falling off even as he floated there. The core in the wheel before him flickered like a dying star, and in front of him was the monster, waiting to devour him last.

Dorian sighed, resting his hand on the core. "It's been a good run."

And perhaps it was just him, but he thought he felt a pulse of agreement in the core, and a grim readiness for what came next.

Dorian smiled sadly, then fixed his gaze. He planted his feet on the deck and gripped the wheel until veins bulged in his arms. His wings fanned out, raining sparks like those erupting from the hearth as another log was fed to the flames. And with a growl, Dorian threw his power into the ship.

The core flared like molten lava. The oars swung and gave a frantic beat. The remaining sails billowed as they caught an astral wind, and with a shout, Dorian drove his ship directly at the monster.

The kraken screeched as it lunged for him, tentacles closing in like the teeth of a trap. The cannons on its crown lit up, raining down fire.

Dorian welcomed it.

He twisted the wheel reflexively, but it was the oars that answered his will. *The Windlass* swung, dipping under a diving tentacle, shooting past the twisting grasp of another. The kraken hadn't expected this. Hadn't expected his speed. Its long reach snatched at thin air. The gunners fired their cannons, their shots going wide as Dorian plowed through towards the monster.

He heard Scarro shout something, but couldn't make out the words. The roar of acceleration howled in his ears as he reached past the *Sky Kraken's* guard. Its bulk rose before him. A great, baleful eye stared down at him.

"So long, friend," Dorian said to the ship.

And for just a moment, he saw the core blink.

Then he leapt.

His wings fanned out, beating once, throwing him clear. Like a comet of fire and gold *The Windlass* screamed straight into the kraken's eye. It punched through, exploding on impact. The monster screamed in terrible agony, writhing in pain, blinded by its own fury as it thrashed. Dorian's wings beat again, throwing him forward. The crown of the ship rose before him. Huge windows filled his view.

Dorian smashed through them, tumbling through the air and landing hard and heavy on wood and metal. He bounced once, twice, rolling across the floor before coming to a halt, gasping with effort and pain.

Red lights throbbed around him. He heard a bellowing laugh, and with a grunt, Dorian planted a hand on the floor and raised his head.

He found himself on what could only be the bridge of the *Sky Kraken*. Crew were racing around controls and wheels, shouting at one another as speaking tubes hooted with alarms and panicked voices. Along the far wall was a great, bronze octopus filling the space with its stretching tentacles. A raised dais with a brass railing overlooked the floor.

And there stood Scarro.

The captain's face tentacles twisted with amusement, his six eyes blazing with cruel wrath. His long captain's coat fluttered as he stepped up to the rail, shoving past several squid-faced crew men. The amulet bounced on his chest, depicting the familiar squid-faced skull crossed with blades, the same as on Scarro's hat and worn somewhere on all his crew.

"Well well! Upon my oath, that was quite a display, boyo," Scarro said, his voice a guttural growl, his gloved hands gripping the rail as he leaned in. "You've caused me no end of trouble, and no end of pain for my poor ship! But what are you doing down there, eh?" he laughed, razor sharp teeth flashing beneath the tentacles of his face. "Kneeling to beg for mercy? Perhaps a quick death?"

Dorian grit his teeth. With effort, he forced himself back to his feet, stumbling a step before recovering. He reached for his sword and drew it, the hiss of steel on leather audible even over the clarion hoot of alarms.

Scarro roared with laughter. "There we go. That's what I like to see!" he said as he planted a boot on the rail and leaped down.

The captain landed with a heavy bang on the lower deck and rose back to his full height, his hands lazily resting on the hilts of two swords at his sides. "Upon my oath, it has been an age since I faced a man like you, boyo! So do try not to die too fast. For after all," he added as he drew the two cutlasses sheathed at his side, "I do intend to make you die slow, for all the damage you've done."

"Then come get some," Dorian growled, his wings flaring with astral light, horns blazing with draconic fury.

"With pleasure!" Scarro roared, and leaped to attack.

Dorian parried hastily, surprised by the alien's speed, and even more so his strength. Dorian knew too well how strong he was in his semi-draconic form, but the pirate's blow put him on his back foot as both blades clashed with Dorian's.

"Ha ha! Not bad, boyo!" Scarro said, his right arm rising, slashing downward. Dorian dodged it, parrying the other blade as it swept to bisect him.

"Not...bad yourself," Dorian growled begrudgingly.

"Oh, I'm just getting warmed up!" Scarro cackled and pressed in.

"What a coincidence," Dorian said, feeling the heat of flames surge up his throat, kindling in his maw. "So am I!"

Dorian opened wide and Scarro's six eyes bulged as the human breathed forth a gout of flame. Scarro roared with pain and surprise, reeling back and flapping his sleeves, suddenly alight as he raised them to block Dorian's attack.

Seizing the chance, Dorian pushed forward, raising his blade.

A flicker of movement caught the corner of his eye and he jerked back with a frantic beat of his wings as a flash of red tore in front of him. He whipped his head around to spot several crewmen taking aim with arcane pistols, their shots cracking through the air as Dorian dove behind a console for cover.

"Cowards!" he barked.

Scarro belted out a laugh, patting out the last embers on his coat. "Cowards? We are pirates, boyo! And upon my oath, that means we don't play by any rules. Blast him, boys!"

Another barrage of fire ripped down on Dorian, chewing up the console he sheltered behind. Dorian cursed, knowing that it was only a matter of time. He prepped himself to lunge out and charge the barrage, knowing it was his only chance. A suicidal run, perhaps, but if he could take down Scarro, it would be worth it. He quickly considered turning into a dragon again, but the confines of the bridge were too small and would leave him easy prey.

Fine, he thought, gripping his sword. So be it.

Dorian leaped atop the console, finding himself facing Scarro and a score of crew, rifles aimed like a firing squad. The squid-man grinned.

And the deck suddenly jerked under them to the sound of riddling explosions.

Shouts erupted from the crew, many losing their footing, most their shots as they reflexively pulled the triggers of their rifles, blasting holes in the deck, walls and ceiling. Scarro rode the sudden bucking, but his surprise was no less profound.

Flashes blazed from beyond the windows, and both Dorian and Scarro looked out and into the void.

Dorian felt a smile split his face as *The Dragon's Wing* skimmed through the void like a silver blade, cannon ports lighting up as they rained down a barrage of blue and red arcane power on the *Sky Kraken*. The monster shrieked, twisting in pain and agony, trying to right itself and face towards this foe, but the sleek ship stayed beyond its range, pummeling the monster with the sort of firepower it was ill equipped to face, wounded as it was.

"Where the devil did that come from!" Scarro thundered.

"Turrets are down, cap'n!" a crewman shouted from the bridge as he clung to a speaking horn. "We're sitting ducks!"

"Whores!" Scarro roared.

A blast ripped apart the ceiling, tearing through and sending pirates flying as it exploded near the bridge. Dorian seized the chance, his wings fanning out and shooting him forward as he leaped for Scarro.

Several pirates hastily brought up their weapons and a few fired off the shots they hadn't wasted, but they flashed past Dorian as the deck bucked under them. Scarro swung his blades in a sudden parry, but Dorian's momentum broke it, throwing the captain back, the tentacles of his face writhing in surprise and anger.

Two pirates on either side drew their swords and rushed him. Dorian ducked the first blade and parried the second, stabbing the pirate in the chest. The squid-man went down with a bubbling groan, and Dorian ripped his blade free, an arc of violet blood splattering the deck as he swung the sword around, slashing the other pirate across the chest and nearly bisecting the man.

Scarro surged into the opening, swords swinging. Dorian parried the first, but the second swiped in low, coming for his chest.

...Only for Dorian to grab it with a hand, the edge of the blade scraping across his gold and crimson scales.

Scarro stared, all six eyes wide with shock as Dorian looked up at him.

"Farewell, captain," Dorian said with a mock salute, then broke the deadlock with a sudden surge of strength, and thrust.

Scarro wheezed as Dorian's blade plunged into his chest, the pirate staggering back, falling against the wall behind him. Scarro stared at the blade in shock as he slowly sunk to the floor, purple blood staining the front of his fine jacket.

"Upon...my...oath..." Scarro gasped, the tentacles of his face quivering with a rattling last breath, and then falling slack as the captain went limp, his gold amulet dropping to his chest.

Dorian yanked his sword free with a satisfied grunt. Another explosion ripped through the bridge, pirates screaming and running every which way. Dorian ignored them, grabbing the amulet dangling from Scarro's throat and ripping it free. Stuffing it in his pocket, he spun around and raced across the deck and back to the windows. He leaped onto the rim and looked skyward, quickly spotting *The Dragon's Wing* as it circled the dying monster.

Here goes.

Dorian jumped from the window, willing his body to change. He felt his aura fill him with a surge of energy. Fill more than him. His wings solidified. His arms stretched and face shifted to a snout. With a roar, Dorian burst from the dying vessel in his dragon form, wings flapping, carrying him swiftly to the circling ship.

Dorian landed on the deck of *The Dragon's Wing* heavily, feeling exhausted from the battle and his frantic flight, already shifting back to his human guise.

"Dorian!"

He staggered as Fable tackled him in a hug, Melia and Emberly soon following as they raced up from the gun deck to join in the embrace. Dorian laughed with relief, hugging them back as best he could.

"Miss me?" he managed to say.

Fable laughed through her tears. "You bastard!" she said adoringly as she nuzzled his chest, not even caring if her antlers knocked against him. "You big, gorgeous bastard!"

"If you hadn't lived, I'd have killed you," Melia growled.

"That doesn't make sense," Dorian said.

"Shut up," she said, flushed with joy and relief.

Dorian smiled at the trio, then looked back over the rail. The *Sky Kraken* burned, the monster's tentacles limp, drifting along with the creature, its hide riddled with holes, blood floating through the void. The crown was in ruins, shattered, and secondary explosions rippled through it as magazines caught fire.

Dorian watched the monstrous pirate ship drift away into the graveyard, another dead vessel joining its fellows.

Dorian could only smile, hug the trio against him once more.

"I'm home," he said.

Chapter 30

By the time *The Dragon's Wing* docked again on Sphere, the buzz of rumour was already in full spin.

Dorian could sense this as they docked, *The Dragon's Wing* sliding into its berth, the silver of its gilt glowing softly with the power of the navigator aboard. The robed security warder stared at their ship in wonderment as Melia tossed him some coins.

"Keep it safe, my man," Emberly said.

The warder bowed low.

Dorian raised a brow as he walked with the trio down Sphere's docks. "What was that about?" he said.

"What do you think?" Fable giggled, hanging off his arm adoringly. "We're big shots now! That ship is the best one on Sphere. Not to mention you, ya big lug."

"Me?" Dorian said blankly.

Fable rolled her eyes. "You got to have noticed how big you've gotten," she said, giving his arm a squeeze.

Dorian frowned. He had noticed he seemed a bit…taller lately. And his arms a bit denser with muscle. And now that she mentioned it, when he'd tried on his old peasant clothes during their flight back, the rough wool hadn't really fit him anymore. He'd assumed they'd shrunk. But maybe he really had gotten that much bigger…

"Do you really think so?" he said.

"Of course," Melia said from his other side. And though Dorian may not have noticed his new size, he surely noticed how close Melia stuck by him, as if it was all she could do not to hang off his arm like Fable was.

Emberly cackled from the lead. "You still have no idea what you are," Emberly said with a sly look back at him as she led the way into the tangled wharves, shops, taverns and whorehouses that made up that level of Sphere. "But don't you worry, big guy," she added with a meaningful wink. "We'll show you. Count on it."

Dorian laughed contentedly, following Emberly and noticing that unlike his first visit, the crowds were quick to make space for them to walk. Dorian wondered if they could sense his draconic nature, then shrugged it off. It didn't matter.

Dorian recognized the *Moonshot* as Emberly led them to the door, the bar being the very same one they'd met Grash in before. The door swung open at Emberly's push, and the four entered.

Dorian slowed in the entrance, looking about in surprise. The common room was cleared out, a stark change from the crammed crowds from last time they were there. In fact, the entire center of the room had been emptied but for a single large, round table loaded with food.

At its head was Boss Grash, the massive orc dressed in his blindingly white suit and necklace of teeth. He was flanked by two of his burly bodyguards, and Dorian noticed a few more of the ogres near the walls.

As they entered, Grash rose from his seat, his toothy maw grinning broadly, the plugs of red stones in his scarred skull glittering in the low light. "Well well!" he bellowed, throwing open his arms, his metal claw clacking audibly. "If it ain't my favourite crew! C'min! C'min! 'Ave a seat round the table."

"Happy to," Emberly barked as she waltzed in and took a seat. Dorian followed suit more warily, eying the ogres around the place as he chose the chair across from Grash, Melia and Fable pulling theirs in close beside him.

Grash settled back in his chair and snapped his fingers, one of his ogre bodyguards hurrying forward with a bottle of beer. Grash fit the cap between his teeth and popped it off with a snapping sound, making Dorian wince and his own teeth ache in sympathetic pain.

Grash took a long guzzle and slammed down the bottle. "Ah, dat's good shit. So!" he said, looking between the four. "Sounds like dat job went off without a hitch, eh?"

"A few hitches," Emberly said. "But nothing we couldn't deal with. Bit touch and go here and there, and we lost our old ship, but we got your goods delivered perfectly."

"Then I suppose youz got my pay?"

"Of course," Emberly said, reaching into her jacket and taking out the lumpy pouch of gems. She passed them to the orc, who accepted it, spilling its sparkling contents into a massive green hand. Grash's eyes gleamed at the iridescent shine of the stones nestled in the leathery contours of his palm.

"Nice," the orc grunted. "Reeeal nice." He poured the jewels back into the pouch and tucked it into his pocket, flashing a toothy grin at the four before him. "I'm impressed. Yes I is. That job was a dangerous one, eh? But you lot came through, so it seems ta me."

"Thank you, sir," Emberly said.

"Yeah! In fact, I feels like I should be da one tankin' you, shouldn't I? But da fing is, I don't think I'm gonna be doin' that."

Emberly's smile slipped. "No?"

"No, I ain't," Grash said as he leaned back in his chair, fingers clasped atop his belly as he eyed them. "Because see, da fing is, I gots word that there was some...mix up with the cores. That one a dem was missing, and instead some crappy piece was stuck in dere instead of a proper one. Eh?"

"Uh..." Emberly muttered.

"Which seems funny ta me," Grash said conversationally, his large green hand ripping a leg off a roasted turkey. "Because see, I happened ta have checked all dem crates before I shipped 'em out. So's I think I'd 'ave noticed somefin' like that if it happened before leaving dese docks 'ere."

"I...I bet you would," Emberly said uneasily.

"And dat gets me finkin' even mores, roight? It make be fink dat if'n I looked at da core in dat shiny new ship a yours, I wonder what I'll be findin', eh?"

Dorian tensed, his eyes skimming around the room, sensing the ogres shifting where they stood, several uncrossing their arms, their beady eyes gleaming from beneath their sloping brows.

"Mister Grash," Emberly said quickly. "This is easy to explain. It was—"

Grash grabbed the edge of the table and flung it out of the way. Plates of food and drinks poured onto the floor with a crash of shattering pottery as the orc lurched to his feet, looming over them, his huge jaw curled in a tusky snarl, his claw snapping like a guillotine. Only Dorian didn't react in fear.

"You fink you're gonna be able ta cheat me?" he roared. "Ain't nobody cheats Boss Grash! Nobody!"

Emberly drew back, alarmed.

Dorian rose to his feet. "It wasn't her fault," he said.

Grash rounded on him. "Oh really? Den who's was it?"

"Captain Scarro," Dorian said.

Grash's eyes screwed up as the orc drew himself to his full menacing height. "Him? What's he got ta do with it?"

"He knew about the shipment," Dorian said. "He tried to intercept us at Asimova's Spire, and even attacked us after we delivered the supplies.

We had to rig up a better ship to fight him off, or you'd have lost both your cargo, and the reward they offered."

"That so?" Grash said, staring into Dorian's eyes, the orc's heavy jaw slowly rolling. "And did youz?"

"We did," Dorian said, pulling out the pirate's amulet and tossing it to the orc, who snatched it out of the air. "He's dead by my hand."

Silence ticked by, the tension so thick Dorian could feel it suffocating him. Grash's red eyes never wavered, his mechanical arm creaking as the orc examined the amulet thoughtfully. The red stones embedded in his head flickered balefully. The ogres shifted where they stood, and Dorian's hand slid towards his sword.

And then Grash laughed.

The guffaw broke the tension like a floor would a mirror. The big orc bellowed with mirth, wiping a tear from an eye.

"Har har har!" he barked, grinning as he tossed the amulet back to Dorian. "So old squid-face bit it, eh? Nice there, humie. Real nice."

Dorian caught the amulet. "Thanks," he said, tucking it into his shirt.

Grash tore a bite from his turkey leg and snapped his claw. Hastily, his ogres began to sweep away the plates, another righting the table. Grash settled back in his chair, still grinning as he polished off the turkey leg. "So!" he said. "Youz done offed ol' Scarro, eh? Nice job. Real nice. Dat one's been a pain in de arse for a long time! Competition's 'ealthy, so long as it ain't with me. I think I likes dat. Sounds good. And a lesson learned. You 'nd me, Dorian? I thinks we'z gonna get along reeeeal nice like."

"Glad to hear it," Dorian said, sitting back down slowly.

"I bet you'z iz. In fact," Grash said as one of his ogres delivered a new plate of steaming steak in front of him. "You'z actually have a bunch a jobs I've been savin' up for our next meetin'. And because I'm such a nice guy, I'll even give you'z a better rate than we agreed on! And as for you'z pay for dis job—Emeritus!"

Dorian spotted the bookish goblin as he shuffled out from the back, hefting a large sack with some effort. The goblin heaved it onto the table with an audible clink.

"Yer pay," Grash said, shoving the sack across the table towards Dorian. "As agreed fer dis job. And when Emeritus stops by tomorrow ta offer you'z up your next one, I'll 'ave 'im bring along a bit extra fer gettin' rid a Scarro like dat."

"How generous of you," Dorian said as several waitresses emerged from the kitchens with more dishes, laying them out in terrified silence. Dorian grimaced, realizing that the entire display of Grash's fury had either been planned in advance by the big orc, or outbursts like this were so common that replacement meals were always available at a moment's notice. Dorian wondered what might have happened if he'd not intervened...

"Go on! Dig in," Grash said. "Your reward, among others, eh? And Emberly?"

"Yeah."

"Just so's you know, you ever pull a stunt like dat again," Grash said, as he hacked off a chunk from his bloody steak, "we ain't gonna have just a chat. I'll 'ave you'z crucified on the docks and let the squags suck your eyes outta yer skull."

"Noted," Emberly said, her voice more subdued than Dorian had ever heard.

"Great! Good ta hear. So glad we'z can all be friends, right ladies!"

"Sure," Fable said, her face ashen.

"Y-yeah," Melia replied as she picked at her own food.

"Dat's what I likes ta hear. And so, a toast!" Grash bellowed, raising his beer. "Ta new friends!"

Dorian smiled thinly and toasted back. Because Dorian did work for the burly orc now, and he had a strong feeling it would be far better to stay Grash's friend than become his enemy...But no one threatened his crew. He'd surely pay for that one day.

One day.

Chapter 31

DORIAN WAS RELIEVED TO get back aboard and out of Grash's eye. The dinner had hardly improved after the initial display, and when they'd finally been able to excuse themselves, it had been with great relief.

Dorian sighed as he wrapped an arm around Emberly, pulling her against his side as they made their way up *The Dragon Wing's* gangplank. "You doing okay?" he asked.

Emberly sighed wearily and nodded. "Sure, sure. Expected something like that, really. But still, wasn't fun. And just know if we do ever end up doing something like that to Grash again, probably better we just vanish to some other corner of the Black. Savvy?"

"Gotcha," Dorian said, giving her a squeeze. "But I wouldn't have let him hurt you. You know that, right?"

"Oh? Thinking you can go around being all protective of me?" Emberly said with a bit of her familiar spunk, her golden eyes flashing as she looked up at him with a grin.

Dorian chuckled. "I think I might," he said. "You are a part of my crew now."

"So now it's *your* crew?" the demoness said.

"Damn right it is," Fable said as she clopped aboard the ship, spinning around with a fey grin, her deer-like tail flicking with delight. "And we're part of that loyal crew! But you better keep us happy, Dorian. Or we'll mutiny!"

"Mutiny!" Dorian said in mock horror. "And what would that look like?"

"It'd be the sexiest damn mutiny you've ever seen," Fable giggled, skipping up towards him with a flutter of her long lashes. "So you better keep us happy, cutie."

Dorian laughed, his other arm looping around Fable, tugging her against his broad chest, his palm filling with the softness of her ass. "Oh really? Any ideas on how I should do that?"

Fable cooed, her hands against his chest as she leaned up. "I might have some...thoughts," she whispered.

Dorian leaned down, capturing her soft lips with a kiss, tingling as Fable quivered in need against him.

Melia sighed at the sight and rolled her eyes. "Honestly," the elf said, striding forward with the click of her heeled boots. "Can't you two go an hour without making out?"

Fable broke off the kiss and gave the elf a knowing look. "Why? Jealous?"

Melia scoffed. "Hardly," she said.

Dorian glanced at her hair, noting the fluttering pink. "Of course she's not," he said as he released Emberly, only to grab Melia's arm and tug the elf in close. "Because she knows she's next."

Melia squeaked in surprise as she found herself against Dorian, the elf pouting in attempted seriousness, but Dorian could feel how her body pressed against him, her thighs rubbing together as her hair and cheeks glowed an aroused pink. "Being pretty forward now, aren't you?" she huffed.

"Sure am," Dorian chuckled, leaned down, and kissed her.

Melia tensed, but almost instantly melted to his kiss, a soft moan escaping the proud elf as Dorian's hand stroked her back, her soft breasts mashing to his chest.

"Hey hey!" Emberly said, grinning at the sight. "Does this mean I finally get to see my threesome between an elf, a dragon, and a faun?"

Fable giggled again, grabbing Dorian's hand. "Damn right you are," she said.

Melia sighed, but grabbed Dorian's other hand, pulling him towards the captain's cabin. "I suppose we did agree..."

Dorian laughed as he let the two women tug him towards the open door. "Well, I do want to keep my crew happy."

Fable giggled and even Melia smiled as they pulled him into the dark room. Light glowed through the windows at the rear, barely illuminating the interior with a dusky blue glow from Sphere's various lamps along the docks.

Dorian heard Emberly shut the door behind them, but he paid little attention to it. All his focus was on the elf and faun before him, Fable slipping in close to Melia, the elf blushing hotly, but not objecting as the pair began to undress each other.

Dorian sat on the edge of the bed, watching as clothes fluttered to the floor, Melia and Fable's pale curves soon revealed, fairly glowing in the blue light which drifted through the windows. Faun and elf turned to him, both blushing softly, but their eyes lidded and smoky with desire.

"Not bad, huh?" Fable giggled, sweeping her hands along her thighs.

"To say the least," Dorian chuckled.

"Damn right," Melia growled, prowling towards him, trying to put forward a forceful front, even as her blush deepened as she sat down on the bed beside him, Fable doing the same to the other. The pair moved in close, Melia turning his head, kissing him. Fable pressed against his other side, her lips gently pushing into his throat.

Dorian groaned as the two women's hands moved over him, peeling off his jacket, undoing his shirt and pants. He shifted, his pants sliding down, revealing his toned, powerful body.

"Oh fuck yes," Dorian heard Emberly whisper, the demoness's golden eyes glowing through the gloom where she leaned against the wall, one of her hands fondling her breast, the other rubbing herself through her tight pants.

The feel of the demoness's eager eyes on them stirred Dorian further. His arms wrapped around Fable and Melia, breaking the kiss and easing the pair off the bed and onto the floor in front of him, his cock jutting up between them.

Fable giggled, stealing an impish look his way. "Now what are we supposed to do with this?" she purred, leaning in closer and delicately pressing a kiss to his shaft.

"Mystery solved, it looks like," Melia said as she pressed a kiss to the other side.

"I do love a crew who looks for solutions," Dorian chuckled as the pair began to delicately lick his cock, their tongues sliding along his shaft.

He groaned as his lust stirred stronger under the adoring lips of the two women, Fable's antlers throwing shadows with every movement, Melia's hair fluttering with their glow.

Dorian was soon breathing hard. Heavy. Watching the pair worship his cock tenderly. "Stop," he suddenly said.

"Too close?" Fable cooed, giving his tip a last teasing press of her lips.

"Yes. And you two deserve it far more inside you."

"Aw, but there's two of us," Fable said, stealing a flirty glance at Melia. "What's the other one going to do?"

"I have a thought," Dorian said, taking Fable's arm and tugging the giggling faun back onto the bed. Dorian fell back, drawing Fable atop him, the faun straddling his head, her eyes gleaming in the gloom as she settled her weight over his face. Dorian grasped her hips, pulling her tight against him. His tongue teased along her slit.

"Oh! Oh mnnnn," Fable moaned, her thighs tightening with unexpected pleasure. Her hips began to rock as Dorian tenderly licked her out, his effort momentarily stalling as he felt Melia crouch above him, his cock teasing the tight slit of her entrance. He heard the elf whimper, then groan as she descended atop him, sheathing him in her hot entrance.

"Oh f-fuuuuuck," Melia groaned, and Dorian could see the sudden flare of her hair as she took him.

"So g-good," Fable panted.

"Guh—It *is*," Melia gasped as she began to ride him, the slick tightness of her pussy sliding up and down his cock, at first slow, as if proving she could, before Melia abandoned such propriety and began to shamelessly bounce herself atop him. "Ah!"

Dorian grunted, his hands tightening their hold on Fable's thighs as he drove his tongue into her, the gorgeous faun moaning as her hips rocked, riding Dorian's face, the three of them moving together. Riding the waves of pleasure on the bed, tension earned at Grash's table finding relief at last as they abandoned themselves to the moment.

"Oh g-gods," Melia gasped. "Gods! Dorian. Dorian, I...I'm...Oh gods, I f-fucking love youuuu!"

Melia cried out, her body tightening on his cock. Dorian groaned as he felt her squeeze him, pushing him past the brink. He thrust up into her a final time, his balls tightening as he gave her all that she yearned for, the elf moaning in ecstasy as his seed filled her in a hot burst.

"Dooooriaaaan," Fable cried as she came atop his tongue, the faun squeaking with her pleasure, her thighs tightening in bliss, the three of them joined in that heady climax together.

Dorian groaned beneath Fable as the faun rolled off him. He lay back there, breathing hot and heavy as Melia eased off his lap and collapsed against his side. He looked at the two blushing women fondly, reaching out and pulling them close against him.

"That was...that was great," Melia breathed.

"Wasn't it?" Fable giggled, then glanced over at Emberly in the dark. "How about it, Emberly? Want some too?"

The demoness's golden eyes quirked with amusement in the gloom. "Really?" she said. "You want some of this?"

"If you're gonna be crew, you should get your fill too. Hate for your bond of loyalty to be tested. Right Melia?" Fable asked with syrupy innocence.

"Althought I kind of hate the idea, it does seem inevitable that things will head this way," Melia murmured, playing with a lock of Dorian's hair. "Fuck it. At least this way, it's on our terms, and she'll know that she's in the fold because we let her be."

Dorian laughed and lazily sat back up. "Well, you heard 'em," he said.

"Is that an order, Captain?" Emberly said saucily.

"Damn straight," Dorian grinned.

Emberly chuckled and sauntered out of the shadows. Her hands moved slowly, shrugging off her jacket and pulling off the thin, black strap that hid her breasts. Her hips swung as she shucked down her pants, ammunition belts clicking as they came to rest on the floor.

Dorian watched the demoness's crimson figure come into view, outlined by the glow of distant lamps. Dorian admired her as the beautiful demoness moved closer, the lazy swing of her hips teasing. Tantalizing. Seductive.

Dorian felt himself harden anew as Emberly moved into his lap, straddling his legs, her folds rubbing against the underside of his cock. Dorian grunted, reaching up, fondling her full red breasts.

"Mmm," Emberly moaned softly. "Those magic hands."

"They can truly work wonders," Dorian said.

Emberly laughed softly, leaning down, brushing her dark hair from her face. "Show me."

Dorian did, kissing her as her body lazily swayed, rubbing herself against his shaft until he was rock hard. She slickened him with her arousal as he played with her nipples. Soft whimpers and gasps escaped the brash demoness as Dorian massaged her breasts, his tongue warring with hers.

Emberly's grinding began to grow more insistent. Needier. Her breath growing hot and fast. Dorian felt stirrings beside him as Melia and Fable sat up and pressed against him from either side, their hands running over the hard lines of his muscles. Their lips kissing his shoulders and neck.

A silent consensus was reached between Dorian and Emberly. Without discussion, she rolled her hips, his hands sliding down her flanks and grasping her rear. His cock bounced, tip coming to rest at her entrance.

And slowly.

Deliberately.

He slid her down.

"Mmmmm," Emberly moaned, her dark lashes fluttering as Dorian stuffed her with his cock.

"Mnnn," Dorian grunted, his hands squeezing her ass as he began to bounce her atop him, thrusting up into her, claiming the gorgeous demoness with slow, loving, methodical precision.

"She good, Dorian?" Fable whispered in his ear.

"Fuck her, star slut," Melia murmured from the other side, the pair's hot breath against him. Their soft bodies squeezing him, trapping him between them and Emberly. The four of them moved together, Dorian thrusting into the moaning demoness, letting her ride his cock with ever growing urgency. "I want to see what kind of undignified face you can get her to make."

"D-Dorian," Emberly gasped between kisses. "Dorian, I'm...oh fuck, I'm not g-gonna last long at all at this rate."

"Then don't," Dorian panted, bouncing her faster on his cock. Thrusting up into her with greater urgency. Feeling the rippling tightness of her nearing orgasm. "Cum. Cum with me, Emberly."

"D-Doriaaaaaan!" Emberly cried, tensing, inner walls squeezing him with her climax. Her hands clung to his shoulder as she came, her high pulling Dorian to his own climax after her with a throaty groan.

Dorian exhaled heavily and let Fable and Melia ease him back onto the bed. He flopped flat onto the soft mattress, Fable and Melia laying themselves out beside him as Emberly settled atop him with a satisfied moan.

Dorian looked at the lovely trio, admiring them. How strange to think not so long ago, his greatest ambition had been to apprentice at an inn watching barrels and dragging out drunks.

And instead, he had travelled the stars, slain pirates, flown ships, and fought battles in the screaming void. Had discovered love with three gorgeous alien women, and now piloted a ship of legends through the heavens. He chuckled, shaking his head.

"What's so funny?" Fable asked sweetly from his side.

"Nothing. Just thinking," Dorian said.

"Too late to be thinking," Melia moaned from beside him, snuggling against his muscular body. "Sleep now."

"Sleep sounds good," Emberly yawned, wriggling comfortably atop him like a tired cat.

Dorian chuckled again, gathering the trio against himself, and let himself drift away with them into the starlit night.

Links

Remember to leave a review before checking out these awesome links! Review counts are the best metric we have for estimating how soon to push sequels up in our schedule! This is the paperback addition, so in order for you to click a link, you have to pinch your nipple and say "Dios mio!" while you tap the link with your butter-soaked index finger. Be warned.

Virgil also just released Solar Dragons Need Love Too, 7! and Three Heads Are Better (book 3 of Monstrous Love) is coming out later this month!

For more Harem Lit and Monster Girl content check out the following:

https://www.facebook.com/groups/haremlit
https://www.facebook.com/groups/haremlitaudiobooks
https://www.facebook.com/groups/haremlit-books/
https://www.facebook.com/groups/monstergirllovers
https://www.facebook.com/groups/dukesofharem
https://www.facebook.com/groups/MonsterGirlFiction/
https://www.facebook.com/groups/1324476308314052
https://www.facebook.com/groups/404822691240858
https://www.facebook.com/RoyalGuard2020
https://www.royalguardpublishing.com

Virgil's Patreon:
https://www.patreon.com/virgilknightley

Jay Aury's Twitter:
https://twitter.com/aury_jay

Their Author pages on Amazon:

https://www.amazon.com/stores/Virgil-Knightley/author/B097P6PSFJ, https://www.amazon.com/stores/Jay%20Aury/author/B079NLYFCQ

And join our Facebook Group!

https://www.facebook.com/groups/pulpfantasy

Printed in Great Britain
by Amazon